The Hon. Rocky Slade

WILLIAM WISTER HAINES

The Hon. Rocky Slade

An Atlantic Monthly Press Book

Boston • Little, Brown and Company • *Toronto*

ATLANTIC—LITTLE, BROWN BOOKS
ARE PUBLISHED BY
LITTLE, BROWN AND COMPANY
IN ASSOCIATION WITH
THE ATLANTIC MONTHLY PRESS

Published simultaneously in Canada
by Little, Brown & Company (Canada) Limited

PRINTED IN THE UNITED STATES OF AMERICA

For F. T. H.

PART I

Chapter One

IT saddens to find old friends lying to you. Legal philosophers like to accord the law pre-eminence in human questing for truth. The practicing attorney deals with people. The limits of their confidence may be measuring him, too.

As I listened to Rocky Slade that afternoon in January of 1947 it was evident that he was telling me less than the truth of whatever had brought him to my office. It was harder to be sure which of us, or whom else, he was trying to protect.

Rocky was not a client of mine, except potentially. He was engaged to be married in three weeks to Lucy Maynard, the daughter of my most important client. Rocky and I were scarcely old friends in the sense of intimacy. We had been lifetime neighbors in our small Midwestern city of Torrent. We had grown up within a few blocks of each other and, in different classes, attended the same grade and high schools and our state University of Wiasota. It happened that I was three years older than Rocky, which can be a divisive gulf through schooling.

After that our lives had diverged before recrossing so that even at thirty-two and twenty-nine we were less than intimate. We had, however, reservoirs of information about each other. Mine was the larger because Rocky had been a state celebrity from high school days and a national one in college. There is still dispute about whether Rocky was the greatest football player ever born but it takes place beyond the boundaries of our state.

At the climax of his career over four thousand of our citizens had signed, with exuberant disregard for the Constitution, a petition to nominate Rocky as legislator at large from Wiasota to the United States House of Representatives. The movement had begun just before a serious ankle injury in his last game had cost Rocky a lucrative contract to play professional football. At the time Rocky had shrugged off both politics and the injury and had finished college.

[1]

After a brief career at coaching, service in the army and a few months in a local real estate office, Rocky had decided to try public life. Time and the war had somewhat eclipsed his renown. He knew it and had been content to enter politics on the local scale. In the early summer of 1946 Rocky had won his first election to the position of Councilor of Torrent County.

It had been evident before the war was over that both City and County of Torrent would be on or near the route of a major freeway of the future. The *Sentinel* admonished its subscribers in every edition that the freeway meant for us the difference between slow death and becoming a minor metropolis. Rocky had seized the issue as his own. It had every merit except opposition. Rocky had created that, over the details of the route, with a fervor that won him indignant criticism and the largest personal plurality ever polled in our county.

Such a victory might have been another man's epitaph. Our County Council is mature, conservative and skeptical alike of youth and transitory pluralities. Instead of ruffling its feathers, Rocky had used his demonstrated strength to free himself from the council. He had easily persuaded its bored elders to designate him our unofficial delegate to our state capital at Prairie, where the major decisions about the freeway fermented in a higher echelon of state politics. There and in the interested towns along the way he had spent most of the summer and fall, beating the drum for the claims of Torrent.

Prairie lies a hundred miles north of Torrent in the newly industrialized part of a state that was once primarily agricultural. His exertions had imposed almost continuous travel on Rocky. He had found time, concurrently, to become engaged to the daughter of our best known citizen. Through the earlier phases of the courtship I had seen a good deal of him. Since the engagement had been announced in November I had seen very little of either him or Lucy. It had been a surprise to me when Miss Premm announced him that afternoon.

Miss Premm had been my father's secretary for thirty years. Long before I was admitted to the bar he used to say that he was never sure which of them ran the office. I think Miss Premm was very sure though she never troubled to say so.

She opened the door every morning at eight except for the two weeks of each summer she devoted to the conventions of her church group. For those she left my father and, after him, me a digest of agenda which she spent her first evening at home checking. The day I returned from the war she said:

"I put your personal things in your father's desk, Mr. James," and that was that.

I could still gauge the nature of most calls by whether she called me Mr. James or Mr. Denton as she opened the door from the anteroom. That afternoon it was Mr. James. There was an undertone of emotion as she added: "It's Mr. Roscoe Slade."

Rocky had fluttered less susceptible hearts than the one Miss Premm thought she ruled. My own height and weight closely approximated the American Average tables but I always felt dwarfed in any room Rocky entered. He still carried his massive shoulders on a thin waist and long straight legs. His forehead was receding a little at the temples but the curly black hair over it was lustrous with vitality. His perpetual smile hid the first faint promise of jowls. His dark eyes flashed down on the neat white hair and frail figure over which he towered until she looked up at him and his face became stern with reproach.

"Miss Premm! Who are you calling Mr. Slade?"

"I might have called you the Honorable," she said.

"Call me Mister again and I quit public life!"

"No you wouldn't," said Miss Premm. "But we'll take no chances, Rocky."

Her eyes were soft as she closed the door on us. He seated himself, looked back toward it and sighed.

"Jim, you're not as dumb as you look."

"I wish you'd convince Miss Premm of that."

"At least you don't have to pat every back you go by. I bet you don't even know that old spook is secretary of the Inter-Church Council."

"She still scolds me every Monday."

"That's only Mondays," said Rocky. "Politics is a rat race in a goldfish bowl eight days a week. I'd trade you straight across for a deal like this. You're smart to keep it staid and shabby."

He would not have traded me. The office was shabby for reasons he knew as well as I. Father and I had considered moving into one of the newer buildings even before the war. Luckily we had not done so. I returned in debt for the modest rent in this one. After the Maynard business had come my way I had been urged again to move uptown. Some day, perhaps I would. Here there were elbow room and library space. Shabby it was, but my grandfather Denton had opened these offices. People still knew where to find the firm.

"How's the freeway coming, Rocky?" I asked.

"In the bag," said Rocky. "I'm just about fresh out of an issue."

"You can always come out against sin."

"You forget my old man," said Rocky.

For the moment I had. Rocky's father was pastor of one of the more vehement of our many small denominations.

[3]

"Thirty years for Christ under a leaky roof; I'll take my sin straight, thank you."

"Communism?"

He shrugged. "Not here. The sovereign state of Wiasota has passed a law against it, remember? It's like adultery; we have a law against that, too. Tell our people to leave each other's wives alone and they'll fight you right now, for civil liberty. But we'll never have adultery or communism, either, as long as farmers get subsidies and cities get relief."

We smiled together and I waited, wondering where all this was leading, until Rocky saw that I was wondering and led.

"Jim, I need help again; you pay a hell of a penalty for being so loyal to me."

"I voted against you, Rocky."

"I'd have worried if you hadn't; this is serious."

"What's your trouble?"

"Have you got Archie Maynard's power of attorney?"

"Yes."

"Will you lend me twenty thousand bucks from the estate?"

"Has Archie authorized it?"

"No. I'm asking you."

"You're asking the wrong man, Rocky."

"He'll authorize it if you tell him to."

"I'd have to know all about it, Rocky."

That was where the lying began. More accurately, it was prevarication. The lies were all omission. Rocky said bluntly that he could not explain his need. Other people were involved. It was all politics; the less I knew about it the better for me. He emphasized that his request was for a loan. He would give me his note. He reminded me that Lucy would inherit everything of Archie's anyway. It was all in the family. He managed to convey a hint that when Archie was gone I should find Rocky's gratitude worth having.

Inexperience had left Rocky naïve about both ordinary business usage and the law. From most men such a proposal would have been insulting. Rocky was in dead earnest. Patiently I reminded him that I could not possibly recommend any loan from the estate without detailed knowledge of all circumstances.

"Duty to clients, eh?"

"Sure. I'm just a legal hired man, Rocky."

"Nuts," said Rocky. "You do everything for them. You're all the brains Archie Maynard has."

"You won't think so when you know him better."

[4]

"Isn't it equally your duty to protect the Maynards?"

"From anything, I understand."

"Jim, trouble for me is trouble for them. You can see that. I'm thinking for them, too."

"All the more reason to consult them, Rocky."

"You know Archie hates my guts," he said.

Archie did not hate him because Archie did not hate anyone, but a tinge of truth compounded the delicacy of this. Archie had never wanted him for a son-in-law. The other side of it was that Lucy was over twenty-five and strong-minded. Archie had sanctioned and announced the engagement. Tension remained. I could sympathize with Rocky's reluctance to ask for a family loan. That did not empower me to make one.

"You won't arrange it on your own hook then?"

"Sorry, Rocky, no dice."

"Will you tell me one thing more?"

"If I can."

"Is that much available, fast?"

The erosion of the Maynard fortune was common knowledge in the city. The details were not. It wasn't my place to confide them, even indirectly. But Rocky's position was unique; his trouble would be the Maynards' trouble.

"If Archie needs it," I said.

"So you *could* give it to me," said Rocky sharply.

"Sorry, Rocky; we've been through that."

"Jim, I'm disappointed; you've always been loyal to me," he said.

I tried to explain myself again without sounding sententious. He tried to dissemble his chagrin. Neither of us succeeded. To change the subject I inquired for Lucy.

"Fine," he said. "She's picking me up at the club in ten minutes to drive me to the airport."

He was still commuting irregularly to the capital and she often chauffeured him to our airport. I asked him to give her my regards but I don't think he even heard me. His mind was on his own troubles. They forced a note of bitterness into his voice.

"One thing you can do, ethically."

"What's that, Rocky?"

"Keep this under your hat, tight."

"All right," I said.

"I'll try to work it out," he said. "But get that dough handy, will you, Jim?"

He was gone before I had time to reply.

[5]

Tom Gilchrist is the owner and publisher of our leading paper. He inherited it from his father, who believed that stability had left this planet with President McKinley. For a generation the *Sentinel* reflected that view to the approval of our end of the state. It had been clamorous for peace, prosperity, piety and independence. When detractors murmured that this translated freely into low wages, high rents and enough bars and brothels to hold the convention trade, the *Sentinel* thundered about radicals and deportation.

It had been a powerful paper and profitable. It afforded Tom an unclouded childhood, a prolonged education in the East and in Europe and a nearly foolproof ultimate legacy. Its revenue from advertising waxed long after it had begun to lose editorial authority to radio and the news magazines.

"I am a fugitive from Sinclair Lewis," Tom used to say. He had matured at an age to be troubled by the epidemic of mockery for everything Midwestern and had been able to afford a long search for perspective. Tom's father had taken subscription charges in corn and traded advertising for shoes. Tom studied his economics and politics in postgraduate seminars.

Side by side in the *Sentinel* you read stentorian demands for One World and earnest assertions that we have the greatest community in the greatest state in the greatest country. Global tumult elbows hog-calling championships in the news columns; local hangnails take precedence over the syndicated accounts of highly placed hangovers in Manhattan and Washington. Neighbors who remonstrate with Tom for printing their parking tickets above the fall of cabinets are solemnly reminded that a free press is the first bulwark of our liberties.

To me Tom will always be much more than a valuable client. Although about ten years my senior, he has befriended me from the earliest days of my practice. We disagree on many things but I shall always be in his debt for a relation he has chosen to make personal as well as professional.

The shadow on his friendly face, as Miss Premm ushered him in about an hour after Rocky left me that day, confirmed my unease. Middle age was then moderating some of Tom's fervors. He still worried more for others than for himself. The *Sentinel*, which meant Tom, had been strongly instrumental in electing Rocky Slade. It had declared him the most promising of native sons and the finest flower of our democratic process. Tom had signed indignant retorts to the opposition's protest that Rocky was a demagogue.

In personal as in public life Tom was always open; even so the bluntness of his first question startled me.

"Jim, are the Maynards giving Rocky money?"

He knew the impropriety of the question as well as I did; with a reflex of belated apology he added:

"Off the records, of course."

"Tom, you know they're my clients."

"And you know they're my friends," he said. "This is to protect them, Jim."

"From what?"

He hesitated and then spoke deliberately.

"Rocky's been spending too much money."

"You wanted that damned freeway," I said.

It was an old argument between us; today he would not rise. He shook his head with an air of weariness.

"I wanted it honestly," he said. "Of course, if it's Maynard money it's all right; it's perfectly all right."

"Why don't you ask Rocky?"

"Can't reach him; he's dodging me," answered Tom.

Piecemeal then, Tom told me what he knew. The *Sentinel* kept a full-time staff man up at the capital. When Rocky had begun his propaganda for Torrent's claims up there the *Sentinel* man, at Tom's behest, had gone out of his way to provide introductions and a veteran's counsel. Rocky had been a tractable pupil through a brief apprenticeship of capital lore. Then, without any open breach, he had withdrawn noticeably from his mentor.

The *Sentinel* man had shrugged over the ways of youth. He told Tom he had seen other fledglings get a big head and get over it. In retrospect he dated Rocky's gradual defection to about the climax of his courtship of Lucy, which consoled his sense of slight.

At about the same time he had noticed that Rocky had begun to spend freely on quasiofficial entertaining. Since Rocky's work amounted to candid lobbying for our end of the state this attracted little attention at first. By the time it became a subject of press gossip Rocky was engaged to Lucy and so under the protective coloration of what had once been a substantial fortune.

In recent weeks, however, the scale of his extravagance had provoked questions on more than Rocky's taste. Belatedly, Tom had learned that Rocky had been maintaining an expensive suite at the

Prairie Plaza in which hundred-proof flowed copiously for other politicians and the local press corps.

Within the week the *Sentinel* man had learned that the Prairie *Times* had quietly assigned a reporter to investigate the sources of this munificence. It was significant that the experienced *Sentinel* man could learn nothing more than that.

Tom had called the owner of the Prairie *Times* at once. Harry Caldwell, like Tom, was a happy man but for very different reasons. Harry despised both parties, all politicians and most men. His misanthropy was incorruptible; it had made his paper a power in the state with national prestige. Ordinarily it ignored the bucolic affairs of our end of Wiasota but that day Tom's call found Harry unnaturally responsive.

Harry had been about to call his old friend in Torrent; he wanted to know whether the Maynards were subsidizing Rocky Slade. Harry had already called Archie Maynard, who told him to go to hell. Subsequently our leading banker had told Harry he could not discuss depositors' affairs. What could Tom tell a colleague? When Tom replied that he did not know, Harry's unwonted cordiality reverted at once to frosty silence.

At lunch Tom had learned that the Prairie *Times* reporter was now asking questions in Torrent. Under normal procedures, Tom told me, a visiting investigator would have utilized the general fraternity of the press for at least a guarded interrogation in the *Sentinel* offices. This one had conspicuously avoided them.

"It's got to be Maynard money," Tom repeated.

"How much is it, Tom?" I asked.

Tom did not know. The *Sentinel* man, now digging quietly himself in Prairie, was already estimating the visible traces at several thousand. Our council salary was three thousand, with no expense account, and Rocky had not yet served a year. All Torrent knew that the Slades were penniless.

Tom had helped to finance Rocky's campaign. The *Sentinel* by rigid policy limited its support to words. Tom, as an individual, often made gifts to both parties. He could be tedious about the duties of citizenship under the two-party system; in other moods he could be droll about its rewards. He called his donations a tithe to vanity. They opened doors, permitted him to entertain visiting bigwigs at breakfasts, bought preferred seats at conventions.

"I'm like a girl who can be had but not too easily," said Tom.

The professionals of both parties distrusted his scruples and courted his support. A word from Tom to the county Republican chairman had been enough to secure the nomination of as popular a young veteran as Rocky. Tom had given three hundred dollars to the general election fund without needing to specify that it be used for his protégé. Rocky's natural drawing power had generated perhaps as much more in smaller contributions.

Tom was sure all of this had vanished in the campaign. Discreet inquiry revealed that our local politicos knew about Rocky's recent extravagances and were irked. Rocky had been a tractable candidate and an independent office-holder. He had never let the professionals forget the size of his plurality. Now every other issue of the *Sentinel* reminded them that he would soon be Archer Maynard's son-in-law. The county chairman had spoken glumly of prima donnas.

"They figure it's Archie or me," said Tom, "and it isn't me."

I think Tom knew as well as I did that it was not Archie but I couldn't say so, at least until I had consulted Archie. On anything except other clients' business Tom and I could be candid with each other.

"Are you thinking of bribery or embezzlement, Tom?"

"I have," Tom admitted, "but I think he's too smart. God knows a lot of money will change hands over that freeway. But Rocky doesn't handle public funds and he won't even vote on them. Naturally every politico makes enemies."

"Enemies who give him money?"

"It's got to be Archie," said Tom.

I said nothing and Tom endured his doubts in silence until they began tumbling out incoherently, half aloud.

". . . think of it; sold papers for my father . . . beat Notre Dame twice . . . in the war, at least in uniform . . . old man's a parson . . . mother president of the All-Torrent Clubwomen . . . just about to marry into our royal family . . ."

"Our paper says we're a democracy, Tom."

"Jim—" he ignored it—"can't you tell me?"

"I can tell Archie you want to know."

He brightened and we discussed the tactics of inquiring without incriminating. It was only a respite for both of us. His next question proved that he knew it too.

"Jim, if Rocky had been, let's say borrowing unwisely, would Archie cover for him?"

"That's a good question, for Archie."

"Jim! This is for Lucy, too!"

"They're still clients."

"Oh for God's sake! So am I," said Tom.

"You're in the clear, Tom," I said and saw, too late, the disappointment in his face.

"Jim, I pushed him into temptation. And for that matter you helped me, at the start. He's our boy."

Of all the men I know, perhaps only Tom would have thought of it that way. Perhaps only innocence ever agonizes about temptation and opportunity but there was an element of truth in his pain. Rocky was our boy. In one way or another we had all helped to put him where he was. I promised Tom I'd find out what I could and walked him out to the anteroom. As we entered it we found ourselves face to face with Lucy Maynard. She and Tom were old friends; he carried off the greetings casually.

"And where is your negligent beau?"

"Flown to Prairie again." She made a wry face. "I'm a freeway widow before I'm even married to the brute."

"Never mind," said Tom. "It'll be nice for commuting to the Governor's mansion."

"Mansion indeed," said Lucy. "Aren't you backing us for the White House?"

"In time," he said. "And don't forget the United Nations."

"Don't *you* forget," said Lucy. "And we'll make you ambassador to Mars."

They chatted a minute more before he excused himself. As I led her into my office his eyes, behind her back, were troubled.

Immediately after the war Lucy had let her hair grow out of the incongruous bob she had worn in the factory. There had been an interim shoulder-length stage, briefly evocative of the child in the wicker pony trap. Once I had told her she should have left it there. She had replied that it was kittenish at her age. If there is an exact point at which unmarried women begin to speak self-consciously of age Lucy had passed it.

That day her hair flamed high above and behind her head. The effect of its deep red-gold, even by the pallid winter light through the window, proved that she had been right about the hair. She knew it, too; the jokes about Lucy's never wearing a hat were envious. Apart from the hair she had never been beautiful except as all young girls are. The bone structure of her face was symmetrical but resolute for a woman. She had clear, inquisitive blue eyes with lovely corn-silk lashes, when she let them alone, and a merry, generous mouth that even lipstick could not entirely disfigure.

She was taller than women like to be but strong and well made. She had the good sense never to slouch, even for shorter dancing partners. From heels to head she stood and walked as straight as a soldier with her shoulders back and her chin up. Yet even through the blurring outlines of the fur coat which she opened on a green wool dress her figure was arrestingly feminine.

Her ordinary manner was so forthright that it handicapped her occasional efforts to deceive. Her grandfather had had guile as well as a callous bluntness. Lucy and her brother had been trained to their father's unblinking candor. As she declined a chair for restless pacing by the bookcase she might as well have told me that her purposes were devious.

"Jim," she asked, "isn't the law dreadfully stuffy?"

"It's people," I said, "and some are."

"You mustn't let yourself become that way."

"We're all part chameleon, Lucy; you have to match your client's mood."

"What if your client is kidding you?"

"You play it straight till you figure out why."

"Can you always figure it out?"

"No," I said. "I can't tell what you're after now."

"So this is how you play it straight?"

"Number Nine professional manner," I said. "What's up, Lucy?"

"Nothing, really, Daddy wants to see you."

I said I'd go right out; she shook her head.

"He said not to interrupt your work."

"This is my work."

"We want you for dinner. Daddy's indignant because you never come any more. The river's pretty clear. If you came early we could skate up to the point and then you and Daddy could talk after dinner. You should, Jim. You're getting pallid in here."

I accepted and she made a pretense of buttoning her coat and then let it drift open and tried to speak casually. When she was troubled her fingers usually toyed with a little gold chain necklace Archie had given her at birth. They were doing it as I watched.

"Jim, can I have some money from the estate, very privately, without bothering Daddy?"

"How much, Lucy?"

"Oh, say, twenty thousand dollars."

"Not without your father's approval."

"Even, say, for just a private present to Rocky?"

"It's still your father's, Lucy."

"I told you the law was stuffy," she said.

"Most people are, about their money."

[11]

"Daddy isn't; he's only stuffy about Rocky."

She elaborated then a well-rehearsed brief. It abraded Rocky's pride to be marrying a girl so much better off. She had been able to find out that with a little capital he could make a killing, through speculation. It was a chance to assuage his self-respect and provide them both with a stake for the hazards of political life.

"Daddy needn't even know about it," she concluded.

"He does before I shovel out his dough, Lucy."

"I knew that's what you'd say!"

"It's what you pay me to say."

"Ethics! They're all self-interest anyway, in the end."

"Why not ask your father, Lucy?"

"Rocky's pride. Honestly! The trouble men make."

She turned and this time fastened her coat tightly.

"Will you just forget this, Jim?"

"No, but I won't talk about it."

"You never talk about anything, do you?"

"A lawyer's tongue is his treasure, Lucy."

"Now you are being stuffy," she said. "But at least, it works both ways. Daddy doesn't know about Rocky and me; I mean, what you know."

"All right," I said. "He won't from me."

"His generation doesn't understand, Jim."

"Lucy, if his generation hadn't understood biology you and I wouldn't be talking about it."

"Jim," she said. "I didn't mean to call you stuffy. Come out about five and we'll have a good skate, the way we used to."

I I I

As I set out through the winter twilight I reflected that I had first gone to River House to help Rocky Slade in Lucy's childhood, perhaps fifteen years before she ever cost me any sleep.

Then in the square I passed the statue of her grandfather with bronze sword, whiskers and McClellan saddle in the pose his generation had considered a link with Sheridan. I remembered that I had been to River House in my own childhood, to steal apples and watch the trotters shod and, as an infant, to attend old Simeon's garden parties. I remembered my father telling me how very near Simeon had come to being hanged in the square he later deeded to our city.

Legend in the state of Wiasota is as elastic as elsewhere. By now it would like to have Simeon one of the pioneers who broke our land in a drought so pitiless that they commemorated it by fastening forever upon settlement, county and river the derisive name of Torrent. Lucy's grandfather was of equal hardihood but in fact he was a land speculator whose techniques are as embarrassing to community as to family memory.

Simeon Maynard appeared in Torrent shortly after the Civil War, already prosperous and mouthing a plausible tale of wanting to grow up with the West. While he made obvious reconnaissances, his confederate, posing as a humble German immigrant, quietly rode the countryside on a condemned Union artillery mule.

Otto Randolph represented himself as a political fugitive from Germany seeking acreage in the new world. He disarmed suspicion by candidly admitting temporary shortage of cash and so made his bargains with the scattered homesteads of the time on an option basis. Against a low ultimate price he offered an enticing immediate fraction, to be forfeited entire if he failed to receive the balance from his remote resources by an early date.

Some of our settlers refused to take advantage of such an innocent. But it is also recorded that when the artless immigrant's negotiations were done, Simeon had options on more than two hundred thousand acres of the best land in the state, cunningly plotted in a nearly solid belt along our main river from the north to the south boundaries of Wiasota.

Then, contemptuously dropping his mask, Simeon went East for a talk with the railroad barons. It was an audacious gamble with the titans of his time. One theory is that Simeon lost by showing his hand too soon. As the railroad men stalled, he had to pick up his options and buy. He did, with both hands. The other theory blames geography for his failure. The great transcontinental roads were finally plotted not to the undulations of our prairie land but to the mountain passes of the Rockies.

Whichever is right, no major railroad spiked a tie in our state for nearly fifty years. They passed us like parentheses and Simeon was stuck with his land and embittered neighbors. Grimly he settled to mastering the culture of the prairie that had trapped him.

The descendants of less tenacious men still whisper about Simeon's luck. He certainly never realized that he was getting bituminous coal, cement shale and limestone as well as our matchless fertility with his tactical purchases. It took more than luck to unify these and the farms into the feudal empire that he made of it.

There was a local saying for years that the difference between Rockefeller and Simeon was that Rockefeller would give you a dime.

The saying itself may have influenced his later benefactions. Every nation on the globe has sent students to the Institute of Agriculture Simeon presently gave our state university.

Simeon's personal consolation for exile in the West was the building of River House. Later generations like to say that it perpetuates the confusion in his mind between Windsor Castle and the LaSalle Street station. Those who knew him recall no confusions in his mind. He said, with his customary tact, that he wanted to show the clover-kickers around him how a gentleman lived; he needed a place large enough to get the whole legislature drunk under one roof. There was a long taproot of truth beneath Tom Gilchrist's half-jocular mention of our royal family.

Through their earlier years in the community Simeon's wife had been pitied as a browbeaten little thing, an opinion widely revised after he began his public benefactions. The wives of the men who envied Simeon could compassionate her because she was apparently barren. Slowly sympathy replaced mockery in the whispers that the seven bedrooms of River House could not produce an heir. Under the same delusion Simeon had extended his largesse from our square, park, hospital and orphans' home to the state university when Torrent was electrified with news of the Maynards' belated blessing.

"Looks like we'll have a crown prince after all," the town chuckled.

Melinda Maynard was nearly forty-four when she bore Archer at River House, a circumstance that revived criticism of everything Maynard. Simeon had just given the town its first hospital; it was not good enough for his own wife; he had brought the consequences on himself. Years later in a despondent moment Archie said to me:

"My first act was to kill my mother."

In fact she lingered until he had passed five. But you cannot look at the portrait of her sad and gentle face, smiling down on his Little Lord Fauntleroy velvets, without thinking how different his life might have been.

Archie was as badly spoiled as a boy could be. By seven he had been given, with personal coachman to attend, the little wicker pony cart his own children drove a generation later until automobiles became too menacing. By nine, in fair weather he often drove the trotters to town under his father's vigilant instruction. A room in the bank building was devoted entirely to the model trains with which he beguiled his waiting. They fill several cases in our Historical Museum today.

Governesses and tutors shielded his erratic hours of study from contamination in our public schools until at about fourteen he began his appalling scholastic record in the most expensive of Eastern boarding schools.

The rest of his time Archie spent with Simeon out of doors, riding their own place and ranging the others throughout the state. His deepest passion, until reading eclipsed it years later, was the broad river flowing past their door.

Long before the spring freshets subsided young Archie knew where the shifted sandbars would attract graveling honkers next fall, where floods had reseeded wild rice and sebago for mallards, where the pools and riffles of lowering water would place bass, walleyes and muskies. My grandfather and father, who often shot with the Maynards along the river or at Widgeon Lake, agreed that young Archie was one of the finest wing shots in the state.

Simeon was equally avid for the open. Before Archie ever set out for boarding school they had extended their collection to the sheep, moose, elk and kodiak heads which nearly covered the walls of the ballroom. They augmented it during Archie's vacations and the awkward interims between his many schools.

Archie was never stupid. He went to boarding school ill prepared, he hated confinement, he soon realized that you can run away from a school you do not like. He did not like several of them. Simeon scolded him, engaged new tutors, scheduled longer trips. But Archie had learned to run away.

The habit may have been confirmed into a career by Simeon's garden parties. They must have been painful for a sensitive boy. Toward the end of his life the old man waxed ferociously patriotic. The Fourth of July coincided with the perfection of his roses. What began as a social function became an institution. At this Simeon, in full G.A.R uniform, presided over flag ceremonies of his own devising and presently took to reading aloud the Gettysburg Address.

This final conceit was variously regarded as ludicrous, blasphemous or both. Simeon had a right to his uniform. As he grew heavier it was replaced by new ones, with epaulettes widened annually to his aging shoulders. Archie must have been as uncomfortable with those as with the whispering they provoked.

Many Torrent families have anecdotes of Simeon. I witnessed ours as an infant but I have heard it so often that I might as well have consciously suffered the humidity, the sun, the muttered resentment among the overdressed guests, the quavering intonations of the red-faced old man declaiming "Fourscore and seven years ago" as his company panted for refreshment.

Simeon always rewarded attendance with champagne for the

ladies, juleps for the men and ginger ale for the young. He was too artful to have these served until he had had his ceremony. That day we sweltered with the others until he finished and began his punctilious tour from group to group. At ours he tempered his civilities with a reproach to Grandpa Denton for not having worn his uniform.

"Mine got dirty, Simeon," said my grandfather. "Now cut out this humbug and give us some whiskey."

My grandmother spent the rest of her days rapturously insisting to anyone who would listen that this was the most mortifying moment of her life. She was very pleased when Simeon called in person to inform her that he would be the speaker at Grandpa's funeral.

After Archie was kicked out of the third college Simeon became restive over his interest in the local belles. Many of our matrons would have been willing to see their daughters presiding at River House. Simeon declared that travel was the only true education and set out with the boy for the grand tour.

He returned alone and dangerously uncommunicative. True culture could not be absorbed by trippers. Archie was remaining in Europe to steep himself in the real thing. Simeon hinted of the diplomatic career. The estate papers of the time record substantial donations to both parties.

Archie worked hard at being continental. The first copies of the *Illustrated London News*, *Sketch* and *Tattler* that ever reached Torrent were open, in the library at River House, to pictures of Archie in appropriate regalia and expensive company at Cowes, Ascot, Biarritz and Nice. The estate papers record payment of a draft drawn by Brown Brothers of London to recompense them for honoring Archie's note to the Monte Carlo correspondent of the Crédit Lyonnais in the sum of one hundred and eighty-six thousand francs. Those were twenty-cent gold francs.

At the outbreak of the First World War Simeon cabled Archie a peremptory summons home. Archie replied at once, demanding a copy of his birth certificate to facilitate his enlistment in the French Army. Simeon rewrote the will he had drawn at Archie's birth and sent the boy a copy. It stipulated that unless he returned at once and thereafter spent six months a year in Wiasota he would be disowned with one dollar. Archie's return cable is in the estate records:

"The problem is not your death but my rebirth. Send certificate at once."

Simeon would not send it and so, instead of the army, Archie joined one of the first American volunteer ambulance units. From this he later transferred to the American Army, which, as he once confided to me, set a more realistic appraisal on the relative values of paper and cognac.

After America entered the war Simon appended a codicil to the will and a dubious document the Tuttlewise office managed to make of it. The evident intention was forgiveness. Implacability still chills the words. In effect it allowed Archie grace for time spent in the service of his country. Otherwise he was hog-tied to six months a year in Wiasota until age forty-five, the estate being placed in trust under the Tuttlewise office and the Maynard National Bank.

This wrinkled brows in our probate court when Simeon died in the summer of 1918 without ever seeing his son again. Fortunately the will was admitted while Archie was still on active duty. He was wounded, near Vigneulles in the Saint-Mihiel offensive in September, and for many months the Tuttlewise office lost all track of him. They are scarcely to be blamed. As soon after the armistice as he could walk Archie had walked out of hospital and army alike. In the sequel it took Senator Gustafson several years to have the matter adjusted.

Drafts, which the trustees continued to honor, finally located Archie at San Sebastián. There despite their protestations he remained for over two years. With the nervous consent of all on this side of the water the codicil of the will was stretched to accommodate his laconic statement that he was recovering from wounds. Horace Tuttlewise and Hewitt Randolph at the bank were considering returning responsibility to the court when they received his cable. Archie was bringing his bride home so that their child could be born in River House. He authorized any arrangements necessary to protect them if he did not survive the journey. In fact they reached River House in ample time for the birth of Lucy and her twin brother Arthur. Dr. Jamison, who delivered them, reported that Archie's first comment was:

"By God, neither of them will be an only child!"

There had been skepticism about Archie's wounds which his reappearance settled at once. He had fled the hospital in a cast to avoid a projected amputation. He had taken machine-gun bullets and grenade fragments frontally. He would always limp and lung scars kept him convalescent for several years. As a hundred-pound boy Archie had stood up to the ten-gauge Bosses, Greeners and Parkers in Simeon's rack. When he resumed shooting years later it was with a custom-made twenty-eight, weighted and bored at full cylinder to reduce recoil.

Those who expected Archie's foreign marriage to turn River House into an outpost of the Folies Bergère were disappointed. Elsie Gaither was an American girl from respectable people in Cleveland. She was energetic, resourceful and high-spirited. She may have been the first woman in Torrent to drive a gasoline automobile. She was certainly the first of her kind to smoke cigarettes openly.

She had gone to Europe as a volunteer for the Red Cross and met Archie in the base hospital, from which she assisted his flight to San Sebastián. Their marriage certificate is in our safe and, as long as I handle the family business, will remain there.

"She said I was worthless but sweet," Archie told me years later. "I hope I was; I wanted to be sweet to her."

Unfortunately there remains of her not even a portrait. She was sitting for the one Archie had commissioned of her and the twins when she was stricken with influenza and died in the first year of their lives.

Archie's devotion to her had consequences as ironic as they were sad. There was no dearth of candidates to replace Elsie. Archie's indifference to them assumed in time the proportions of a climactic affront to our community. The women of Torrent, as I have cause to know, will tolerate anything in a man but singleness. Archie would not remarry.

This reanimated the old gossip with new malice. No man could rear children of that age, history was repeating itself, River House could produce only grief and profligacy, Archie was keeping a milliner in Chicago and the proprietress of a thread shop on Fourth Street, he was a drunkard, an idler, an atheist, impotent and worse.

In fact Archie kept a suitably aged trained nurse in the house throughout the twins' infancy and an exemplary Swedish couple through their childhood. His importation of a mademoiselle for Lucy provoked a fresh outburst until her arrival. Unfortunately for everyone Mademoiselle resembled a bottle with a mustache. She soon, however, provided a secondary grievance by taking the twins to Mass. Torrent is widely divided in religious views. It remained for Archie to offend a score of convictions with one shrug:

"All religion is the same."

He would never attend church; he waited for his children outside a variety of Sunday schools in all weather. One of the Protestant phases produced another storm. Lucy astounded an abstemious sect by precocity in Bible lore. She explained innocently:

"Daddy reads it to us after dinner with his brandy."

There were other differences at River House for those willing to see. The twins drove the wicker pony cart with only casual supervision from the aging McClintic. They harnessed, fed and currycombed the pony themselves. They drove it often to the neighbors'. Archie kept his house swarming with their friends.

There were never any tutors. The twins attended public schools and dancing school in town. They were punctual and attentive and got good marks. And they and the children for miles around adored Archie.

From his own contemporaries Archie remained much withdrawn. After some disastrous experiments with the handling of his affairs he abandoned them again to Hewitt Randolph and the Tuttlewises. He would work with patience and skill at anything unproductive—carving decoys, tying flies, splicing rods, training the dogs, shaping stocks and intricate amateur gunsmithing. He did these things in solitude.

He was always good for cards or billiards at the Torrent Club while he waited for the children to emerge from school, doctor or dentist. He dined occasionally with a diminishing circle of friends. Simeon's cellar could still make River House a beacon in the long darkness of prohibition.

More and more, however, Archie retired into personal seclusion. A community that had looked to River House for cotillions as well as authority shook its head over the shuttered windows behind which he played happily with his children until their bedtime released him to books and more brandy.

Gossip remembers more of the cognac than of the library in which he drank it. Archie came late to his education. He pursued it most of every night, matching its stimulus with larger drams than other men could carry. He carried them at home and abroad with unbroken dignity.

Archie was drinking brandy and water the afternoon of my first formal call on him. I disliked him that day. Explanations are usually excuses. Archie needs none. For myself I can say only that it was easier to dislike him than to admit despising myself for the errand to which Rocky Slade's mother had committed me.

I V

Rocky Slade had come by his football prowess naturally. The Reverend Luther Slade was a massive figure with an organ of a voice, a great leonine shock of white hair and a serenity said to derive from his inner peace. In his own day he had been a halfback of renown at a neighboring county high school and later at State.

There, between his last football game and mid-term exams, he had acknowledged the call. With divine assistance he hoped to renounce the university and temporal life. Our church of his faith became the

[19]

first instrument of this assistance by sending him through Torrent Divinity School. While attending it he met Winifred Parmenter.

Winifred was a contemporary of my parents, perhaps two or three years older than Archie. Her father had been a farmer and then a dealer in grain who owned elevators. Winifred had grown up to advantages which, unhappily, had not survived Mr. Parmenter's prophecies of wheat prices.

Some people date her disillusionment with all things temporal from that time. Others speak of the coincidence of Archie's departure on the grand tour and Luther's appointment to our local church. She married Luther that year.

Their sect was small, devout and fiercely proud of its humility. When she embraced it Winifred had loudly relinquished the social vanities of her youth. A realistic experience of humility in the dismal rectory soon expanded her views. It became obvious to her that no life could be a power for good until it was a power.

She began her new consecration by vigorous activity for woman suffrage and extended her triumph with that through the entire orbit of female civic Torrent. Red Cross, Parent-Teachers, Visiting Nurses, Welfare Board, Ladies' Aid, Protestant Council, Inter-Faith Group and City Planning found her successively a hard worker and a firm president. The All-Torrent Clubwomen was nearly her single-handed creation. Many questions were asked about it; no one ever doubted who would be its permanent president.

Concurrently Winifred bore and raised five children, of whom Rocky was the oldest. They were not pampered. From the cradle it was impressed upon them that while they were just as good as anyone in town the life of service must not expect its rewards in this world's goods. They must learn to do for themselves and get on.

From childhood Rocky sold papers, cut lawns, tended furnaces, understudied the janitor of their church. His sisters did such housework as was done in the maelstrom of the rectory. Winifred did not escape criticism for their hectic home life. She ignored it for concentration upon their adjustment to the outer world, which she supervised from vantage posts in the Parent-Teachers, Neighborhood and Motherhood Leagues.

Slowly the rest of us learned that it wasn't fair for the scouts to hike before Rocky's work was done. It was only fair for teammates to help with the star pitcher's chores. It wasn't fair to plan picnics or parties while he worked. It wasn't fair of adults to hire lawn mowing from boys whose parents had more of this world's goods. The town rule against freshmen on varsity teams was changed the year Rocky entered high school; it wouldn't have been fair to him.

Being three classes ahead of Rocky removed me a little from these general strictures. My turn came a few weeks before my graduation from high school. Winifred ambushed me one day by stopping the Welfare Board's car, which she habitually drove, across my way home.

"Jim," she said, "I hear you're showing wonderful leadership in school."

I would like to plead youth; my trouble was vanity. If I dimly realized that flattery always wants something, I had had little enough to find it heady. I had led nothing. My grades were acceptable; my rating on scrub teams was lower.

"Leadership," said Winifred, "can make you of great service, Jim."

Before I realized it I had agreed to discuss this glittering possibility at the rectory next afternoon.

"Just you and I," she said. "Rocky will be at track."

It was raining when Winifred received me in the parlor. The windows had to be shut; strings of laundry brought indoors permeated the disorder with a pallid stench. Through the open kitchen door Maybelle Lou squawked in her crib. Thelma and Veronica quarreled over the breaking and washing of a monumental pile of dishes, peering out at us as they wiped the sturdier ones. From the closed study door came the unmistakable rhythms of the Reverend's regular snoring. In a corner of the parlor Hazel, then about ten, squinted sullenly under a flickering light as she hand-addressed a hundred and fifty notices of a P.T.A. meeting.

"She won't mind us at all," said Winifred and seated herself close to me on the sagging sofa. She was a large woman with black hair and bold coloring. The heat of the room added a little mustache of beads to her floridity. I moved as far from her as possible.

The times, Winifred told me, that Rocky had already made in the hundred- and two-twenty-yard dashes would have won both events in the previous year's Regional Interscholastic Meet in Chicago. I could see for myself what that would mean to Torrent, to all of Wiasota.

The hitch was financial. Unfair as it was, our athletic budget could not send a contestant to Chicago. The raising of a subscription fund was a clear challenge to my leadership.

An unworldly boy like Roscoe could not go to Chicago alone. Winifred and the Reverend would make the sacrifice of accompanying him, even though it meant being away from their other darlings. She showed me a budget to cover the trip for three.

I don't think I ever did accept. I didn't have to. She had progressed to selected contributors when the door opened on Rocky in the varsity sweater and school baseball cap that were then practically his uniform. He greeted me negligently and then his eyes narrowed on Winifred.

"What are you after Jim for?" he asked.

"Never mind, dear. Why aren't you practicing?"

"Rained out," said Rocky. "You deaf or something?"

Winifred's mind had been in Chicago; now she nodded.

"So it is. Put the pans in the study, Roscoe."

"Why can't Dad do his own damned pans?"

"Roscoe! Don't swear at your mother. Your father is meditating on his sermon."

"He's snoring," said Rocky. "Why do I have to do everything around here?"

"You don't!" screamed Hazel from her corner. "You never have to address these stinking cards."

"Children," said Winifred, "what will Jim think of you? Your grandfather Parmenter was a close friend of his grandparents."

"If Grandpa was so good why don't we have a car?" asked Rocky.

"Roscoe," said Winifred, "put those pans in your father's study this very minute—or something nice that only you and I know won't happen."

Hazel burst into wailing screams.

"Why don't I get something nice for these cards—I hate them— hate them—HATE THEM."

Rocky made a face at her. She threw a handful of cards at him. He began to throw them back. I reached the front door while Winifred was getting them out of the room. She caught me on the porch.

"One little hint, Jim," she said. "Archer Maynard would never miss the whole amount."

That night I took my first lesson in fund raising at our dinner table. It is one thing to know you've been coerced, another to admit it. I represented the idea as spontaneous.

"What made you think of it?" demanded my father.

"It would be good for Torrent," I lied.

"The only good thing for Torrent would be sending those damned Slades to Patagonia," said my father.

"James!" said my mother.

"I've told you before about earning things or doing without them," said my father. "It still applies—to you and the Slades."

A glance from my mother stopped him. As I went upstairs to study I heard it come up again in the parlor.

". . . a generous impulse," said my mother.

"We'll have to put him in the government," said my father.

Next morning she gave me five dollars. Father gave me a considered permission to contribute as heavily as I chose—from my own allowance.

"It'll buy you a good lesson in other people's business."

At school I formed an apathetic committee. We rang doorbells and waited in anterooms downtown. Enthusiasm expired fast, leaving me fifty-six dollars short.

I bicycled the seven miles out to River House along the Ridge Road with reluctant legs. It seemed a bad omen to encounter old McClintic with the wicker pony cart at the head of the lane. The twins went to our school by a co-operative car system among their neighbors then, but they could sometimes wheedle McClintic into meeting them with the cart at the lane. The last time he and I had met was in their orchard and he remembered it. I explained with dignity that I was calling on Mr. Maynard himself.

"He won't be in the strawberry patch," said McClintic.

I wheeled down through the oaks, maples and pines of the upper woods and paused at the clearing for final assault.

Simeon had placed his fieldstone and slate monolith well down the long slope of the moraine. The site gave him blizzard shelter to the north at his back, a five-mile reach of the river, which there ran nearly east and west, at his feet and a fourteen-mile view across the valley, of which he could once say that he owned every visible inch.

By then ivy had softened the harsh rectangularity of the house. Gothic north windows reflected fifty years of mowing and rolling on the parklike lawns of the upper yard. Paired oaks and elms along the winding bluestone driveway spread an avenue of shade to the north porte-cochere.

On the upstream side, from well above the house, sloped a meticulous succession of vineyards and orchards that ran down to the greenhouses and rose gardens, threaded with a gravel path to boathouse and dock. On the downstream side ranged kitchen gardens, poultry sheds, stables, paddock and pastures.

Before the house itself emerald terraces descended to the river's edge. Swallows and martins cut glinting arcs around the white flagpole. A seasonal aroma of cutting beds and greenhouses mingled with the sweetness of honeysuckle and the aromatic scent of pines. Doves cooed from them; beyond a plaintive bobwhite reproached the fickle hens of his covey.

The long valley across the river was ripening corn and wheat as far as the eye could see, broken only by the white smoke plume of a chugging train. Every few years those flats flooded the train tracks, to the distress of shippers and stockholders alike. This had been foreseen when Simeon had put them on the lowlands. He would no more have considered trains on the firm slope near his house than I, that day, could have imagined the state would one day project a freeway through his rose gardens.

I have remembered often the beauty I saw then, ordered, serene and secure. At the time my thoughts were not aesthetic. I dreaded the impending interview.

I knew Archie Maynard as a rare guest of my parents and the most considerate of hosts when Father and I shot the Maynard river shores or fields. Twice, at his explicit suggestion, I had been taken with the older men to the Maynard place at Widgeon Lake.

"It's time that boy got started right," he had said to my father. There was more than hospitality in it. One fanatic knows another; Archie could understand my passion for shooting.

Unobtrusively, almost diffidently, he had unfolded to me his knowledge of boats, blinds, winds, loads, leads, decoys and inexhaustible information on fowl themselves. At night I had lain sleepless with excitement in the unheated upstairs rooms of his lodge. I had savored the frosty air and the scents of cigars, woodsmoke, shell wax, gun oil and kerosene lamps and listened to the occasional explosions of laughter from the poker table below. I knew I owed Archie more than any mortal could ever repay. I was about to beg from him.

Old Weicker answered my gingerly twitch of the door pull with more surprise than pleasure. I had encountered him in the orchard as well as McClintic. That afternoon his hands were stained with brass polish. Finger marks from it showed on the white coat he had buttoned hastily askew. He was doubly vexed to have buttoned it for me.

"Mind your feet on my parquetry," he said sternly.

Except for the library the formal rooms at River House are dark and oppressive. The hall has an austere and gloomy chill. You emerge from it to the crowning amenity of the south verandah, to sunlight on the sparkling river, to dappling leaf patterns on greensward, to a vista of far fields under blobs of heavy cumulus.

There I found Archie seated beside a small inlaid table. On it were a copy of Gibbon, a decanter, carafe, cut-glass tumbler and small mother-of-pearl box. In his lap was a mass of proxy notices from which he was tidily scissoring the stamps into the box. This was his favorite, and very nearly his solitary, economy. Years later when the companies began metering postage he told me that technology had terminated his career.

At an hour when every other man in the state was working Archie lounged in white linen shirt and tennis flannels. He was immaculately shaved and pomaded. His flaxen hair lay tight under waxy restraint of the natural curls he hated. His clear skin would never sunburn. Summer reddened it unbecomingly and inflamed a little the penetrating gray eyes behind his black-ribboned pince-nez.

He arose to offer me a ceremonious handshake and inquire gravely if I would join him in a glass of brandy. The flicker of amusement at my hasty refusal was sympathetic.

"The more for me," he said. "How are your parents?"

There are people who complain of derision in Archie's easy urbanity. Formal he was, but I never knew him unkind; no man I ever met could accord you such a flattering entirety of attention. We spoke a little of shooting. Then I got to work and he listened with concentration before taking a thoughtful sip of brandy.

"Fifty-six dollars is a sizable deficit."

I spoke of civic pride.

"Your troubles are the measure of that," he said.

I spoke of prospective glory for city and state.

"I'm thinking of the boy," said Archie.

There had been many excuses for not giving. This was a new one. I couldn't help contrasting the opulence around me with the Slades' parlor. I hated what I was doing; I wanted to blame Archie. I repeated my rehearsed arguments.

"Jim, do you know what an ethic is?"

"No, sir."

"You should taste before you swallow," said Archie. "Three times now you have said: 'fair to Rocky.' I'm not sure whether this nonsense is by Christianity out of Democracy or vice versa. Either way it's a bad horse to bet."

I didn't understand; this seemed dangerously afield from our duty to Rocky.

"He has a right to an education, sir."

"You've changed the subject," said Archie patiently. "But let's call my refusal to subsidize this nonsense part of his education."

"You won't subscribe then, sir?"

"Not a cent. Where are you going to college?"

He heard my plans and sipped again, thoughtfully.

"That is many years in one state."

His observation probed an old family issue. My mother had urged a change for either college or law school. Father had pronounced it ostentation. Once in my hearing he had asked her how much good four prep schools and three colleges had done our leading educational exhibit. I was resentful enough to think of quoting it to Archie; I thought twice and cited my father's argument that I had been born in Torrent and would live here.

"Moses was born in the bulrushes and Columbus in Italy," said Archie.

Then we both heard the patter of the pony's hoofs on the bluestone change to clump-clumping as they hit the sod. In a second Lucy drove the wicker cart around the box beds and straight across the velvet lawn to the verandah steps.

As she tossed the reins over the dashboard we could see tear stains and dust marring the pinkness of her young face. Her hair flamed out of its one blue ribbon as she hit the grass and bounced up the steps to Archie. Then she saw me. Emotion and discipline struggled briefly; she was still a child.

"Daddy, I bit Mrs. Slade and made her hand bleed!"

"Lucy," said Archie, "we have a caller."

"It's only Jim Denton," she said. Then, at his look, she dropped me a perfunctory curtsy. Lucy could throw a hard snowball in those days; she could also understand Archie's quiet inflections. The check had restored her composure a little; elation lingered.

"Why did you bite her?" asked Archie.

"She slapped me," said Lucy. Then, after a defiant look at me, "About sex."

Ignorant as I was of what Archie called an ethic I had the going local convictions on sex. Her very use of the word violated our ethic. Our high school had nice girls who never spoke of sex and often enjoyed it. We had hot numbers who spoke of little else and often refused it. But no boy or girl I knew would have breathed the word before a parent. Archie chuckled and replied as to an equal.

"That's interesting; Mrs. Slade slapped me about sex once."

Lucy exploded into laughter.

"Did she? Tell me about it."

"Some day," said Archie. "What happened today?"

Then Lucy remembered me again and he saw her quick uncertain glance.

"It's all right," he said. "Jim's old enough."

She looked at me once more and then forgot me. Archie had told her it was all right. She plunged into her story eagerly. Lucy had stayed late at school to swap pictures for her collection of movie stars. Ordinarily this exchange operated at private houses. That day Hazel

Slade was involved and had to wait at school until her mother finished a Parent-Teachers meeting.

Trading had been brisk and apparently loud. Lucy had refused to scissor her scrapbook before agreement on her terms of her Ralph Graves for Hazel's Ramon Navarro. Stalemate switched the talk from commerce to marriage. The girls were asserting their choices among the stars when Mrs. Slade arrived to invite them all to the rectory for cambric tea.

She had overheard enough marriage plans to remind the girls firmly that moving picture stars were common vulgar people no nice girl would think of marrying. Nice girls, said Mrs. Slade, built lofty dream castles. Then, if they were good, a real Prince Charming from a fine old family in Chicago would propose to them and make their dreams come true.

"Will he give us babies?" Lucy had asked.

Mrs. Slade said that nice girls didn't talk about having babies. Lucy must say she was sorry unless she wanted her mouth washed out with soap. Lucy had not wanted that. She said she was sorry but how could they have babies without talking to Prince Charming about it?

Mrs. Slade said God would attend to that. If they were good girls and said their prayers regularly, some morning they would wake up to find the babies waiting, perhaps behind a beautiful rose bush in the garden of the castle.

"And that's a lie, isn't it, Daddy?"

"That's a lie," said Archie. "Did you tell her so?"

"What I really said was: 'That isn't true!' Then I started to tell her what you told Artie and me and she slapped me and held her hand over my mouth and I bit it and Gretchen and I ran out to Aunt Madge in the car but we didn't tell Aunt Madge."

"Do you often play with Hazel?" asked Archie.

"No. She cries and throws things."

"Do you know her brother Roscoe?"

"Everyone does! Gretchen has a crush on him!"

"Has he a crush on Gretchen?"

"Of course not; he's too old for our class."

"Would you like to see Roscoe run in the Interscholastic Meet in Chicago?"

"Oh! Daddy! *Could* we, and see Aunt Victoria and try on all the hats?"

"Perhaps. Now bring my checkbook from the desk and then take Bucephalus to the stable. Your piano lesson is at four-thirty and you must wash up."

She sped about the errands with the happy resilience of her age. Then, reins in hand, she looked back to the verandah.

"Daddy, I *was* right, wasn't I?"

"Not to bite people."

"But if that's true why did she slap me?"

"Some people don't like the truth."

"Then why do I always have to tell it?"

"So you won't be like them. Do you want to be like Mrs. Slade?"

"Not for anything!" said Lucy and drove off, laughing.

Archie sighed, opened the checkbook and squinted over the top of it at me.

"Your ethic of being fair to Rocky presupposes knowing what *is* fair. Are you sure about this?"

"No, sir," I said.

"Nor am I," said Archie cheerfully. "And we've just had evidence of a Higher Confusion than ours. I doubt that Chicago will square it but we can try."

He began to write a check. Then we both heard the voice of Weicker in the hall and the click of heels on the parquetry. Archie closed the checkbook as Winifred Slade burst out onto the verandah. Her face was as red as the stains on her handkerchief-bound hand.

"Winifred," said Archie, "may I offer you some brandy?"

"You may certainly not! I have to see you alone."

"It happens," said Archie, "that I have company."

"Then I will tell you in front of Jim. You're ruining Lucy!"

"By not slapping her for intelligent questions?"

"Archie! She is not old enough!"

"She was old enough to ask."

She gave an angry gasp and her nostrils flared.

"I did not come here to talk sophistries!"

"Winifred," said Archie. "I must advise you solemnly not to slap Lucy again."

"I was wrong about that," conceded Winifred.

"I'll give your apology to Lucy," he said.

"Archie, you'll cut her off from decent children."

"Do you mean that you will?"

"There will be talk about this; I can't lie."

"Winifred," said Archie, "the truth is much too precious for either of us to be reckless with it."

They stared at each other in silence, perhaps three seconds. Then Winifred turned and vanished into the hall, slamming the screen door behind her. Archie seated himself, resumed his writing in the checkbook and handed me a check. The fifty-six dollars were payable to me personally.

"A condition, Jim. Don't tell where you got it."

"Sir, people might think it's from Father."

"No one who knows him will," said Archie, and smiled. "It would be droll if they do. He's always refused to represent me."

"I guess the office is pretty busy, sir," I said.

"So he tells me," replied Archie dryly. "I hope your addition will enlarge its capacities. Come and see me when you're ready to practice."

The dictionary at home said that ethic was the rare singular form of ethics and related to the whole field of morals. It was a field I still associated exclusively with sex. I was still a little shocked by Lucy's candor on that topic. It was many years before it occurred to me to wonder whether Mrs. Slade had always slapped Archie about sex.

My fund was raised and I was glad to drop the whole matter. Rocky won two medals in Chicago and that summer Hazel began the screaming fits which kept her, intermittently, in the county hospital until her elopement.

Chapter Two

BY winter moonlight the River House I approached that January evening fifteen years later might have seemed the same place. Snow has a kinship with sleep and death. A heavy fall of it had shrouded in white silence the neglected ruin of lawn and gardens. A puffy frosting hid the scaling roofs of stables and sheds.

The dark block of the house still cast a firm shadow on the white serenity around it. The river still wound its silver scar of ice through brooding stoical trees and endless plain. Eastward, through the leafless branches, I could see the blaze of lights at Hewitt Randolph's place and beyond them the distant glow of the city. Westward, snow hid the jungle that had been vineyards and masked the underbrush choking the old orchards.

Beauty the place still had, or took from the mercy of the snow. My heart was heavy with knowledge of its inner wounds. I had been managing the Maynard affairs for over a year then. Neither words nor arithmetic could make Archie and Lucy understand as I did the remorseless fiscal combustion that was devouring it from rusted guy wires in the top-heavy elms to unfathomed catastrophes maturing in the pipes.

Looking down on it then I knew it would be a blessing if Rocky did steer the freeway right through the rose garden. But euthanasia is comforting only in the abstract. An instinct stronger than duty still wanted to defy the bulldozers.

Old Weicker no longer polished brass or answered the doorbell. The place had consumed the energies of his life. Now, with nine others on the pension payroll, he was helping to consume it. His grumbling Frieda insisted on continuing her lifetime struggles with the old coal stoves in the cavernous downstairs kitchens. Only death would end her forty-year quarrel with Douglass, who answered my pull at the bell with a frigid curtsy. She, too, was more liability than help; she was still up to letting me feel her indignation at the new economies.

[30]

"He's in the library, sir. And Allen says without more pressure in the pipes he can't be responsible about the west wing plumbing."

After the glacial hall the library glowed with warmth and light. Its two fireplaces had preceded the age of central heating; their dancing flickers mocked the decay of that upstart innovation. Lucy herself kept the brass on screens and irons gleaming.

Bookcases hid most of the stains and cracks on the old wallpaper. The inside shutters sustained an illusion of impregnable security. The old portraits smiled, or, in Simeon's case, glared down from the half-light of the primitive electric fixtures. These, and the radio which Archie had finally accepted to hear war news, were the only discordant elements in an atmosphere already past its threescore years and ten.

Archie sprang from his chair and limped briskly half across the room to wring my hand. His flaxen hair was white by then; the notable difference was in his manner. He had drowsed away his active years in languid indolence. Age had brought him a peppery briskness. Many people remarked it with approval; it reminded me of a conversation with the man we had consulted about the orchards:

"They flower wonderfully just before they die."

He waved my briefcase contemptuously to the table.

"After dinner; Lucy says you're skating."

"Come on," said Lucy from the door, "before you get too warm in here."

"I'll make sidecars while you're gone," Archie beamed.

He spoke rarely of that earlier World War; his limp and a passion for brandy above all spirits were what remained of it.

"Sidecars," said Lucy, "are probably why Jim never comes out any more. I'll have one with you but Jim prefers bourbon."

Upstairs I put on skating pants and sweaters and then we walked together down the winding paths to the boathouse. It was much more than that. Simeon had built it for shooting and skating parties as well as bathers. In their childhood it had been a second home for Lucy, Artie and their friends.

Canoes and duck boats filled a lower extension of it with pilings and slips right out into the water. The upper part was a spacious all-weather playhouse, open on three sides in summer to lovely vistas of the river. In winter its huge fireplace had been a haven for three generations of skaters and gunners.

I had spent happy moments there and there, also, I had spent the worst ones of my life. We were both stiff with constraint at the memory of them as we went down the path. I had wondered if she would enter. She did and flicked on the light by the door as naturally as if neither of us had ever been there.

Inside we said nothing. She would not accept my help with her skates and had them on before mine were ready. We emerged into snow-reflected moonlight so bright you could have read a paper. As we stepped out the door she looked suddenly at my face.

"Why, James! You *are* blushing, just to be here. You're a worse Puritan than Rocky. Come on; I'll beat you to the point."

She did, too. She and Artie had inherited Archie's passion for the river in all its guises. Either of them could swim upstream for miles. She skated with an easy, expert sweep of long legs, jumping clean over the snowdrifts and turning sometimes to float before me with elusive rhythm as she skated backwards.

We rested at the point, keeping our conversation entirely on the ice and moon and night, and then skated back down the river together, moving more slowly through the white silence.

Just before we reached the boathouse she took a long final look around and skated over very close to me.

"When I do this I always remember Artie and Vinty; they loved it too, Jim."

After we had changed from skates to shoes and started up the path she spoke again, too casually.

"By the way, I asked Daddy about the money; he'll tell you it's all right."

At dinner she was unnaturally vivacious and as perverse as Archie himself. They always enjoyed teasing each other; tonight her merriment was a mask for the troubled mood she had shown me in the office. By tacit consent their teasing always excluded Rocky; the rest of his family was fair game during Douglass's absences from the dining room.

"Mother Slade sent you her love today, Daddy," she said demurely.

"Tell her I don't want it," said Archie.

"She wants a little talk with you, about Grandma's linen."

"She can steal it all, the day I die," said Archie.

"The Reverend still wants a church wedding."

"Do you?" He was suddenly serious.

"No; I'm sorry about Jim but if we break the family rule we'll have a mob scene."

Archie had been perturbed; he enjoyed his revenge now.

"Perhaps we should, dear. That female chiropractor could hand out cards."

"Daddy! You know perfectly well Hazel is not a chiropractor; she just married one."

"At least she got out of being a Slade."

"Now, Daddy, you're not marrying them."

"Remind Mother Slade of that or I'll keep my threat." He turned to grin at me. "I hope to get her and the Reverend drunk at the wedding."

"You will not," said Lucy. "You can save up and disgrace our first reception in the Governor's mansion."

She had coffee in the library with us and then, as we progressed into cigars and brandy, excused herself.

"I'm going to pine by the phone till Rocky calls," she said. "Remember your promise about skating soon, Jim. You're in that office too much."

I watched her kiss Archie's forehead and vanish into the hall. We smoked in silence for a minute before I reached for my briefcase. There were always things for him to sign but he waved the case away.

"Just routine, aren't they?"

"Yes, sir."

"Then you sign them and stop calling me sir. You all had too much rank this time but even so I was only a lieutenant."

"Very well, Lieutenant," I said.

He grinned and then it faded from his face and he looked back to the door Lucy had closed on us.

"Jim, that halfback's in trouble."

"What kind of trouble, Archie?"

"Money, of course. Heard anything about it?"

"Some gossip," I said, wondering if he could see the reddening I felt in my face. I could tell him what Tom had said. Lucy and Rocky had both asked my confidence.

When I took over the Maynard business I had privately blamed much of its calamitous condition upon Hewitt Randolph and Horace Tuttlewise, who had managed it before me. Neither of them ever made Archie face the facts. Now I was preparing to withhold facts of concern to him. I thought of my father's dinner table long ago and of other times since. Somehow everywhere you touched Rocky Slade you wound up lying a little.

"It's more than gossip," said Archie and launched into explanation.

Lucy had gone to Prairie that week, for trousseau shopping and to dine and dance with Rocky, who was approaching the climax of his freeway lobbying. She had planned to spend two or three nights, depending on the duration of fittings. She had returned after one, visibly disturbed.

Archie forbore questioning, as he systematically did about the engagement. Then abruptly she had raised the question of money, expressing her hope that Archie would subsidize the marriage substantially.

They had skirted the subject before with embarrassment. She knew even better than Archie the crippled condition of the estate. She did not want to impose on him. He cared nothing about the estate, everything was for her anyway. His instinct opposed any agreed subsidy. He thought the long-range effect on Rocky and the marriage would be bad. He cited our local tradition of self-reliance. He hoped that she and Rocky would live with him; everything would be theirs anyway when he was gone. He thought she seemed as relieved to drop the subject as he was.

Rocky had returned to Torrent later in the week but to stay with his parents instead of at River House, where he had often week-ended since the engagement. Though she was much with him, Archie saw that she continued tense and disturbed. Then, out of a clear sky, Harry Caldwell had called Archie from Prairie to ask if he was already subsidizing Torrent's most talkative County Councilor.

Archie had barely enjoyed the satisfaction of telling Harry to go to hell when Harry's reporter from the Prairie *Times* had appeared at River House.

"Mr. Brady," said Archie, "tried to humbug me about what he called the romantic angle, the poor-boy rich-girl nonsense, but every other word was fishing about Roscoe. He wanted a picture of them together under the Sargent of Father. He wanted to know if Father would have approved Roscoe's efforts to run the freeway through my rose garden; he wanted to know if I was backing Roscoe for a permanent career in politics."

Luckily Lucy was absent, driving Rocky to the airport. Archie was wondering whether to tell her about the reporter when she had returned to the house quite upset. She told him she wanted to make Rocky an immediate present of twenty thousand dollars. She had asked me to dinner, knowing he would want to consult me. He had told her that if it was serious she could have it, of course. He would instruct me to raise it. She had thanked him, hurried to her room and not come down until I appeared.

"Did you tell her about the reporter?" I asked.

"No. Nor about Harry's call."

"What did you tell the reporter?"

"I told him if he clicked that damned camera on this place I'd get a gun and blow it out of his hands."

"I wish you'd called me, Archie."

"The time has not come when I can't put a whippersnapper off my own place," said Archie.

I did not reply and after a moment he sighed. The remembrance of the newspaper's snooping had revived his spirit briefly. When he spoke again the indignation was gone; he was plaintive.

"All right. I didn't put Roscoe off in time. How could I? Nature abhors a vacuum, Jim."

He had used those words to me the first time Rocky ever went to River House.

I I

"Montagu and Capulet all over again!" exulted Winifred at the time of the engagement.

The allusion dignified the Slade position. It extended the protective mantle of romance over the blunter summation that ran like a counterpoint through Torrent's amusement.

"Rocky's really hit the jackpot now."

Most of the chuckles were sympathetic. We had all partaken vicariously of the football fame Rocky had brought our town and state. Nine tenths of the county delighted in his political pyrotechnics; a certain incongruity in the match enchanted people who knew neither Rocky nor Lucy.

Equality in Torrent is as sacred as the Decalogue and perhaps as remote from many of our tacit arrangements. The *Sentinel* addresses fervent editorials on Democracy to Our More Responsible Element, preaches brotherhood and prints more society than world news.

The society it reports is straticulate, with lines blurred by the passion or indifference of those concerned, but its dimmest markings would leave the rectory a long way from River House.

In childhood this mattered not at all. Later Lucy used to boast that she, like all the other girls in the combined grade and high school of the time, had had a crush on Rocky. He was three classes ahead of her; his celebrity was general, impersonal and remote. She was still an adolescent in pigtails while he had gone on to State and his three field goals against Notre Dame.

Their college years widened the gap. Rocky was at State; Lucy and Artie were already responding to the gravitational pull of what the *Sentinel* called the Younger River Set.

This was more of a geographical than a social entity. Simeon's house had begun to draw courtiers up the river in the days when he would sell its frontage only as a personal favor. A measured generosity to associates had been part of Simeon's genius. His old confederate, Otto Randolph, ended a prosperous life on the place adjoining River House. Otto's son, Hewitt, had succeeded to more than a subordinate position. Archie's indifferent default had given Hewitt the presidency of the bank. His place was larger than River House now; his Vincent and Gretchen were almost exactly the age of the twins.

They with Lucy and Artie and the young Inglises, Howards, Perkinses, Gregorys and others whose families share the sunny slope of that long moraine above the river had grown up as a group. High school graduation dispersed them to various colleges; on vacations they returned to the unity of their childhood.

Archie's amused indulgence made River House their storm center. There and in the boathouse no matron wailed over stained rugs, broken glasses or records or curfew. Archie and Madge and Hewitt Randolph often said they weren't sure which kids lived where. It didn't greatly matter. They danced, skated, skiied, swam, shot, caroused and flirted in a homogeneous group, mingling freely with other elements of the town at the Country Club or more general gathering places but coalescing slowly into the faintly secluded pattern of their parents.

They did not escape gossip. The lack of feminine chaperonage at River House was deplored by the mothers of youngsters not invited there. Envious puns were made about their hay rides. Every generation delights to call the next one wild and so these kids were called by those who knew them least.

Age had placed me several years ahead of them. In my observation they were an improvement on either my contemporaries or the half generation ahead of me. There had been an age bracket in Torrent which considered prohibition the greatest menace liberty ever knew and the bootlegger its symbol of freedom. These kids could just remember the last of that with distaste. Most of them had felt the depression; they had not been hungry but their youth and warmth had felt the havoc around them. They were sensitive to the popular thesis of the day that good fortune in itself was guilt. They matured with unemployment around them and conscription ahead.

Artie Maynard was a firecracker of a kid. He was too high-strung for organized athletics; he played them all with reckless energy and led the rest of the crowd in more imaginative deviltries.

It was for Artie and Lucy and young Vincent Randolph that I first

[36]

broke the family rule that Dentons do not represent Maynards. In the early days of my practice, the summer before we entered the war, all three of them appeared one morning in our office. Vinty had more of bone and muscle than Artie; those who thought less of his brain forgot that it had the good sense to defer in most things to Artie's quick intuitions.

The very sight of them brought springtime, with its hint of happy, impenitent guilts, into the tired summer air. The boys stood straight and firm in white T shirts under their sunburned crewcuts. Lucy had on a printed dress, mostly of white that contrasted wonderfully with her long freckled arms and gleaming hair. I was no graybeard myself at the time; their presence made me think of a basket of puppies. It strained my new professional manner to take them seriously at first.

"We need a lawyer," said Artie.

"Very confidential," said Vinty.

"You've got to help us, Jim," said Lucy.

I reminded them that for legal matters the Maynards belonged in the Tuttlewise office; they shook their heads.

"Not a family thing," said Artie.

"That old bastard would faint," said Vinty.

"This is important," said Lucy.

I still wasn't sure of the professional proprieties; I was beginning to be very sure they needed help. I told them to spit it out and we'd settle jurisdiction later.

"It's really just about a fight, Jim," said Artie.

"Unless they did drown," said Vinty.

"If they did you've got to get me hung too," said Lucy. "You've got to get us married before you surrender Vinty or whatever it's called; we're engaged and you're the first person except Artie who knows it and they have to hang me too."

"That has nothing to do with it," said Vinty.

"It has everything to do with it," said Lucy. "If they hang you they hang me and Jim will get us married first."

"They don't hang you unless it's premeditated, do they, Jim?" asked Artie.

That summer the gossip about the Younger River Set was enlivened by stories that it swam naked in mixed company from the Maynard and Randolph docks. All three insisted that it was untrue. Some of the boys did swim at night in jockstraps only. The girls said it was disgusting but not enough so to absent themselves. As the story spread they became indignant. Lucy had led the other girls into getting flesh-

[37]

colored bathing suits; they left the dock lights on so that to passing boats or peekers from the far side it might seem true.

Two boys known to them all, who resented not being of the usual company, had vowed to prove it. On the previous night they had floated a canoe in close to the Maynard dock before rising up out of it with cameras and flash bulbs.

Artie and Vinty had been so far ahead of the others in pursuit that they insisted on sole guilt. They caught the canoe and capsized it, sinking the cameras. In the scuffle with its occupants they all became separated. Artie and Vinty found each other easily by calling and drifted on down to the Randolphs' dock.

They had given the other boys repeated duckings. After they got their own wind it occurred to them that they had not seen their victims again. They scoured the river the rest of the night in canoes without finding a trace. By daylight they found the photographers' canoe smashed on the riprapping of Baker's Island, three miles downstream from the fight. They were wondering what to do when they heard an early newscast over the radio in the Maynards' boathouse. It announced the photographers as missing from an evening's fishing on the river.

"We thought we'd better know the law," said Vinty. "I ducked mine pretty hard."

"I ducked both of them again, after you were clear," said Artie.

"I started it all with that damned bathing suit," said Lucy. "That makes me accessory, doesn't it, Jim?"

I called a police lieutenant for whom I had been arranging a marital separation. Terry Banion knew the professional alignments of the town better than I did and would never think of associating me with Maynards. I told him a friend of mine had correlated the newscast with a stove canoe he had noticed at Baker's Island and wanted to know if the boys were still missing.

"Jim, who in hell are you fronting for?" asked Terry.

"None of your business, Terence," I said lightly. "Do you broadcast everything you do up the river?"

"Fishing," said Terry. "It's always innocent boys fishing in the middle of the night before you begin finding the river full of drownded girls without their pants on."

"I don't know any drownded girls, Terence."

"I'm glad to hear it," said Terry. "Tell 'em next time their fun will last longer up on the bank."

Fortunately my father was pleading at Prairie. Miss Premm would not have opened her mouth if clients had carried a body into the office. I put Lucy and the boys in Father's room and then went into the library to refresh myself on manslaughter. It made grim reading until Miss Premm told me Lieutenant Banion was on the phone.

"Them corpses just walked home along the tracks," said Terry. "But tell your female friends what I said about canoes. This weather I could lose half my force dragging that river in bathing suits for a lost cat."

"Jim," said Lucy, "I'll remember all my life that you saved Vinty, and Artie too, of course."

"We'd like to pay you right now," said Artie.

"Whatever you say," said Vinty.

I had a hard time making them realize that I had done nothing but make a phone call.

"All right," said Lucy, "but you'll be our lawyer when we're married only we're not telling anyone about the engagement yet; it's too wonderful even to share. You ought to get married yourself, Jim. Everyone should."

That night I found Mother waiting at home with that faint exasperation women always accord a mystery.

"Who on earth sent you a case of champagne?"

Late that summer Archie announced Lucy's engagement to Vinty Randolph. Female Torrent purred. The parents were as pleased as the kids. Archie could mock Hewitt Randolph's occasional pomposities to his face but there was a lifetime of intimacy between them. Hewitt had long since eclipsed Archie in local significance. He would never quite forget that his father had been Simeon's subordinate. Now he would have Maynard grandchildren. The day they told him, Hewitt engaged David Gregory to plan a house for them, on the boundary between his place and Archie's.

Lucy, from the few glimpses I had of her, seemed already to have taken up residence in that dreamy contentment which is the sphere of engaged girls. The details sparkled around her like bulbs on a Christmas tree; she glowed from the inside out.

It was Vinty who stood out against immediate marriage. He had two more years to finish at Amherst, where he and Artie were then rooming together. Lucy and Gretchen ostensibly had been attending Smith; the intimacy of their schooling projected the parental thesis that they were not sure which kids belonged where. Neither did they care.

Vinty had always seemed a happy-go-lucky, irresponsible kid. Perhaps the engagement itself sensitized him to the long shadows of that summer. Whether Lucy felt them or not, he did. Vinty insisted that they all return to college for another year, to see how things turned out. Back they went and three months later we all saw how things turned out on Pearl Harbor Day.

Torrent had been as skeptical of the Second as of the First World War. Our draft board reflected more than our apathy to global woes. Without naming names it could be said that our people knew they would be living with each other long after the current administration ran out of emergencies.

Pearl Harbor changed that, too. The old board met that afternoon. Its first official action was to ask Archie Maynard to become its new chairman. Men who would have shuddered at his opinion of a bond, farm or automobile requested him, unanimously, to judge their sons. The news of his acceptance sent a chill through the town; by then Torrent was ready for it.

Rocky Slade's deferment was one of the first the new board reviewed. Everyone knew about his ankle injury. It had cost him a professional football salary larger than the bank paid Hewitt Randolph.

Medical advice had held out hope that he might be able to play again in two or three years. In the interim Rocky had been appointed coach at our high school. It had made some feeling because the old coach had developed Rocky. The problem was solved by keeping him on, too. As Winifred reminded the other members of the school board, Rocky had done a great deal for Torrent and the laborer was worthy of his hire.

Rocky had given us winning teams. He had found time to be scoutmaster as well and was widely admired for leadership of youth. Everyone knew what full recovery of that ankle would be worth to him. In the peacetime draft he had been easily deferred.

Bud Huston, who was on the board, told me Rocky made a good impression at his review. He said he intended to enter service as soon as he was sure about the ankle. He wished to remind the board that his very promising basketball team was in a critical phase. With a few weeks more he could leave Torrent another championship. He was already putting out feelers, through contacts at State, for a direct commission in the army's over-all physical training and recreation program, where he believed he could be of real service. The other members were nodding sympathetically as he finished; Archie was not.

"Your country has been attacked, Mr. Slade," he said. "The army will judge your ankle."

Winifred was wild. Now the draft board was not fair to Rocky. Her hatred focused on Archie; it was an outrage in our democracy for a rich man who'd never done a stroke of work in his life to be sitting in judgment on boys whose whole lives had been of service to the community. If Archie didn't send his own son she would get a court order to have him removed from the board.

Archie did not send his own son. Artie and Vinty had enlisted from college the day after the attack. Lucy returned for the Christmas vacation with Gretchen but in spite of Archie's protests she would not go back to college. That spring she worked in the Red Cross in town. When the first of the new factories opened in Torrent she was near the head of the line in overalls.

She was working in the factory the day the news came. The telegraph office should have sent it to River House but everyone in town knew where Archie was. The boy carried it right into the draft board meeting. Archie read it and folded it and put it in his pocket. Then he thanked the boy and faced the board.

"We will proceed, gentlemen," he said.

Everyone in the room knew what it was; the boy was the only one who could speak.

"Mr. Maynard, aren't you going to tell Lucy?"

"When she's through work," said Archie.

The boy went out and Bud Huston got his voice back.

"Archie," he said, "let's adjourn for the day."

"At our regular time," said Archie.

No one else could say anything. They wound up the work in hand as fast as they could and had just finished when Hewitt Randolph came through the door with a telegram in his hand. He gave it to Archie, who read it in silence and then handed Hewitt his own. For several seconds they just stood there, looking back and forth between the telegrams and each other.

"We'll have to tell Lucy," said Hewitt.

"I'll do it," said Archie. "Her shift is over at four. We won't ride the pool car tonight, Hewitt."

"I thought of that; there's a taxi waiting, Archie."

That was the only day from the beginning of rationing until the end of the war that either of them used gasoline for personal purposes. The next morning they were waiting at the lane for the pool car as they did every day until it was over.

Rocky Slade was the victim of a cruel irony. No one ever doubted his courage. That was not what the caprices of the armed services wanted of him. In his first training camp his name was recognized. The C.O. of the camp wanted winning teams for morale. Rocky spent the war coaching in a sweatshirt in America.

Nobody cared. The war had given Torrent more than football to think about. By its end the town was yawning over Winifred's assertion that the army was not fair to Rocky. Perhaps it was not but time had put one element of truth into her ethic. Whoever was or was not fair to him, Rocky would be measured forever, in Archie's eyes, against the first two names on the new monument in our square. In a sense they were the price of Rocky's admission as a suitor at River House.

I I I

The war cost Rocky more than frustration. He emerged too old to begin professional football. He might still have coached; he said that the army had taught him a lesson. He was not going to spend the rest of his life in a sweatshirt.

Of his available opportunities real estate looked best because of the imminence of the new freeway. A ripple of speculation was already following the Highway Commission's surveys of various routes. There would be early profits somewhere; the long-range consequences would benefit the whole county.

Rocky went to work in Freddy Eastman's office as a salesman. He took the real estate course in the City College of Commerce by night, became active in the Junior Chamber of Commerce and addressed the younger service clubs on the dynamic future of Torrent.

He soon found this future more general than personal. The informed speculation on freeway probabilities had been done before Rocky heard of it. He had no capital. The golden prospects he preached at first did not materialize, perhaps because all the other communities in our end of the state were trying to be dynamic too. We did keep two of the war factories to accelerate the ruin of the river downstream and Rocky was eking out a thin living on commissions.

No one in Torrent at that time felt the groundswell of the coming postwar boom. The prophecies of boosters were wryly discounted. Older heads could remember other booms and the forty-cent wheat that followed.

My first solid clue to the new prosperity in the country came from Mr. Franklin. He registered quietly at the Maynard Hotel, drove the county at his leisure and asked such naïve questions at the larger real estate offices that they scarcely bothered to be polite to him. Then he went back to Rocky, who had bothered, put that certified check on the desk and told Rocky to buy him River House.

Mr. Franklin had chosen Rocky for more than his personality. Older men would have told him he might as well bid for the White House. Mr. Franklin knew a dynamic younger man when he saw one. He told Rocky it had been his experience that anything was for sale at a price; he believed that check was a price.

Mr. Franklin knew that River House was a white elephant in these days of no servants. He did not care. All his life he had dreamed of living in peace and quiet on his own acres. The place, as he had first seen it, advertised distress. In the first week of peace Archie and Lucy had set to work vigorously, mowing, trimming, scything, pruning and repairing the long wartime neglect. The graver decays had to be budgeted to the new wage scales for skilled mechanics. First and last Archie and Lucy put their hands to everything else.

Lucy was a daughter of the mechanical age; she had run outboards and held the tools while Artie and Vinty rebuilt flivvers. The factory had enlarged her knowledge of machines and much of this she taught Archie. Either of them could operate the little tractor. They teamed with the scandalized Allen and McClintic on cultivator, chain saw, power mower and posthole digger.

Mr. Franklin had seen them at work. He may not have understood their deeper compulsions; he could scarcely have failed to hear the sympathetic muttering:

"Bringing back the place won't bring back Artie."

Archie called me the night Rocky took him Mr. Franklin's offer. He had refused to interrupt his afternoon in the box bushes but had agreed to see Rocky after dinner. When I reached River House he and Rocky were alone in the library. Lucy had excused herself from what seemed only a routine business session. The men had been having coffee while they waited for me. The brandy tray was close at hand.

"At least you'll get a drink for this imposition," said Archie. "Mr. Slade refuses to join me."

"Just business, Mr. Maynard," said Rocky. "Would you want me drinking if I represented you?"

"Jim manages it," said Archie, "but perhaps only because I insist. Please don't let me strain your scruples."

"Maybe I'll have one later—to the deal," said Rocky.

"That may be much later," said Archie, "but please tell Jim exactly what you've told me."

My first inclination was to accept immediately. It is dangerous to think you know more of a client's business than he does. I had then been several months with the Maynard estate. The first week had convinced me that if I didn't know more about it than Archie did it was doomed.

The offer was more than generous. It would trade a nightmare of continuing liabilities for enough cash to relocate Archie and Lucy in dignified comfort. It would reduce the corrosive encumbrances on every productive asset in the estate. It would diminish the specter of the ultimate inheritance taxes. In every way it was so much too good to be true that I had to repress my eagerness.

"Why does he want it, Rocky?"

"He's hurting to be a country gentleman," said Rocky.

"Are you sure about this check?"

"That's the beauty part," said Rocky. "I phoned the bank in Chicago myself; it's okay."

"What do you think, Jim?" asked Archie.

"You should accept at once, sir."

Rocky had come to River House expecting to be declined in a word. As Archie hesitated, Rocky's knuckles whitened on the chair until I thought its old arms might break.

"I couldn't without consulting Lucy," said Archie.

"Then get her, please, sir," I said. "You might wait twenty years for another offer like this."

He vanished into the hall. Rocky exhaled a long sigh and then whispered tensely to me.

"Can you make her do it, Jim, can you?"

"I don't make them do things, Rocky. I'll advise it."

"Then we're in," he whispered. "We're IN. I'll never forget this, Jim; you were always loyal to me."

"Save it, Rocky. I'm representing them."

"No," he whispered again, "you're on my side. You always were, Jim. What's the angle to use on Lucy?"

"Relax," I said. "There aren't any angles."

"I would have come to you first," Rocky apologized, "but that Franklin's an operator; he insisted on my slapping Archie right in the eyes with the check. I told him he was nuts but he said everything's for sale. I guess he's got something, Jim; everything is."

Then he jumped to his feet as Lucy came into the room with Archie. She had on blue silk lounging pajamas, cut tightly above the waist, that night. The effect of her figure and the glints of firelight on her hair and face made me wonder if Rocky could keep his mind on business. It was going to be an effort for me, as most of our encounters at that time had become.

"Lucy," said Rocky. "That is a gorgeous creation."

[44]

"Thanks," said Lucy. "It's nice to see you again, Rocky. How is all your family?"

"Real fine," said Rocky. "We miss Sis but I guess everyone gets married sooner or later."

Then he began to color; she saw his confusion and smiled.

"Sounds as if you had plans of your own, Rocky."

"Not me," said Rocky. "I'm going to be set right before I take on any load like that."

"I read they're still besieging you to turn pro."

"Paper talk," said Rocky. "I couldn't get peanuts, now."

"*Sic transit gloria* Saturday." Archie smiled at him.

"Pardon me, sir," said Rocky. "I never took languages."

"Daddy just means none of us are getting younger," said Lucy. "He says you have some business to discuss."

"One thing I'd like to say first," said Rocky. "I already told your Dad how bad this whole town feels about Artie. That was a real tragedy. I always said, light as he was, I could of made a real running back out of Artie."

"Thanks, Rocky. He admired your playing."

"I guess those days are over for all of us, Lucy. Now I gotta admit my interest in this deal is selfish 'cause it would mean so much to me and the old folks but I do think it's a real break for you and Mr. Maynard and Jim says so, too."

Lucy knew more about the estate than Archie did, or, at least, I had been able to make her pay some attention to the inexorable details. She heard Rocky attentively.

"Heavens, what a sum! Have we uranium here, Jim?"

"No."

"Mr. Franklin," said Archie, "is purchasing respectability."

"He's hotter than a pistol for it," said Rocky. "He figured psychologically to knock you both over the head with this check instead of chiseling around. He's real dynamic."

"What do you think, Daddy?"

"Jim says to sell," said Archie.

Lucy looked slowly up to where Simeon glared at us from above the fireplace. The wallpaper on both sides of the portrait was waterstained from the latest plumbing disaster.

"How do you feel yourself, Daddy?"

"Our agreement with Jim was to do what he said," replied Archie.

"You wouldn't quit us if we didn't, would you, Jim?"

"I would not; I didn't anticipate this," I said.

[45]

"Then you can decide independently, Daddy."

"My independence has made the place what it is," said Archie. They looked at each other and then they looked at the water stains again. Her eyes lingered there and Archie saw it.

"We'll sell," he said, "subject to two conditions."

Rocky was taking long, even breaths. He leaned forward now, straining not to seem too eager.

"First is the freeway; after all, we can't take advantage of this man. Have you considered that, Jim?"

I had considered it as minutely as I could. Only Archie could have imagined a bidder ignorant of such a well-known probability. In my own mind I had already conceded that Mr. Franklin knew things about the freeway that I did not. I had the best knowledge available to me. In the light of it I was more than willing to leave him the rosiest mirages of subdivision or condemnation proceedings. I had already told both Archie and Lucy we would be lucky to keep the place from winding up as a roadhouse full of jukeboxes. I told Archie that Mr. Franklin certainly knew of the freeway and I still considered this a desirable sale.

"You believe the freeway is coming, Roscoe?" he asked.

"Cinch, Mr. Maynard." He smiled knowingly. "Cement wants it, petroleum wants it, Detroit wants it, Pittsburgh wants it, Akron wants it. Good God, even the people want it."

"Rome wanted roads, too," said Archie, "and so, if I recall, did Hitler. Provided Mr. Franklin knows about it we'll consider this point satisfied."

"He does," breathed Rocky.

"Now, where did Mr. Franklin get this money?"

"I'm glad you asked that question," said Rocky. "I checked that with the bank, too. This Franklin is an operator. He had a big war deal in electronics, contract to make some gizmo by the millions for twenty-eight bucks a time and he wound up stamping 'em out for sixty-nine cents. They're still fighting renegotiation but this check's good no matter how they come out."

"So we'd be war profiteers, too?" asked Archie.

"I wouldn't think of it like that, sir," said Rocky.

"Perhaps not," said Archie, "but you may tell Mr. Franklin that Gresham's law does not operate here."

"You've got me on that law," said Rocky. "It wasn't in the City College course."

"It was expounded before we became so dynamic," said Archie.

[46]

" 'When good and bad money circulate concurrently, the bad drives the good out of circulation.' "

"Don't worry about that, sir; the check is good."

"I'm not worrying," said Archie. "Please return it to Mr. Franklin."

He had turned pale and looked, suddenly, very tired. Rocky rose, reddening and controlling himself with effort.

"Rocky," said Lucy, "I'm sorry, but this *is* our home."

"Lord," said Rocky. "I been friends with you before I ever saw this Franklin; I just hope you're not mad."

"I hope you'll forgive us," said Lucy. "It's getting warmer now; would you like to come out and swim some day?"

"Why, sure," said Rocky. "Thanks very much."

"Good; see if you can tear Jim out of that office any afternoon. I never can."

Archie's glance detained me as Lucy walked Rocky out to the door. He sat white and silent until we heard it slam and she rejoined us.

"Sorry to put you through this, kitten," he said.

"Daddy! I agreed with you entirely. Are you going to abandon us to the Tuttlewises again, James?"

"No."

"Then bring on your jukeboxes. I guess concrete is the tendril that flowers into neons."

"You don't really mind, kitten?" Archie asked again.

"No; the Ushers stand as one." She laughed, almost convincingly, and then added: "I'm only sorry for Rocky."

"That is one pain that is spared me," said Archie.

"Daddy! He's pathetic!"

There always has to be a beginning and that was it. Pity can be enough. Lucy told me long afterward that she had been unaware of any other emotion at the time. Perhaps she was. I had certainly seen nothing more than that in the meeting. I think Archie had. When Lucy left us again he shook his head.

"Jim, does State teach anything besides dropkicking?"

I was exasperated with Archie. I'm afraid I let it into my voice.

"They didn't teach him dropkicking, sir; they hired him to dropkick us into amateur championships."

"Yes," said Archie. "I guess Mr. Franklin could call us all hypocrites."

"He's probably calling you worse, right now," I said.

"And so are you," said Archie. "Am I a quixotic damn fool?"

"About this you are, Mr. Archie."

"We're making progress," he smiled. "Hitherto, I've only been a plain damned fool. And stop calling me Mister."

"This was total war, sir, and all the money in the country was part of it; you never will sell except for war profits of some kind."

"Jim," he said suddenly. "We've got to sell; Lucy can't go on being a yardman."

"I'll get Rocky on the phone, sir," I said.

"No." His voice was firm again. "No dynamic operators, thank you. And I've got to get her used to the idea first. All her old crowd is married or moved away; there's no one here for her. Perhaps I'll sell, to someone else, in the summer, and then take her traveling. The whole business is really out of my line, or would be if I had a line. Do you ever read the Psalms, Jim?"

"No, sir."

"'The fire consumed their young men and their maidens were not given to marriage,'" quoted Archie.

I said nothing; he was silent and then sighed again.

"Keep your eyes open for another offer. We can't go on like this. Nature abhors a vacuum."

From my house that night I telephoned Rocky and, after warning him about false hopes, asked him to bring Mr. Franklin to my office next day. For the moment I knew it was hopeless; I didn't want to lose touch with so solvent a prospect.

My first sight of him showed me why Mr. Franklin had preferred operating through Rocky. It would take more than property to make Mr. Franklin a country gentleman and he was smart enough to know it. Even in the seclusion of my office he looked back over his shoulder from time to time as we talked. I did my best to mollify him; he was a man who did not take defeat lightly.

"Wait till inflation's worked on that sucker's governments awhile," he said.

At the beginning of the war Archie had exchanged all of his best securities for government bonds. It was one of the few financial impulses on which both Hewitt and Horace Tuttlewise had tried strongly to overrule him. He had insisted on doing it without publicity. No one else in town knew about it, but Mr. Franklin knew. When he had departed Rocky sighed.

"That's big dough, even if he does look like a gangster at Mass."

"You get around, don't you, Rocky?"

"So I've never been to Mass," admitted Rocky, "but the last time I lost a big solid chunk of dough it was to some gangsters just like him."

I told him I hadn't heard about it.

"You don't hear a lot of things in an office like this," said Rocky. "Just before the last Illinois game some of the boys from Chicago offered me fifteen thousand bucks, in hundred-dollar bills, to sprain my ankle. I socked one of them in the nose. So all they did was switch their bets and I still made them a pile by beating Illinois for a sixteen-buck sweater and an assistant librarian's salary. Next game I tore all the ligaments out of my ankle anyway. That's what you get for being an amateur."

He scowled and shrugged and scowled again.

"That's the trouble with those Maynards. They're amateurs, but the difference is they can afford it, so maybe Archie isn't the fool he looks."

That sale would have made a big difference to Rocky. I tried to speak consolingly.

"There's a lot more to Archie than fool, Rocky."

"There must be," said Rocky. "Look at the parents he picked himself. The only sensible thing Archie ever did was fire those Tuttlewises and hire you. You got a real lock on him, Jim. How's about coming out there for a swim with me this afternoon?"

I told him I had to work.

"You're another," he said. "Why don't you get wise and marry that girl instead of just fattening her up for some Ivy League fairy?"

Enough people were saying the same thing to me, in different words, at that time so that I had evolved a stock answer.

"They hire me to look after their property."

"She doesn't know they have property," said Rocky. "What she needs is a man."

"What makes you so delicate, Rocky?"

"I'm telling you." He shrugged. "She could get over those hoity-toity manners very fast. Stand 'em on their heads and they all look alike."

I said nothing and in a minute he rose.

"Jim, I'll never forget you tried for me. Will you try something else?"

"Sure."

"I'd like to speak on that panel of Tom Gilchrist's."

That spring Tom had persuaded the Chamber of Commerce to sponsor a series of luncheons at which younger businessmen of the town spoke on the future of Torrent.

"Are you serious, Rocky?"

"Sure," said Rocky. "I'm strictly minor league to them but I could wake some of those complacent bastards up."

"I'll call him, Rocky; he'll be delighted."

[49]

"He won't be delighted," said Rocky, "and don't call him. Wait till he starts bleeding about civic apathy over there at your club. Then bring it up casually."

"All right. I'll let you know."

"He'll let me know if you do it right," said Rocky. He took a long look around the room.

"Don't overstimulate yourself with these books."

When he had gone Miss Premm put her head in the door.

"Do you want that other person with Rocky entered in the office diary, Mr. James?"

"Of course."

"Very well. Do you know his name?"

"I told you this morning: Mortimer Franklin."

"I have that," she said. "I wondered if you had his real name."

There is no wisdom like hindsight. At the time I told myself I had gone as far as I dared to make them sell. I should have insisted. Archie's whole life had been pointed toward a worse ultimate shock than that. The next day he had his heart attack anyway.

He had complained of fatigue while he and Lucy were raking in the morning. He knocked off early and then fainted at the lunch table. Lucy called me as soon as she had reached Dr. Jamison. He had insisted on taking Archie to the hospital and there, several hours later, made his report to Lucy and me.

"I've seen 'em live twenty years after one of these but it's not percentages, dear."

Jamison had known Archie all his life and had delivered the twins. They had begun learning the alphabet from the faded initials on his bag. There were devotion and practicality as well as medicine in his gray head.

"Is there anything we can do, Arby?"

"You can spend a lot of money learning the same thing at State or Chicago or Rochester."

"We wouldn't think of taking him away from you. I just meant . . . anything Jim or I could do?"

He shook his head a little wryly. "Ordinarily in these cases we speak of overwork; we're probably wrong. You can be very careful to keep him from getting angry or excited."

"Arby, did this come from worry?"

"Lucy," said the doctor, "people worry too much about worry. There's only two kinds of it—hunger and the others. People with enough to eat make it up other ways so it's all about even. What this came from, I don't know; the trouble is degeneration of tissue."

He instructed us patiently in his proposed regimen. Archie would be under sedation for a few days and immobilized for several weeks, after which the injury would be reassessed. Momentarily there was nothing to be done. He didn't even want us to see Archie again that day. When he had left us, Lucy spoke.

"It was worry; it was that damned offer."

"That's over now, Lucy."

"Jim, you must see that there aren't others."

"That's not entirely in my hands."

"Then get it there; he trusts you."

I explained that that very fact limited the responsibility I could assume. She shook her head impatiently.

"He didn't want to sell. He thought he ought to take me out into the world to win friends and influence people and buy me a nice bridegroom."

"It's more than that, Lucy; he knows the tax and legal problems."

"Can taxes and laws keep him alive? Then to hell with them. I'm a big girl, Jim. I can tidy up afterwards but no more offers."

"No good comes of deception, Lucy."

"Life is organized deception," said Lucy. "If you force us back on the Tuttlewises they'll kill him next week with exasperation."

I finally agreed to alert the other real estate offices to channel everything through me, officious though it seemed.

"That's your penance," said Lucy. "You be officious and I'm going to be frivolous so he won't worry about my lorn estate. I'm going out and buy some new bathing suits."

As matters turned out, Archie made an excellent limited recovery from the attack. It took him the rest of the summer, however. His hope of travel had to be postponed. By the time he might have resumed it nature had begun to fill the vacuum with Rocky Slade.

I V

A log in the fire broke into a shower of sparks. We blinked at each other and Archie sighed.

"Whatever he's done involves Lucy."

"Not necessarily, sir."

"You mean not legally."

He had a layman's impatience of the law. Simeon's force and guile had made it his own instrument. Archie found it one long restriction.

"Depends on what he's done, Archie."

"What is the gossip you mentioned?"

I told him the substance of Tom Gilchrist's conversation.

"That fits," said Archie and shook his head again. "Tom was just the fool we needed to put Roscoe where he is today."

"We all had a hand in that, sir."

"I had more than I've told you, Jim. After the engagement Roscoe asked me pretty bluntly for a subsidy. He said it would be helping democracy by underwriting a career of service for high stakes. It made a painful scene; he talked of loyalty, I of self-reliance—extortioner and hypocrite. I did tell him the estate was badly crippled. I don't think he believed me. He said if he couldn't count on help from me he'd have to find it where he could. Apparently he has."

"Any idea where?"

"Yes, but my knowledge is confidential."

I felt a little comfort. At least I wasn't the only one withholding facts. The rest of the pattern still fitted; you started to help Rocky and wound up in deceit.

"It's enough if you know, sir."

"It's not enough," said Archie. "I've got to help him."

"How?"

"With the loan, of course. Didn't Tom say it would be all right if it is my money he's been spending?"

"He did; but it isn't."

"Have we that much available, Jim?"

"Not in cash."

"Then get a loan from Hewitt tomorrow."

I thought a minute about the loan and about the pattern.

"Archie, it's your money. You can do it yourself. Before I do it I'd have to know more about it."

"To satisfy your legal doubts?" he asked dryly.

"That's what you hire me for."

"Any licensed rascal can tell you the law," said Archie irascibly. "What I'm hiring, as you so bluntly put it, is your common sense. The law is house rules devised by pedants to circumscribe custom. Where it fits custom it works; where it doesn't it's ludicrous.

"Observe that pillar of an admiring community, the estimable Hewitt. His bank pays us gratifying dividends by circumventing the laws on usury. Hewitt even has some personal renown for flouting the law on two counts we both know about: prohibition and adultery. Prohibition is over, of course, but its laws never troubled him or any of us. He prospers like the green bay tree because we all accept the fact that regardless of law, people are naturally improvident, greedy, thirsty and licentious.

"But Hewitt would rather assist at a discreet murder than lunch at the Torrent Club in a bathing suit. Anything so sensible would outrage custom. The law you're so sentimental about would probably allow his family to certify him as lunatic if he did.

"I wish Roscoe's troubles were legal. Lucy couldn't marry him in a penitentiary. But I agree with you and Tom that he's too smart for bribery or embezzlement. He doesn't handle public funds; he won't vote on the freeway. His difficulty is ethical and I've got to cover it."

"You still haven't said why, sir."

"Lucy would never quit him under fire," said Archie.

"Are you assuming she wants to quit him?"

"I'm assuming," said Archie wearily, "that she's a woman of character and taste, unfortunately infatuated with this Neanderthal relic. When she gets over it you can get her a discreet divorce. There are law and custom again for you, Jim. Under the law we're monogamous. Thank God for custom. In the meantime I'll have to buy off this mess. Will you see Hewitt in the morning?"

I studied his fatigue and remembered what Dr. Jamison had told us about excitement and anger.

"I'd rather ask Rocky some questions first."

"He's at Prairie and it's urgent," said Archie.

"I'll take the morning plane up there."

"Would you, Jim?"

"Of course."

"Thanks, Jim," he said. "Scandal is the one thing that could bind her to him."

I arose at once. Then, as I was saying good night, Lucy hurried into the room.

"Jim, Uncle Hewitt's been trying to find you all over town. He insists that you stop in there on your way home, no matter how late it is. Honestly! He thinks the world revolves around that damned bank."

She had called him Uncle long before the brief engagement and she was very fond of him, but tonight her mind was on other things.

"All right," I said. "I'm just going."

"I'll show you out," she said. "Don't you come, Daddy. It's cold in the hall and I may kiss Jim good night."

She closed the library door behind us and we walked together through the hall, chill and dim with the feeble reflections of its antiquated Victorian chandelier. By its light I could just see in the west parlor the glitter of silver and white tissue on the tables piled with wedding presents.

"Jim, did you get it settled?"

"I want to talk to Rocky a little."

"He wants to talk to you. He just phoned that he'll be down on the morning plane."

"Oh, good; tell your father, will you? I was going to Prairie to see him."

"Jim, I'm afraid he's in trouble; something about a speculation. You'll get him out of it, won't you?"

"Anything for a fee, Lucy. Lawyers live on trouble."

"Stop it; I'm very serious."

"All clients are. The beauty of it is they never realize that most trouble never happens."

"You will help him, won't you?"

"We'll bury the body in my back room."

"Jim, I am going to kiss you good night."

She did, too. I drove out the lane and down the Ridge Road to Hewitt's lane with the faint fragrance of whatever cosmetic it was lingering on my left cheek. Before I went into Hewitt's I checked with the car mirror for lipstick. There was no trace of it.

Chapter Three

"I DIDN'T ask to be the big frog in this puddle," Hewitt Randolph told me once.

The disclaimer has become a standard phenomenon of success but there was more than modesty in Hewitt's wry remark. He had a tender pride. It would always know that he had been appointed to the presidency of the bank as a second choice in consequence of Archie's contemptuous default of commercial life.

Hewitt had more than justified his selection. Simeon and Hewitt's father had made the bank a landmark in the state. Hewitt presides over deposits from half the states in the country but it is still the Maynard National Bank.

As a matter of policy the bank has always divided its legal business. After Simeon's death my father had represented it many times at Hewitt's request. The first case I ever handled was given me by Hewitt.

Two sisters named Chegwidden had maintained for years a joint savings account. Shortly after her seventy-fifth birthday Miss Lucille had had a series of dreams which revealed to her that Miss Emily was squandering their savings in support of an illicit relation with their yardman. The informant of her dreams had warned Miss Lucille that naked assertion would not sustain her suspicions. Under the same guidance she had stolen a bottle of the green ink the tellers used and adjusted the entries in their passbook to confirm her views.

"It isn't even law, Jim," said Hewitt. "What will be remembered is not that we beat her but how we treated her."

We got it settled without scandal, for which Hewitt expressed a gratitude out of all proportion. When, a few months later, Miss Lucille's further revelations persuaded her to kill the yardman with a hatchet, Hewitt phoned me at once.

"The bank isn't even in the paper. Well done, Jim."

From the day when he was committed to it, every step in Hewitt's life has been measured in terms of its effect on the bank. For that he has been honorary chairman of the Greater Torrent Committee and the Civic League. For that he has been an enduring pillar of Red Cross, Chamber of Commerce, Community Chest, Y.M.C.A. and Hospital Board, a diligent vestryman of St. Mark's.

The suppression of Hewitt's youthful dream of larger puddles was not entirely voluntary. His father had put him in the bank, after college, as a frankly interim step. In those days Wiasota had been invincibly Republican. Before long we had begun to see photographs of Hewitt far from his desk, husking corn or ploughing in borrowed overalls. The only conjecture had been as to whether, after proper seasoning, he would pause in the Governor's mansion or proceed directly to Washington. Archie's refusal, upon his return from Europe, to enter the bank at all had extended Hewitt's stay in it. The New Deal had closed its doors upon him in more ways than one.

"You couldn't elect an honest banker poundmaster in this state now," he used to say.

His perception had understood the magnitude of the change. As we settled to the long Democratic years Hewitt had accepted the inevitable with outward flexibility. He retained an invisible touch with Dennis Flynn, the state Republican boss, and he continued discreet support of that party through its long eclipse. Personally as well as locally he abandoned all political activity. Simeon and Otto Randolph had practically appointed the chiefs of our Police, Fire, Park, Education and Tax Departments. Hewitt was more than content with a quiet backstage veto over city supervisors and County Council.

He kept adroit step with the tunes he could not call. When the diehards of the Torrent Club thundered about socialism, Hewitt was already talking of social justice. When they fulminated against usurpation Hewitt could discourse on "the realities of partnership with Washington." When they spoke of revolution he spoke of expanding democratic concepts. When they told him he was becoming as hairbrained as Tom Gilchrist, Hewitt pointed to his dividend record.

He ran the bank with sensitivity. He always had a Catholic vice-president, a Jewish vice-president and, with an eye to the farmers on whom we all lived, at least one German and one Scandinavian officer. For years an ebony chief watchman greeted half the depositors by name. When he died, he was replaced by an Italian. Within a few months two Negro girl graduates of our local College of Commerce were working machines on the first floor.

Hewitt had taken me up because I represented to him a new generation in the business life of Torrent. He had given me other work after the Chegwidden case. Upon my return from the war, he had been instrumental in my assuming the management of the Maynard estate.

"You can lean on my shoulders, Jim, they're broader than they look."

Ironically, my duties had put Hewitt and me into brief opposition. Archie had told me confidentially that he wanted to make a clean sweep of the change and sever all connection with the bank. It would have been folly; the bank was the core of Torrent business. After examining the estate I had asked Hewitt to sell it back some of the bank stock Archie had insisted on exchanging for government bonds. Hewitt had hemmed and hawed about values. I reminded him that those could be adjusted.

"You could wind up with no Maynard on the board of the Maynard National," I said.

"Personally," said Hewitt, "I could regard that as less than catastrophic. If you'd ever tried to steer Archie through a meeting . . ." He sighed and stared out through the door of his office.

Then I saw his face change; following his gaze, I realized that his chair was still placed where he could see the portrait of old Simeon, glaring down from the wall of the main lobby upon depositors and bank personnel alike.

"You've got half an idea," said Hewitt. "I'll deal with you for the other half."

"What's that?"

"You come on the board yourself; we need young blood."

Archie had snorted happily over the news: "Hewitt is trying to kill you—with boredom."

Archie seldom bothered to attend the meetings. He did come to my first one and sat solemnly through the preliminary business. That day after Hewitt had introduced me formally to the others, he touched, in his official manner, upon another change.

"Old Tobias will always be a venerated memory here," he said. "But in his way he was a symbol of the past. I am sure you will understand your officers' feeling that the two new young women of his race downstairs are a living proof of your bank's harmony with new social sentiment."

"Will we get a Russian, too?" asked Archie.

"We're waiting," said Hewitt, "to see how they work out in the other United Nations."

He smiled to remind us that humor had its place, even in board meetings, and then resumed his official cadences.

"I know you all share my views that there is more to banking than reserve laws, just as we all know there is more to our country than all its laws put together. The plus," he concluded, with a casual glance at Archie, "is human people, working together, constructively."

"Amen," said Archie. "All God's bankers got wings."

Hewitt led the laughter to show us that it was all right because Archie was Archie and still the founder's son. Then he got to work once more.

"We come again," he said, "to the question of public relations counsel."

"For God's sake why?" demanded Archie.

"You missed the previous discussion," said Hewitt patiently. "The smart boys in Chicago are getting 'em."

He enumerated some of the larger Chicago banks, respectfully.

"Do they have more special charges than we?" asked Archie.

"We do our best," Hewitt smiled, "but I'd still trade balance sheets with some of 'em."

"Then let's get a special charges officer," said Archie. "The only function of public relations is to boast or apologize. Our business is usury; why complicate it?"

"We live in a complex time, Archie," said Hewitt. "Banking is increasingly a public business. I'm not sure we don't owe the community a constructive presentation of our activities. One of the tests of management is keeping abreast of new ideas."

"This idea," said Archie, "was old when our forefathers wrote into the Declaration: 'a decent respect to the opinions of mankind . . .' just before they started shooting their cousins. They got it straight out of Cain in Genesis. Now, instead of saying: 'Am I my brother's keeper?' you hire professional soft soapers to say: 'Am I not my brother's benefactor?' Cain still killed his brother. It's still our business to work every fool in this county to death, paying us interest on radios and cars he doesn't need, but we don't have to insult him with pious humbug."

Hewitt's faint half smile ignored Archie for a long circuit of the other faces; it stopped abruptly at the unconscious scowl on Bud Huston's.

"Your views, Bud?" he asked easily.

Bud has spent a long life making a notable success of the hardware and implement business without public relations counsel. He was skeptical of Archie but he could always listen.

"Archie's got something, Hewitt; sounds to me like cold cash for hot air."

Sentiment crystallized instantly into other nods, which Hewitt did not miss.

"Merely sounding you," he said. "We should congratulate ourselves on having the benefit of such erudition."

"I must disclaim this compliment," said Archie innocently. "It's just that unlike the rest of you industrious gentlemen I do not waste my time upon fiction."

"Fiction!" Hewitt protested. "I never read it."

"Nonsense," said Archie happily. "What do you call corporate reports?"

The autocratic principle has to work two ways. Hewitt enjoyed setting the community an example of tolerant indulgence to Archie. A prime minister loses no honor for loyalty to the most wayward of princes. The intimacy of their children had strengthened the lifelong bond. The brief engagement of Vinty and Lucy had proclaimed a final equality. The caprices of politics had doomed Hewitt to being the big frog in a puddle that measured eminence by Simeon's shadow. The war had extinguished more than Hewitt's name; it had denied him grandchildren who would have had Simeon's blood.

The Hewitt who opened the door for me that night carried his scars with jaunty vigor. He was enough below the average stature to be self-conscious about it. He stood and walked aggressively erect, his strong shoulders spread wide. Faultless tailoring helped him to make the most of an active, well-exercised body. His abundant hair, now graying, still split his head with the straight part and symmetrical pompadour of his collegiate days. A small, trim mustache over white teeth and a strong jaw enhanced the impression of confident energy.

"Good of you to stop, Jim. I appreciate it, young fellow."

In his younger days Hewitt had been brusque. Confidence had eased his formality. He could still be distant when he chose; his normal effort was for familiarity. Sometimes it could seem a little forced. He did appreciate my stopping; he was asking me to help him pretend it was a casual courtesy.

"Madge left you her excuses," he said. "I'm sorry to tell you that even at this barbarous hour this is business but I see no reason not to conduct it in civilized comfort. I assume Archie's been giving you brandy?"

He was bustling me, as he spoke, out of my coat and down the long hall to the den he sometimes called his sanctum. Its knotty pine paneling, heavy leather furniture and Navajo rugs advertised masculine informality. The guns in the long rack were excellent; only the shade of their bluing testified to the infrequency of their use. An elk head and a well-mounted greenhead and honker validated their presence.

On the mantel there were some small silver trophies and an enlarged picture of a younger Hewitt flattening a tennis ball in expert service. Then, as you turned from the ornaments you saw the big desk and filing cabinets. The bookcases in reach of the swivel chair ran to Standard and Poor's, Moody, the nightmares of the Dow Jones disciples and leather-bound copies of *Fortune*.

On the low table before the hearth there was a freshly set grog tray with ice brimming out of a chromium bucket. A stately rank of decanters and glasses reflected the reds and golds of the fire. Hewitt drank sparingly himself; his nimble hands flashed through the details with loving care.

"Put out both kinds of glasses," he said, "in case you'd rather go on with soda. I find Archie's habits a little Spartan."

"Thanks. What's the business, Mr. Randolph?"

"Jim," he said, "I still wish you'd call me Hewitt. I'm getting sensitive about this gray hair."

"All right. What's on your mind, Hewitt?"

"Rocky Slade," said Hewitt, "is in money trouble."

"Can't you manage some crocodile tears?"

He flashed me his quick, white-toothed grin.

"I'm sparing you the one about the mills of the gods," he said. "Perhaps I should pretend to cry that he won't be able to keep his promise to run that damned freeway through this room because that was evidently the will of our sacred majority. But seriously, James, management has to view some aspects of our politics with a certain sophistication. As you should be learning, some of us have to think for the community as a whole, regardless of personal feeling."

"What do we think for the community?"

"Don't be so damned edgy," said Hewitt. "You and I are on the same side of this one, young fellow."

"You haven't even told me the trouble yet."

"Rocky," said Hewitt, "accepted some financial assistance that never went through party channels. If you'd interested yourself in politics, as many of us wish you had, you'd know that isn't unusual. If he'd behaved with discretion no one could have peeped. But getting engaged to Lucy turned his head. He's made enemies who'd be glad to crucify him."

"Whose money was it, Hewitt?"

"Jim, I learned of it in confidence because it went through the bank. You'd better think of it as misguided admirers. It was strictly legal but it could make some red faces neither of us would like to see. I won't deny to you that I wouldn't mind seeing Rocky chastened. I don't think either of us wants him destroyed. Archie and Lucy would be stigmatized."

"Where's the stigma if it's all so legal?"

"I'm lame on Scripture," said Hewitt, "but there's something about avoiding the appearance of evil. Every do-gooder in the state would want a Roman holiday out of this."

"A County Councilor isn't much burnt offering, Hewitt."

"Nineteen forty-eight," said Hewitt, "is closer than we think. Dennis Flynn really expects a Republican sweep for a change. In strictest confidence, Jim, Dennis phoned me tonight that old Herman Brodbeck will not run for the Senate again."

"Are you seriously suggesting that Rocky might?"

"Probably not," said Hewitt, "but that plurality gives Rocky a high nuisance value in this end of the state. Dennis will have to field his strongest team. There are fifteen House seats and a whole state legislature to elect and the fight for that Senate seat will be wide open."

"Surely Dennis isn't afraid of a County Councilor?"

"Jim, it isn't that simple. If Rocky got sore and ran independently down here it could drain off enough votes to hand it to a Democrat. And Rocky is just the boy to know it."

"I should think Dennis would want him destroyed."

"Privately he might. Between ourselves Dennis is disenchanted with Rocky. He told me that politics is the art of the possible and Rocky has been trying to out-lie the New Deal. But Dennis had to take him up after that plurality down here. He even took him to Washington with that gaudy presentation of Rocky's to fish for federal dough and meet the boys. A scandal for Rocky rubs off on the whole party now. And Rocky could be a dangerous dog in the Republican manger. So you and I," Hewitt concluded dryly, "are elected to forestall scandal."

"I'm no politico, Hewitt."

"You represent Archie," said Hewitt.

"Have you talked to him about this?"

"Jim," said Hewitt, "if I open my mouth to hiccough Archie starts saying no."

That was true. I asked Hewitt what he wanted me to do.

"Harry Caldwell phoned me today," said Hewitt, "to ask if Archie is subsidizing Rocky. Apparently that general supposition has quieted curiosity so far. By good luck, when Harry asked Archie the same thing Archie simply told him to go to hell. I gave Harry some double talk about privacy of depositors but I left him a strong implication that

Rocky's prosperity did come from Archie. It would be easy for me to call Harry tomorrow and tell him I had permission to confirm that. But I won't do it until it's so; I'd like to be able to ask him to call Archie and check for himself."

"What would this cost Archie, Hewitt?"

"Twelve thousand will pay off Rocky's obligations," said Hewitt. "I know this isn't peanuts and I know Archie's troubles as well as you do. But money is not the crux of this, Jim.

"Madge and I have always thought of Lucy as our own. We've been intending to do something substantial about a wedding present. I feel strongly enough about it to pick up this tab myself, if it comes to that. But I'm not sure Archie will play ball unless he *has* put up the money."

"He wouldn't, Hewitt."

"If it comes to that, Jim, he can afford it. All politics is *quid pro quo* and I hope I'm not quite as naïve as I look. Dennis Flynn understands very clearly that if we take him off this hook, the freeway goes over the ridge and leaves us alone down here. It's worth that to Archie in cold cash. Now that you know all, perhaps you'll permit me to mention the mills of the gods," said Hewitt comfortably.

He was right, at least about the value to Archie of keeping that freeway off the place.

"Are you sure about the freeway, Hewitt?"

"On Dennis's word," said Hewitt, "and he'll keep it, to me."

"What about Rocky's promises?"

"Jim, that campaign is over. Dennis doesn't mind trimming Rocky's sails a little. And as long as we get the freeway the voters don't give a damn about routes. If it costs a bit more on the ridge, who pays this state's taxes, anyway? We don't owe those socialistic fairies on the Park Commission a scenic target for tourists' beer cans. The whole deal is solidly in Archie's interest but you're the only man alive who can make him see it. You and I can adjust the money thing in twenty minutes, once we've got his moral support."

There were still things about it that I didn't understand but that was always part of the pattern when you were dealing with Rocky Slade. The rest of it was running to form. Hewitt wouldn't tell me where that money had come from; the silence was shrieking with the things I had not told Hewitt.

"I'll see Archie in the morning," I said.

"Jim," said Hewitt, "I knew I could count on you."

At home I found that Mother had left a note for me to call Tom Gilchrist, no matter what time, upon my return.

"Jim," he asked, "can you answer my question about Archie?"

"I think I can tomorrow, Tom."

"What time tomorrow?"

"I'm seeing him in the morning," I said. "Anything new?"

"Our man in Prairie called this evening," said Tom. "Unless the hypothesis you and I discussed turns out to be true, the Prairie *Times* is going to charge that our friend has been living on two payrolls."

"What County Councilor is not, Tom?"

"This is different," said Tom. "Bud had his store and the other members had their jobs and businesses *before* they were elected. The voters knew all about it. This is sudden and unexplained prosperity *after* the election."

"That isn't necessarily criminal, Tom."

"Jim," he said wearily, "stop hiding in your damned law. Whatever it is I gave him his start and you asked me to. Morally you and I are at the bottom of this."

I I

When Rocky asked me to get him a place on Tom Gilchrist's panel I had been more than willing. Tom had begun his project with enthusiasm. He very soon found that the men with ideas on the future of Torrent were not confiding them to Chamber of Commerce luncheons. His desperation had extended even to me. He was not rancorous about my refusal but I was pleased to be able to offer him a prospect.

Rocky's instructions about how to approach him had irked me a little. Subtlety usually defeats itself. My own instinct had been to call Tom at once, settle it and forget it. I had humored Rocky, made a note on my pad, and then, in the excitement of Archie's heart attack, forgotten it without settling it.

It was the easier to do because the back of my mind knew that Miss Premm never forgot anything on that pad. She had her own ideas about subtlety; they amounted to giving me a reasonable period of grace. The end of this coincided with the abatement of our excitement about Archie; she lingered after dictation one morning.

"Would Rocky make a good public official, Mr. James?"

"I doubt it. Why?"

"I happened to think of it when he was here the other morning," she said. "Miss Holcomb at the library just happened to mention to me that he's been reading handbooks on politics."

"Did she happen to say anything more about it?"

"We discussed sincerity," said Miss Premm. "Miss Holcomb and I have often wished more young men took interest. Of course, Rocky may just have been doing research for a speech or something."

That was what she had made of "Tom about Rocky" scrawled on my pad. After lunch at the club that day Tom sought me out to inquire about Archie and then asked me to step into the library.

"Jim, I hate to ask again but I wish to God you'd speak to that panel of mine."

"Tom, I'm no speaker."

"You're part of this community," said Tom.

"You need someone who believes the whole is greater than the sum of its parts."

"There," said Tom, "that's exactly the kind of thing. Instead of hot air and mutual admiration we need fresh ideas."

"If I give you one will you take it?"

"I'd take Novocain the way it's going."

"Why not ask Rocky Slade to speak?"

His face lit up with that reflexive enthusiasm which makes you like Tom and then it sobered.

"Jim, Rocky's a lightweight in business."

"He's part of the community."

"By God, he is," said Tom. "It's kind of a shame the way this town's forgotten Rocky; I'll think about it, Jim."

A few days later Rocky called me on the phone.

"Jim, you hooked him through both gills. Will you give me a little rundown on what it's like?"

"Sure," I said. "You'll be in the Gilt Room of the Maynard Hotel at twelve twenty-five. At twelve twenty-eight you'll be singing 'God Bless America,' off key, with forty or fifty other men who are thinking about selling each other insurance or fertilizer or cement. Then you'll eat some tired fruit cup and dried-up creamed chicken and a scoop of wet mashed potatoes with a side dish of peas dissolving the bottom of a little paper cup. When that's over, Tom will tell your peers that you're the hope of the future and you'll tell us that on projection of the latest census and Department of Commerce statistics . . ."

"Never mind my part," said Rocky. "Just get me through that gate and I'll call my own signals."

"There isn't any gate."

"There is for me," said Rocky. "Will you walk over with me when I crash it?"

Tom had expressed the current estimate of Rocky accurately. He was a lightweight in business. Memories in a small community have to be long. The same men who had cheered themselves hoarse for

Rocky's touchdowns could remember his father's inertia, Winifred's intrusive zeal and Mr. Parmenter's judgment of wheat prices.

At the peak of his fame Rocky had turned down a dozen lucrative jobs at selling. The war had eclipsed that fame; when he went job hunting people remembered that he had been a good high school coach. He had had to settle for a salesman's desk in a second-rate real estate and insurance agency.

It was second rate precisely because Freddy Eastman still believed that Rocky was the greatest thing that had ever happened to Wiasota. Freddy ran a declining business and a disorganized life on the principle that money isn't everything. For him athletics were the horizon of a happy existence. He always knew who would be catching for the Cardinals next year. He could tell you exactly why the horses he bet to win ran second. He could remember more details of Rocky's career than Rocky did.

"You were on the *fourteen*-yard line," he would say furiously. "My God, I saw it, didn't I?"

The day of the speech I found Freddy with his feet on the desk in the fly-specked little office in the painless-dentist district. He was scratching his head with one hand and holding up the sports page with the other.

"Coming to see the fireworks, Freddy?"

"Hell, no," said Freddy. "Those guys in the Chamber already got houses. I'm going down to the Grille, where they got this new television; double-header today."

Rocky came in while we were chatting. He had on a blue serge suit, freshly pressed, a pale green shirt and a tie of our state university colors. He didn't have to tell us he'd just come from the barbershop; Freddy sniffed approvingly.

"My boy!" he beamed. "All stunk up like Easter in the whorehouse. Knock 'em over, kid."

"Freddy," said Rocky. "Mercer Gamble called twice more about that claim."

"I knew there was something I had to do," said Freddy. "Is he sore?"

"He's going to be," said Rocky.

"Imagine that?" asked Freddy. "Nine chain stores and getting ulcers because some jerk burned three squares of roof off one of them!"

"Maybe that's why he's got nine," said Rocky.

"He's not a bad guy," said Freddy, "just eager."

We started to go and Freddy suddenly stirred.

"Jim," he said. "Old Rock and I sure appreciated your co-operation on that Maynard deal."

"It wasn't a deal, Freddy; close but no cigar."

"Just like I told Rocky," said Freddy contentedly. "He was all burned up. I told him what the hell; you lose one deal you make another. It all figures."

"They don't all figure like that one," said Rocky.

"I guess they don't at that," said Freddy. "Boy! If we ever hit one like that I'd close this joint for a week and take the whole family to the Derby. Give 'em hell, Rock."

Until Rocky began to speak, Tom's fourth luncheon ran exactly to form. Only the rule about departures kept the members through the ice cream. We had already heard from an actuary that Torrent's future was brighter because we were going to live twelve point three years longer than our grandfathers, though not necessarily in the individual case. We had heard from an advertiser that it was no longer enough to make a better mousetrap in this new era of modern communications. We had heard from the county agricultural agent that the soybean would revolutionize both agriculture and industry.

Rocky got a cordial hand after his introduction. Then you could see the room slump back to drowse over its cigars. Here and there livelier arms stretched on the table until wristwatches showed.

"Gentlemen, I feel like a con man after the nice things Mr. Gilchrist said about me 'cause he asked me here to talk about the future of Torrent and from where I sit, Torrent hasn't got any future.

"The reason it hasn't is because half you well-meaning gents are going to sleep right now while we're supposed to be talking about it and the other half will go back to their offices and sleep after we have. None of you men really care whether Torrent has any future or not as long as you eat regular. The men who do care are those big shots over there in the Torrent Club. They aren't asleep. They're sitting there right now, making damned sure Torrent never will have any future that lets other people eat as well as they do."

The half dozen members of the Torrent Club who were sitting in the room reddened angrily. The three dozen nonmembers looked around at each other and then attentively back to Rocky, unaware that their heads had begun to nod in approving unison.

Once he had established the sinister presence of an oppressive plutocracy in Torrent, Rocky had the sense to switch from the Torrent Club itself. As he knew, its membership was nearly as heterogeneous as that of the Chamber he was addressing. The only real difference was a slightly higher mean income bracket, to which most of the men at the luncheon confidently aspired. By the same token, most of them had not made it yet; Rocky rubbed their noses in it.

[66]

Then he adverted, in rapid succession, to older local grievances, real and imaginary. Without ever naming Simeon he declared that the dead hand of property had kept Wiasota from having an adequate railroad system. Without naming Archie and Hewitt he pointed out that we were the last city of our size to have gas instead of electric street lamps.

". . . because you were indifferent to the safety of wives and kids? Oh, no! *Ostensibly* it was cheaper to use gas from local bituminous coal that just happened to keep some of our people in Cadillacs and others in the dark. Wasn't it a fortunate coincidence that the army engineers, in *some* administrations, insisted our river couldn't be dammed? Cheap hydroelectric power for all might have changed the water levels in some of our most exclusive front yards—not that most of us ever get into them!"

Our airport was primitive because certain property owners of adjacent lands wanted profits instead of progress.

"You can call this past history," Rocky thundered, "but the past is what makes the future and now history is repeating itself. This state is as good as committed to spending sixty million bucks on a freeway system. Theoretically that's only about thirty bucks a head for our population. As a practical matter I don't need to tell productive, constructive businessmen like you who carries our tax loads. All the parasites in this state are going to be riding on your shoulders and on your children's.

"There aren't enough really rich men in this state to pay a load like that and no one's heard the ones we have volunteering extra help, either. Oh, no. You're going to pay for it. Is it going to do you any good? Is that freeway even coming to Torrent?

"You all hope so. Perhaps some of you think so. For my dough it's time we think about that again; I've been doing some hard thinking about it. In the first place that freeway doesn't have to come here. It could pass thirty miles east of us and all we'd ever see of it would be a tax bill.

"There are only two tentatively surveyed routes that can bring it into Torrent. One is up along the ridge. It would cost more dough up there. It would either bypass or cost extra for extensions to give service and get political support from the three county seats north of us—if it goes along the ridge. Finally, neither the Highway Commission nor the Park Commission wants it on the ridge.

"The other approach to Torrent would be along the natural contours of the riverbank. It's cheaper; the Highway Commission wants it there, the Park Commission wants it there, the towns north of us want it there. Everybody wants it there except our River Set.

"To bring it along the river would cut right through the rose gardens of some of our leading citizens. It would cut across the private bridle paths on which they like to ride horseback. It's a great thing to ride horseback; if it means that the people around you have to live in the mud, what of it? If it means the merchants, who rent your inherited property in town, won't ever expand enough to buy their own competitive property, what of it? If it means the whole community around you never gets a freeway at all, what of it? It's still a great thing to ride horseback through your own gardens, while your tenants and neighbors are taxed for a freeway they never get.

"Now, if this makes you sore, I'm glad. It makes me sore. But there's no use blaming the people with the rose gardens. It's natural for them to want to protect their property; it's natural for them to want to keep Torrent where they've always kept it—fifty years behind the times. The only people to blame are yourselves. It's well-meaning, easy-going people like you who have spent those fifty years patting each other on the back instead of developing a leadership with the guts to get a freeway to set Torrent free!"

He stopped abruptly, bowed to Tom and sat down. There were angry cries: "Communism!" "Socialism!" "Un-American!" They were engulfed in a tumult of applause. Tom had to wait two or three minutes before he could speak. He was smiling as he waited. One meeting had come alive.

"Rock," said Tom paternally, "we might have expected a blast from a guy who used to hit the line the way you did, but that was a humdinger. Thing is, to accomplish anything, a man's got to be *con*structive as well as *de*structive. Maybe some of our generation have muffed leadership around here. Would yours take it up if we got behind you?"

Rocky had been vehement in his speech; as he rose again his manner was meek.

"I can't speak for a generation, Mr. Gilchrist. You just asked me to speak on how I felt."

"Fair enough," said Tom. "Would you yourself take up this fight if we got behind you with votes?"

Part of the room broke into indignant cries: "No politics, Tom." "No politics here!" "What the hell is this?" They subsided in expectancy as Tom raised a moderating hand.

"This isn't politics, boys. I'm asking this for the whole community. How about it, Rocky?"

"Mr. Gilchrist," said Rocky, "I'm not sure what you mean but I hope you all know that I've always done my best for Torrent and always would."

It took Rocky several minutes to get out of the room. Some angry stares followed him, a few men lingered to expostulate furiously with Tom, but Rocky's departure was a triumphal exit of handshakes and hearty claps on the back.

I had come to yawn. I walked down the street with Rocky, trying to see the Torrent I had always accepted as the norm of a comfortable universe through his eyes. I was still three years older than Rocky but all of us had matured through the heyday of the New Deal. Rocky had known no more of hunger or oppression than Lucy and Artie and the young Randolphs, but the emptiest oratory might have sounded very different under the rectory's leaky roof.

"You're pretty quiet," said Rocky. "At least I woke those other bastards up."

"They aren't bastards, Rocky."

"Okay," he said, "so they're just dopes. But they're getting along. I got to make a change, Jim. You know Freddy."

"Are you thinking about politics?"

"What I think won't fetch it," said Rocky. "Politics is what you make other people think."

"Where did you get your freeway information?"

"Freddy," he grinned. "How wrong was it?"

"Pretty wrong," I said.

"I figured that," he said. "Freddy's always going to be wrong. But so are the other jerks in that meeting and the men who do know aren't talking, so who cares?"

"Most of what you said isn't true, Rocky."

"Most of everything isn't true," said Rocky. "You ought to try life, liberty and the pursuit of happiness and all that hogwash about the Four Freedoms and our glorious standard of living in Freddy Eastman's office awhile."

"You can change jobs, Rocky."

"To what? I damned near paid for that new stadium at State, for an assistant librarian's salary. 'Good old Rock! Just kick those goals for us, boy. We'll see that you pass economics.' So I did and they did. But you don't pass economics in Freddy's office, Jim."

"You aren't passing yet, Rocky. Hatred and fear and envy aren't economics in spite of the New Deal."

He grinned suddenly. "So who knows that but six-thousand-buck-a-year economists? I never thought about those things at the time. When

I started wondering all I could remember was people saying: 'Damn that New Deal; it won again.' "

"Its winning days are about over, Rocky."

"So who cares," said Rocky, "whether you call a good play a criss-cross, a spinner or a reverse? It's all the same old play and it got old because it's good if you play it right."

I found myself wondering if fear and hatred and envy and self-pity had become old because they were good. At my corner he offered me his hand.

"Don't take things so seriously, Jim. We'll all be dead a hundred years from now and you'll have a swell tombstone. If other people were as loyal as you maybe I could get one, too."

"I'm not loyal to that hot air, Rocky."

"Don't talk so loud," he laughed. "Disloyalty to hot air is un-American, Jim."

Tom Gilchrist called me on the phone in mid-afternoon. He was jubilant and wanted to thank me again for having suggested Rocky. The speech had surpassed all expectations. His phone had been ringing ever since with praise and with indignation. His panel was justified. He kept saying it was good work.

"I'm not so sure it's good, Tom."

"Controversy is the lifeblood of democracy, Jim."

"I hope you're not serious about backing him for politics."

"I certainly am," said Tom. "He's coming to dinner to discuss it tonight. Will you join us?"

"I will not and I wish you'd think twice about it."

"Jim," said Tom, "I know he's crude. Youth and vigor always are. But they're just what that council of ours needs."

Two days later the *Sentinel* announced Rocky's candidacy for the County Council with an endorsement signed by Tom. Side by side with it was a cartoon by Tom's staff man that set the key for the campaign. It showed Rocky in football togs carrying a ball labeled "Victory" as he plunged over a line labeled "Forces of Reaction" to a touchdown zone lettered "Freeway for Torrent." Two of the ineffectual defending linemen bore recognizable similarity to Hewitt Randolph and Archie.

I called on Archie late that afternoon. He had the paper beside the chaise longue on the terrace, where he was then spending most of his convalescence. He produced it for me with delighted chuckles.

"This is very droll, Jim," he said. "The Emperor Commodus descended from the throne to the arena but it has remained for us to start a gladiator toward the White House. Is he practicing the violin or will he just put another nickel in the jukebox when he's ready to burn us?"

"I'm glad it hasn't disturbed you," I said.

"Disturbed me? It's practically cured me. When Rocky is President he can make that chiropractic sister a major general in the WACs and household physician."

"How are you feeling yourself, sir?"

"Shattered," said Archie.

I began to speak encouragingly of his condition and his chuckles exploded into laughter.

"Nonsense! All citadels crumble, Jim. I can stand the coronary. What shatters me is missing Hewitt's face as he saw this cartoon."

Hewitt was so angry he had taken pains to conceal it. The day the cartoon appeared Tom had obviously made a point of being early for lunch at the Torrent Club. He took his place, as he always did, at the big round table. His smiling defiance accepted the immediate outburst of kidding cheerfully.

There was as much laughter as indignation in the club. Adult Torrent still couldn't take Rocky seriously. Two of the members had propped fresh copies of the cartoon conspicuously at the side table where Hewitt usually lunched with one of his relatively small circle of intimates. That day, however, Hewitt entered alone, came straight to the round table and motioned to Harvey for another chair. He indicated the dollar lunch negligently before turning to the others.

"I trust an economic royalist can still join you princes of privilege," he said, looking at Tom.

They had been friends all their lives.

"Hewitt," he said, "I hope you understand this is not personal."

"Of course," said Hewitt. "I'm going to save you a place in my tumbril."

"I should apologize about that cartoon," said Tom. "I didn't see the final proof on it and I admit the boys in the shop corned it up a little. But you'll have to admit yourself that the council needs new blood."

"This isn't new blood," said Hewitt. "This is just a new leech looking for some drops the New Deal forgot."

"Hewitt, for God's sake! This is purely local."

"Cancer begins locally," said Hewitt.

"Won't you admit we need that freeway?"

"Of course we need the freeway," said Hewitt. "We need faith, hope, charity and salvation, and we'll probably get them, too, with a new cabinet commissar apiece."

"Well, if you admit we need it . . ."

"I have admitted it," said Hewitt. "What I sat down here for is to tell you the facts of life about that freeway."

The table quieted respectfully. Hewitt had been noticeably close-mouthed about it up to then. He spoke with judicious restraint.

"The primary fact is that we're going to get that freeway anyhow. We would have had it from the New Deal except for the war short-ages. Those gave Dennis Flynn his first chance in fourteen years to out-Santa Claus the big white father himself and he isn't going to miss it. He's going to elect a Republican state legislature on the strength of it, this fall, every man of them frothing at the mouth to vote the appropriation.

"The technical planning has been well done by the only two honest and capable agencies in the state, Parks and Highways. It won't be quite so honest when the legislature gets through corkscrewing it past every voting bloc in the state. But we'll get a well-built freeway for only two or three times what it should cost. It will come to Torrent because by-passing us would hand southern Wiasota back to the Dem-ocrats for another twenty years.

"So the freeway for Torrent is in the bag. There was only one thing more we needed. We couldn't get it with all of politics, all of technol-ogy, all interested business and every boob who can mark a ballot pulling for it—until you, Tom, handed it on a silver plate to this obsolete halfback to step up and put his name on it."

"Hewitt! You know there's opposition!"

"I should," said Hewitt calmly. "I am the opposition. But if you'd let that paper of yours deviate into common sense just once, you'd spell it out in capital letters that I am not opposed to the freeway and neither are my neighbors. We oppose a choice of routes that will run it through our parlors. On a showdown, I'd rather have it through my parlor than not have it. It's worth more to this community and to the bank than my residence is worth to me.

"But the actual route is not going to be my choice and it's not going to be Rocky Slade's. It's going to happen in three steps and we can't affect a damned one of them because I've already tried.

"Firstly, Dennis has to elect his legislature and he will. Secondly he's got to vote the appropriation before he declares the route. De-cision on that will create so many disgruntled soreheads among the by-passed that he couldn't get the appropriation through if the ma-jority saw how thin the gravy will be for most of them. So he's got to hide behind Parks and Highways till he gets his dough voted. Then he'll cork up all his scorpions in the same bottle and let them choose a route. He told me himself he'd let them run it throught Saint Patrick's

Cathedral on Easter morning if he has to. He knows he's going to make six enemies for every friend that gets his snout in the trough. Neither he nor they are going to be reading your editorials or asking my wishes or Rocky Slade's advice. You're just giving Rocky a free ride on a sure thing."

Tom looked troubled. Hewitt could be irritating; we all sensed the truth in what he had been saying.

"Hewitt, would you explain this, in a quoted interview?"

"And get Rocky more votes? No thank you."

"All right," said Tom. "You've answered yourself. That's the whole trouble with America; keep your neck in and let George do it."

"The only trouble with America is Americans," said Hewitt. "Your sacred majority still believes it can get something for nothing by votes."

"I might have agreed with you once," said Tom. "I went abroad full of cynicism about our imperfections. I saw people plowing with oxen outside the game parks of those lovely castles and châteaux and then I went on to the Orient and saw women pulling wooden plows with shoulder harnesses. Baseball may be a silly national pastime but it beats hell out of blood baths. I came home glad to be a booster. Maybe we are young and gauche and new . . ."

"There is nothing new," said Hewitt, "in the idea of two and two making six as long as you can steal the extra two from your neighbors or grandchildren."

"Our grandchildren will use that freeway, Hewitt. Do you expect scientific advance for nothing? Granted it's not free; what other civilization has ever equaled our mastery of our environment?"

"Environment isn't gadgets," retorted Hewitt. "Rocky is *our* environment and if you think electing him is mastering him . . ."

They argued for an hour with one result beyond the usual stalemate. Tom had come into the club embarrassed and a little sheepish about Rocky. Hewitt's arrogance drove him into making a crusade out of a mistake. The *Sentinel* did temper its editorial tone after that first issue; but looking back, I think Rocky could have coasted to victory on his Chamber of Commerce speech.

Rocky did not choose to coast. The born contestant in him plunged into politics as he had plunged into football. It took little publicity to revive the memories Rocky had made synonymous with victory against odds. Fans of his playing days and youngsters he had coached, who were just reaching voting age, remembered old Rocky with the nostalgic glow of happy times.

Rocky Slade clubs blossomed in every precinct, short on experience, long on zeal. The service clubs, athletic associations and church groups welcomed him. And toward the end of the campaign he had a spectacular piece of luck. Two farmers came into town to celebrate the end of cultivating. Their zigzagging course home collided head-on with a car full of picnicking teenagers on the Ridge Road. Winifred could still convene any women's club in town with three phone calls; she went to work before the bodies were cold.

"Has your agony borne the children of Torrent to become statistics in the tragic toll of our highway massacres?" demanded Rocky.

Next evening he was shaking a furious fist at the South County Grange:

"Are you peasants and serfs, to be denied decent roads to the hospitals, libraries and churches your honest work feeds?"

He could adjust his minor keys to any particular audience; through them with endless variation ran the major themes of fear, envy and hate. It mattered not at all that there was no opposition to the freeway. Rocky created one in toto out of the glum silence of the River Set and vanquished it several times a day from sound truck, street corner, rostrum and microphone.

"Old Rock isn't afraid of any of 'em," said our elevator boy.

Our county elections were concurrent with the state primaries in late June. The only surprise in them was the size of Rocky's plurality. Prior to then he had had no real opposition. That plurality automatically created a dangerous one. The vote had been counted in Prairie as well as in Torrent. Dennis Flynn could speak glowingly of a landslide over the Democrats. In private he had to reckon with a new factor in southern Wiasota Republicanism.

The consolidation phase of his victory should have shown the most skeptical of us that Rocky had outgrown dropkicking. His first act was to propitiate the other members of the County Council. He had no intention of upsetting their normal deliberations. He regarded his election as a mandate to crusade for the freeway. With their concurrence, he proposed to devote himself to that.

They were delighted to be rid of such unpredictable energy. Their approval enabled him to go, hat in hand, to Dennis Flynn at the capital with what amounted to a double endorsement. There, after a Delphic acceptance from Flynn, Rocky got down to hard work.

At the university he found two master's candidates in civics. In the city he found an advertising agency. From the fusion of these talents with his own he produced what came to be known as the Slade presentation.

It amounted to a lecture, illustrated with multicolored graphs and charts and maps, on Wiasota's need for the freeway. Tax trends, population trends, birth rates, crop production, manufacturers' billings, truck loadings, auto licenses, accident statistics and land values were all accommodated to one persuasive argument.

From the heavy-implement dealers and the Highway Commissions of other states Rocky got film of their freeway operations. Then he took it to a film laboratory that understood its business. The film ran for only twelve minutes. What you remembered of it, even more than vistas of finished freeway and miles of machinery smoothing mountain, desert and forest, was Rocky Slade himself, supervising it all. He hadn't been out of Wiasota since the war. When the cutter got done with that film you saw him brooding like Napoleon on a hilltop or pointing imperiously to activity in California, Pennsylvania and New Jersey. He even had humor in it:

"Here's one detail I'll try not to repeat for you," he would tell audiences just before they saw a tractor and carryall rolling crazily down the side of a fill. While the audience was still gasping, a reversed section of the film rolled the equipment back up the fill and into its starting place.

"Can't keep a good program down, though," said Rocky.

With his presentation mounted and rehearsed, Rocky hunted up his audiences as methodically as he had created its elements. Elections for the state legislature were coming up that fall. Before them, Rocky and his show appeared in every county seat in the state, in every crossroads between Torrent and Prairie. He was always under the auspices of the county chairman; he always shared the platform with the local candidate:

"My old friend, Thorwald, wanted you neighbors of his to see with your own eyes what aggressive action in other states has got them to show for their Washington dollars. Thorwald is just as determined to pull Wiasota out of the mud as I am."

Rocky always gave a good show. He departed with the personal gratitude of chairman and candidate, with a widening knowledge of state politics, with a cumulative accretion to the fame of Rocky Slade.

These activities kept him much away from Torrent but his immediate need for Torrent was past. It would always vote for him. His absences reduced jealousy on the purely local plane. It was out of sight, out of mind in county affairs and Rocky, in his own mind, was already through with county affairs. Even Dennis Flynn did not realize, until the momentum was rolling, how solidly Rocky was building himself into state affairs.

The gratitude he won from obscure legislative candidates was not immediately negotiable. All of them were already pledged to vote for the freeway. Rocky himself would never vote for it. For his purposes none of this mattered. Long before it was voted he had ridden it to state-wide personal fame. It had taken hard work and, as I realized by hindsight, it must have taken a lot of money too. Somehow you never thought of Rocky in connection with money. He was always the underdog who presently made the touchdown.

Chapter Four

YOU can know a man all your life and see him in forty or fifty changes of clothes or background but the recurrent thoughts that bring him back to you will usually carry a single image. Consciously or not I had always thought of Rocky as the adolescent in the high school varsity sweater and baseball cap.

When he appeared in the door of my office the morning after my talk with Hewitt, it took a conscious effort to see him afresh, to weigh the visible evidence of whether I was looking at a convict or a senator.

He towered over Miss Premm's gray head as imposingly as he had on the previous afternoon, the same easy downward smile was still insuring her vote.

"Mr. James," she said, "it's the Honorable Roscoe Slade."

"So you *do* want me out of public life," said Rocky.

Her mouth smiled back; her eyes were gentle and grave. I had learned a good deal in the twenty hours since Rocky's previous visit. Miss Premm learned more than I did in every hour we both lived.

"No," she said, "I want to continue thinking of you as the Honorable, Rocky."

She closed the door quietly and left Rocky and me staring at each other. You can carry general as well as particular images. My notions of a senator would never be quite rid of the broad-hatted, synthetic planters and ranchers but they were obsolete and I knew it. The new trend in appearance was to what Hewitt always called management and Rocky knew it.

That morning he wore no pale green shirt and college tie. Even before her engagement ring had licensed proprietary henpecking, Lucy had gone to work on Rocky's rough edges. He already looked more like New York than Torrent. His dark tweeds, white shirt and navy knitted tie were modeled somewhere between Hewitt's fastidious elegance and the advertising men in Prairie. The gold watch Lucy had given him for Christmas set off an immaculate cuff. Convict he might be; the potential senator was scowling over Miss Premm's remark. He shook his head at me wearily.

"Jim, did you ever see a woman without a needle?"

"I never did."

"Lucy had hers waiting at the airport. I have to be very nice to you because you're going to help me. What the hell did she think I was going to do, come in here and punch you?"

"I hope not, Rocky."

"Don't worry—" he flashed me his best smile again—"if they were as loyal as you this never would have come up. She told me you talked Archie into the loan last night and I'll never forget it, Jim."

"She's mistaken, Rocky; we talked and Archie instructed me to handle it."

"Don't kid me, boy. I know who did it and I'm grateful but I'm in a hurry, too. Let's get on with it."

"Rocky, handling it means I understand it."

"Jim, believe me, you're better off not to. All you've got to do is give me a check. You've got Archie's say so and you're in the clear."

"I've got his orders to handle it, Rocky."

"Jim, it's just politics. Some sharpshooters think they've got me cornered. That's always when you win games. Remember Michigan? We were on their ten-yard line and I practically stuck the ball through Red Kennedy's navel and the idiot fumbled and that ten-second end of theirs had it while I was getting up. Everybody in the stadium thought that was the ball game. I got him with one hand on one ankle on our five-yard line. I made two of the three tackles that held them and I ripped off a fingernail knocking down their last pass.

"There were sixty-six thousand people in the stadium who figured I had to play it safe and kick . . . and that Michigan quarterback was one of them. Well, the next play—"

I didn't have to follow it because I had seen it. At the time it was hair-raising. Now I was thinking of Lucy's "He's pathetic." Perhaps in extremity all of us remember brighter moments. He was reminding himself, as much as me, that he had snatched triumph out of disaster before.

". . . they chased me seven yards behind our goal line while that boob was getting free and then I hit him right between the elbows with a forty-nine-yard pass and that *was* the ball game. This is just like that, Jim. Those sharpshooters are out on a limb; with a family loan I saw it off under them."

"We're wasting time, Rocky."

"Jim," he said, "I've never had anything from Archie but Latin double talk and sour sidecars. I've got to have this and all you've got to do is what he said: give it to me."

"We're still wasting time, Rocky."

"All right," he said. "I've been operating on an expense account. It's perfectly legal but it might stir up a publicity stink. A loan from Archie makes the whole thing a family matter and leaves my enemies up a tree."

"Whose expense account was it, Rocky?"

"Believe it or not, I'm not supposed to know."

"I've got to know, Rocky."

"Okay," he said, "the bastards never came clean with me. It's that gang out along the river. The ringleader is Hewitt Randolph."

Our County Council is a vestigial relic of rural days. It still exercises supervisory powers over county problems but direct elections and the extension of the city have gradually relegated these to compromising ambiguities of surveys or jurisdictional blind spots. The council meets irregularly as these problems arise and functions with its eyes on the clock.

Rocky went to his first meeting surging with zeal. He had been in the high-ceilinged old room in our courthouse before. It was different to enter as part of it. He felt the presence of the flags behind the desk, the solemnity of the gray-headed neighbors around the U-shaped table, the rap of the chairman's gavel in Bud Huston's firm hand. Rocky's voice was husky as he took the oath of office and accepted the handshakes of the others.

As the gavel rapped again he glanced around, raised a hand and then, at Bud's quizzical nod, rose to his feet.

"Mr. Chairman, I have a memorial for this council, based upon the obvious mandate of the people about the freeway . . ."

"Rocky," said Bud, not unkindly, "the election's over. Miss Elphinstone will put your memorial in the record, if you like—"

"Why sure, Rocky," said Miss Elphinstone, "tomorrow, right after my permanent."

"Mr. Chairman," said Rocky again. Bud shook his head patiently but with finality.

"Rocky, the freeway is state business and we got work to do. Is counsel for Wiasota Power and Light ready?"

"Ready, Mr. Chairman," I replied.

"Okay, Jim, what's your beef today?" asked Bud.

Rocky sat silent and smoldering through an hour's discussion about whether a change of power poles on South Cherokee Street might infringe the limits of the easement. At the end of it, Bud appointed him, as freshman member, to form a committee of one and check the width of the sidewalk.

"I'll lend you a tape from the store," said Bud. "That damned surveyor would charge the county sixty bucks and do it wrong."

The county did not even provide Rocky with an office. There were three desks for seven members in the little back room where Miss Elphinstone kept records and did correspondence.

"You can share any of 'em, Rocky," she said brightly, "but it's safer to keep anything nice in your own office. Those girls from Sheriff's steal every pencil in the building."

Rocky walked back to Freddy Eastman's office in sagging, anticlimatic dejection. The hullabaloo was over. The Rocky Slade clubs had dissolved. The freeway was a long way from Cherokee Street.

"Freddy," he said, "I knocked myself out getting into an old folks' home."

"So what?" asked Freddy. "You still get three Gs a year for a couple of long naps every week. How about putting a barb in the council's butt to get us a class A ball team?"

Rocky was pondering his future when Miss Temple at the bank telephoned him. He supposed that he was overdrawn. He had thought he had about sixty dollars left but he had written a blizzard of small checks during the campaign. On top of them he still owed a job printer a hundred and ten dollars. He had begun to explain when Miss Temple informed him that Hewitt Randolph's personal secretary did not call customers about overdrafts. She had called to tell him that Mr. Randolph would like to see him at his convenience.

Rocky walked to the bank with his muscles flexed for a fight. Hewitt had preserved an ominous silence through Rocky's campaign assaults. Rocky knew that Hewitt was a good friend of Bud Huston's. It could be easier to tame a councilor than to silence a candidate.

Hewitt had received him with congratulations and cordiality. He said that he understood political necessities. He did not deny that he had disapproved of some of Rocky's tactics. But no one could deny that they had produced victory.

Rocky, said Hewitt, was at a turning point in a promising career. He could go on singing his soak-the-rich theme to the envious, but he would soon find that the election had dispersed his audience, that electorates were notoriously forgetful. People understood what it took to get into office. His real future would be measured by what he did in office. It would be measured by the substantial element of the community that did not forget.

Most of those thoughtful people regretted that their own responsibilities precluded an active part in political life. It was one of the tragedies of democracy that too often responsibility went, by default, to the people least capable of exercising it for the true public good.

It was another tragedy that too often a man of proven capacity for victory and leadership was so hampered by his financial position as to be incapable of independence in statesmanship.

Hewitt and other farsighted members of the community had considered this through Rocky's campaign. They had even considered lending their support to his opposition, as they always would have to do in any situation that threatened the true public welfare. But they remembered what Rocky had done for Torrent in the past. They had been impressed by the size of his plurality. They had seen in it a force that could be of effective use for the public good, with proper support. They had considered it all very carefully and they had authorized Hewitt to say that they were ready to make a disinterested contribution toward a constructive public career.

"In exchange for what, Mr. Randolph?" asked Rocky.

"I'm glad you asked that question," said Hewitt. "It shows the intelligence and scruple we admire."

Hewitt had gone on to insist that this offer was in no sense a deal for anything. The men for whom he spoke were resolved to remain anonymous. Rocky should never know who his benefactors were. It was their guarantee, and his, of the innocence of the offer. They would naturally watch with interest to see what use he made of their gift. They were confident that he would show the kind of judgment they would hope to back for larger public trusts in time.

"How much are you talking about, Mr. Randolph?"

"You can count," said Hewitt, "on twelve thousand dollars, to begin."

He had thought Hewitt might be talking about five hundred. To Rocky twelve thousand could mean only one thing.

"What if I can't keep the freeway off the river?" he asked.

That question, Hewitt said, disappointed him a little. It showed Rocky was still taking a narrow view. It illustrated the kind of personal pressures from which his admirers wished to free him. Hewitt did not deny that many responsible members of the town didn't want a freeway through their front yards. But that was only one way of looking at the problem.

The same men emphatically did want a freeway for Torrent. There could be no question of bribery; they knew Rocky would vote on neither the freeway nor the route. They believed that the energy and vigor he had already shown could be expanded to serve a more constructive vision of the community's true needs. Those could be served quite as well by a freeway on the ridge as by one on the river.

A man with the vision to lead a unified effort for that instead of a divided and rancorous grandstand play for the river route would be serving his whole community as well as his own true interest. Time and money to carry his work to the other communities preferring the ridge route would solidify him with the whole state picture. He could make friends of county chairmen and candidates for the legislature on terms of a dignified joint effort. He could make himself a public figure not only in Torrent but in Wiasota.

"Mr. Randolph," said Rocky, "I think you got something."

That was the origin of the Rocky Slade presentation and the money that underwrote it. Hewitt had given Rocky three thousand dollars at once. He had given him much more than the cash.

Their understanding had enabled Hewitt to telephone Dennis Flynn that regardless of appearances, which can be so deceptive in practical politics, the substance of southern Wiasota was solidly behind Rocky. It was Hewitt who had sent Rocky to the advertising agency in Prairie. It was Hewitt who had helped him get films from the road equipment people. It was Hewitt who had put Rocky up for the Torrent Club and for the Country Club that summer.

Rocky and Hewitt had agreed that evidences of intimacy between them might be misunderstood. He had never gone to Hewitt's office in the bank again. For counsel, as long as he was accepting it, he had driven out to Hewitt's house after dark.

Both had preserved the original condition that Rocky should not know the names of his other benefactors. It was a protection for him as well as for them. There could be no question of bribery or improper influence when he didn't even known the sources of his assistance. Hewitt had given the others, as well as Rocky, his word that their names would not be known.

"You'd take Hewitt's word, wouldn't you, Jim?"

"Yes," I said, "and you took the money, too?"

"Natch," said Rocky. "Between ourselves, I'd kind of expected a deal from Hewitt to hush me up in the campaign. That would have been peanuts; this was jackpot while it lasted."

"How long did it last?"

"All twelve thousand bucks' worth," Rocky grinned. "He was sore by the end but I'll say for the bastard he paid off."

"You made no promise about the freeway?"

"Of course not; I don't even vote on it."

"But you took this money after the election?"

"That's the crux of it," said Rocky. "It was just expenses for propaganda but theoretically I'm a public official. It gives the Prairie *Times* just enough toehold for a stink."

"How did the Prairie *Times* get hold of it, Rocky?"

"Search me," said Rocky. "In politics you make enemies. I never even met Harry Caldwell; Hewitt always coached me to stay away from him. But I have been operating high, wide and handsome in Prairie. A lot of this dough went for keeping a permanent suite at the Plaza.

"It's expensive and it's a very good investment. It gives me a lot of front when I'm there. When I'm not there I've been lending the key to a lot of small-time politicos with big-time ideas. Some of them had some very lively evenings there. They'll either remember it when they get to voting the freeway route or they'll wish they had.

"Then I've had charge accounts at the Broiler and the Fandango Room and the Acme Liquor and I've always got plane tickets through the Modernage Travel—I wasn't trying to hide, Jim. I was building myself, big. A few days ago a friend of mine who reports politics for the Prairie *Times* told me on the quiet he'd been ordered to run a tape on my expenses. He said he already had enough to hang me unless I could do a lot of explaining."

"What day did he tell you this, Rocky?"

"I don't remember, exactly; last week some time."

"Could it be the Democrats after you?"

"Hell no," said Rocky. "They don't want any more talk about quiet money than we do."

"Who else knows?"

"Hewitt, of course. But he's screaming for you to get me under Archie's wing. He's sore enough to break me but he wouldn't dare do it this way."

"Why's he sore, Rocky?"

Rocky scratched his head thoughtfully.

"Jim, Hewitt is as phony as a cotton tit. He was just playing king-maker with me. While I buttered him up and asked foolish questions, I was his boy. When he began to see that I had better answers than his, he was miffed.

"The personal gripe started with that damned Cadillac. There I was plugging a high-speed freeway in a second-hand jalopy. Ed Delany was always a fan of mine and he started one of the first Rocky Slade clubs in the election. When he first spoke to me about that car I thought he was kidding. He talked about advertising value to him

[83]

and keeping up appearances to me. And Ed gave me a deal that was practically a gift. I didn't find out till after the deal was over that one reason he'd done it was to spite Hewitt.

"Even second-hand Cads were hard to get last summer. Hewitt was after that one for a present to Gretchen but he figured Ed wouldn't dare sell it to anyone but our leading banker. He was chiseling with Ed about price and Ed's got just enough Irish in him to tell our leading banker to stuff it.

"So I turn up driving the car Hewitt wanted and he was sore as hell at me: 'That's pretty ostentatious, Roscoe, I'm disappointed in your judgment!' all very pious and lofty.

"The thing that ripped it between us was Lucy. He figured she ought to mourn her life away for his heroic son. When I started taking her out it was presumption. You remember that night at his damned Halloween party?"

"Yes."

"He was like that in private, too. And then he was sore about the way I handled Flynn, upstate. We tangled on a detail or two and Flynn phoned Hewitt I was getting too big for my britches. That's my idea of progress but Hewitt thinks he's the only man alive who can handle Flynn, or anything else for that matter.

"So when Lucy and I got engaged, Hewitt lowered the boom on me. His friends no longer saw the need of helping anyone with such strong family backing. It caught me short just when I was beginning to get somewhere. I had to brace Archie for dough. For all I knew he'd been one of Hewitt's gang, though I didn't mention it. Archie told me to paddle my own canoe but now he's going to help me and he's going to like it."

"Could Flynn have tipped the paper on you, Rocky?"

"He could," said Rocky slowly. "I've worked hard on Flynn but you just don't get chummy overnight with eighty-year-old state bosses. He knows that I know where a lot of bodies are buried. He knows he's either got to help me or ditch me pretty soon. And he's told Hewitt he wants this thing hushed up fast."

"Why twenty thousand when you only accepted twelve, Rocky?"

"My election," said Rocky, "was a fluke. I was just a new face with the old tricks. People remembered my football and it was strictly local. The next one can't be. I've learned to operate and I'm going to keep operating.

"Last night I found out for sure in Prairie there'll be a Senate seat open in 'forty-eight. Flynn's known it longer than I have and he didn't tell me. I'm probably going to be needing a professional campaign manager. I can get the same guy who's been told to expose me. He hates his paper but he can't leave it for nothing. And then, with or without Flynn, I'll need dough for an office and printing and promotion and radio time and travel and—the works, Jim. I'm playing for keeps.

"But I'm trying to think of the family, too. All of this doesn't have to come from Archie. Between ourselves, Hewitt is scared enough to pay Archie the twelve himself, if you handle it right, so that Archie and I can start fresh. But we've got to have the formal loan from Archie, fast."

"How will a loan now cover last summer's spending?"

"Oh, I forgot," said Rocky easily. "Hewitt says it's got to be retroactive."

"Retroactive? You mean a false date?"

"What the hell is a date?" Rocky shrugged. "As Hewitt says, the world uses half a dozen calendars; we use our own."

"Not through this office, Rocky."

"Jim," he said, "you'd better think a little harder."

"I've thought. This office falsifies no records."

He stared at me a second and then he looked around the office. He was angry and he was taking his time to control it. When he spoke again it was patiently, persuasively.

"Jim, the world isn't run in ivory towers like this room. America is run by lobbies. You can't hold a union job or raise a bushel of corn or own a share of stock or eat a meal or drive a car without supporting lobbies. Maybe it's not what the Constitution says; it's what America does. If Jesus had seen as much trading in the temple as I've seen over one lousy freeway, He'd have thrown away His whip and taken out a license. If people wanted ethics they could have sent Archie up to quote Gibbon in that snakepit at Prairie. They wanted a freeway and they sent me. I've been lobbying and it's perfectly legal."

"Then why hush it up with false dates?"

"Jim, we're hypocritical people. Bastards who wouldn't give a dime to get us a freeway will crucify me for taking help where I could get it. They'll be hollering about ethics and quoting Scripture about my serving two masters and being on two payrolls."

"You were, Rocky."

"Jim," he said. "If you can't be loyal to me you might think about the Maynards."

"I'm trying to, Rocky. I'll get you the loan this morning, but not with false dates."

He had been angry. Now as he hesitated I could see the anger draining out of him. For the first time since I had known him Rocky was scared.

"Jim, you don't understand yet. This is for keeps. God knows Archie never did anything for me. I'm going to enjoy his funeral but I don't want to kill him. You know what Jamison said about anger and excitement. If we don't get this thing stopped it could even come out in public that I've—well, what you know about Lucy and me."

PART II

Chapter Five

"YOU needn't look censorious," Lucy said to me once. "It's all your fault."

That was some time after her engagement to Rocky had been announced, so that we had begun to be natural with each other again, or as natural as we could be in the new circumstances. She enjoyed teasing me and she was doing it then, about my having blundered into them in the boathouse, but there is always a needle somewhere in feminine teasing.

My intrusion may have precipitated the engagement; its roots were not accidental. Rocky was more disconcerted that morning than I. His assertion that they were already engaged was not a chivalrous lie. He wanted to marry her. They both knew that I would not speak of what I had seen. And Lucy would have told me about it anyhow as, first and last, she told me almost every detail of their courtship. She had no one else to talk to and confidences were inherent in our intimacy.

This had begun with my assumption of the management of the Maynard estate in the fall of 1945. As soon as I could get out of the army I had taken the first available plane back to Torrent. It had been nearly four years since I had written a brief. Once I would have thought such an interval disastrous, even to a well-established practice. The war had given me perspective on disaster; I knew I was a lucky man.

I was alive, unimpaired, and chafing to return to productive work. It awaited me on terms that were a stimulus in themselves. The practice was lost, as I knew, and I should have to rebuild it alone.

This was only in part a consequence of the war. I had scarcely cut my teeth in Father's office before he left it for good. He had never wanted to be a judge but our family had lived by the law for three generations. He regarded the Governor's appointment to our Superior Court as mandatory.

The relinquishment of private practice was, for him, implicit in the appointment. But for the war I might have held some of his clients. My long absence had left those with active business no choice but to change. Some, I could hope, might return in time. My immediate future was a formidable and welcome challenge.

My father had died during the war, leaving little property. His life insurance would keep Mother comfortably in our house while she lived. The office, Miss Premm and my future were up to me. The day I returned I had to borrow from the bank to pay the arrears in salary about which Miss Premm had lied to my mother.

"It would have worried her, Mr. James," she said, "and I had my savings."

"You were gambling with them," I reproached her.

"Keeping the office open made us sure you'd come back," she said. "We'll manage nicely now, if you're a little more prudent. You never should have started paying Mr. Randolph interest until it became a tax deduction."

I never told her that I had thought of that myself. Our debt to her was long overdue; you don't start taking tax deductions until you have a taxable income. That still seemed remote the morning she broke the silence in Father's old office.

"Mr. James, it's Mr. Archer and Miss Lucy Maynard."

They had not gone into mourning for Artie but that day they seemed more formal than I had remembered them. Archie limped in wearing a full suit instead of the jacket and slacks he customarily wore to town. Lucy's hair was still short from the factory. She had on severe tweeds that seemed mannish until you noticed her figure. As I did, I remembered Vinty. The glowing carefree girl who had sat in that same chair and said: "You ought to get married yourself, Jim; everyone should," was now a mature, self-possessed woman.

"We came on business," said Archie, "but I hope you'll allow us to say first how deeply we all miss your father."

"He was so sweet under that austerity," said Lucy. "I always thought if I did a crime I'd want him to sentence me and then I'd know everything was done right and I could quit worrying about it."

I said what I could about Artie and Vinty. Mother and I had intended calling at River House that week.

"You must bring her out to dinner," said Archie.

"Artie and Vinty were so fond of all of you," said Lucy. "Artie always said when he took over our things he'd fire Mr. Tuttlewise and ask you about everything."

"That, in fact, is why we came," said Archie.

Their proposal astounded me. It was known in town that there was friction between Archie and the Tuttlewises. There always had been but they had represented him, and Simeon before him, for over sixty years. When I reminded them of this, Archie shook his head.

"You'll find him as eager for change as we are," he said. Then he smiled dryly. "As soon as we knew you'd be back, we started making sure of that."

"Mr. Horace is senile," said Lucy, "and Leonard would be subnormal in a room full of cockroaches. He says we can't have horses any more and may have to sell Widgeon Lake."

"I might say the same things, Lucy."

"If you said them we'd believe them."

"That isn't just, kitten," said Archie. "This is not a question of trust, Jim. Most of it is my own fault. I could never bear details; I'd always thought it would be good for Artie to handle things when he was old enough. I'm sure the Tuttlewises have done their best but what we need is salvage."

"I'll help," said Lucy. "I'll learn all the details. I'll get an accounting book and find out which are debits and which are credits. It can't be any worse than Italian and I almost learned that."

"You did, except for the accent," said Archie.

"We won't accent the accounts," said Lucy. "I'll even learn about debentures if you say so, Jim."

"I believe we ate the debentures," said Archie. "But Horace will give you the records. I won't bother you about details, Jim; in fact I can't bear them."

He scowled at the remembrance and then his face brightened happily; his work for the day was done.

"Now that that's settled," he said, "I got four drakes and a hen bluebill just off the northwest corner of Baker's point this morning with number six shot in the twenty-eight. I had about twenty miles of southeast breeze over my left shoulder and I only put out seventeen blocks. If you'd like to use Artie's boat with me tomorrow—"

"Mr. Maynard, this is not settled. I'll have to speak to Mr. Tuttlewise."

"Do it this afternoon," said Archie. "The wind is hauling east."

"Jim," said Lucy, "we need you, badly."

Mr. Horace Tuttlewise received me with great civility. He was over eighty and time had made him the patriarch of the Torrent bar. He had always been dilatory and he could be exasperatingly opinionated. He was also a man of scruple and self-respect. He was by then almost inactive; for a decade he had used his hearing device as a shield from a world that had begun to bore him.

Mr. Horace had been twenty years older than my father. They had spent a lifetime on opposite sides of the court and often lunched together. He had come, in person, to our office the day I reopened it and had spoken with sincerity of his wish to return some of our straying clients.

In his own office he seated me ceremoniously and scowled while he toyed with his hearing aid, tapping a bony knuckle on his desk until the sound suited him.

"Hundred-and-seventy-dollar swindle," said Mr. Horace. "You've come about Archie?"

"I've come for your counsel, sir."

"My counsel won't help you," said Mr. Horace. "You need a doctor with guts enough to commit him but you'll never find one. Archie would be very dangerous in the chair, Jim. At large he's only dangerous to himself, as you will discover."

"I'm not discovering without your approval, sir."

"Jim," said Mr. Horace, "he's yours with my approval and compassion. I might have got Archie to the grave without bankruptcy proceedings but I'm eighty-one and he won't even speak to Leonard on the telephone. He just sends us his overdrafts and someone's got to look out for Lucy."

He shook his head wearily and frowned at me.

"Perhaps I should apologize for the condition of the estate. You won't understand until you know Archie better. Simeon gave me my first case . . . and he kept me on after your grandfather beat us. There was only one rule: if Archie wanted it he got it."

"It was bad enough while he was chasing those fancy women around every roulette wheel in Europe and trying to lose his citizenship by joining the French Army. It was worse when he came home. Some Frenchmen had filled his head with ideas about the brotherhood of man. The first thing he did was insist on building playgrounds for our miners just when every heel in Texas was kicking the top off new oil wells.

"Then a man he'd known in one of those goddamned colleges explained short selling to Archie in nineteen twenty-seven. The same man sold him most of an investment trust in August of nineteen twenty-nine.

"When that rascal who sold us the helicopter factory killed himself, Archie told me he should have paid more attention to Sir Isaac Newton. A year after he insisted on those tenant-purchase agreements that made us the laughingstock of the state, he said he'd read further into Tolstoi and wasn't sure it would work. Just before Wiasota passed the first comprehensive road program, Archie sold both cement works. A friend had told him about a reef of solid cadmium in New Mexico. We never even got a clear title but it didn't matter because the cadmium had apparently moved. The day the war was declared—"

He stopped and readjusted the hearing aid and shrugged.

"Jim," he said, "a little biography beats a volume of counsel. Hewitt can tell you the rest. Now tell me more about the war. Did the British really make our vehicles drive on the left side?"

"In England they did, sir."

"Arrogant," said Mr. Horace, "arrogant and insular."

At the bank Hewitt Randolph gave me his approval and warm encouragement. "The Tuttlewises are honest, Jim, but . . . you can lean on my shoulders, young fellow; they're broader than they look."

At home I encountered a different ramification. My mother heard me out with that bright semblance of attention women accord any subject on which they've already made up their minds. Then she smiled sweetly.

"Your decision, dear, but Dentons never have represented Maynards."

Somewhere we all have our crutches. Winifred had been a Parmenter and Rocky had beaten Notre Dame and Archie had a libraryful of negative wisdom at the end of his tongue and Dentons never had represented Maynards. My mother's tone of voice made it sound like an eleventh commandment. In fact it had been a sound professional policy. Grandfather Denton had told my father that no attorney in Wiasota could ask for more than a case against the Maynards with the Tuttlewises across the court. Father had repeated it to me. My mother's mind would always be oriented to the past. Now the times had changed; the estate was respectable business.

"This is not business, dear."

"What else would it be?"

"Archie has decided to marry you to Lucy."

"Mother, please! This is serious."

"It won't be serious until she decides," said my mother, "and then you'll have to do their business anyway."

All mothers are fatuous about their sons and all women are obsessed with marriage. Forty-odd months in the army had dimmed my recollection that the world is half women. From then on I began to catch up fast. My next taste came the following day when I began to explain our new duties to Miss Premm.

"It will probably make a lot of changes," I said.

"Of course," said Miss Premm, "but it's time you were married, Mr. James."

I categorized it with my mother's remarks as another proof of feminine absorption, not only with matrimony but with the obvious. The six-year gulf between our ages had fixed Lucy in my mind first as the red-haired child in the pony cart and then as the engaged adolescent who had insisted on being hanged with Vinty. I had always liked her; we belonged, in my mind if not in fact, to different generations. Propinquity the new relation would certainly give us. It was inevitable for women to leap to obvious conclusions about that. Perhaps it is as inevitable for men to imagine they can resist the obvious.

I I

Sometimes I think back upon the six months that followed as the happiest time of my life. I was plunged at once into work so multifarious that every phone call brought a new problem. Nearly every one of them involved discussion with Lucy, which, in its turn, brought me presently the unique exhilaration that vibrates through the whole process of falling in love, long before you realize you are doing it.

It began the next morning over their breakfast table. I had insisted on cutting our shoot short to get down to work. Archie said that was absurd; we could stay half an hour longer on the river and more than make it up by working at the breakfast table; there was time for everything if you used it efficiently. At the table Lucy was waiting for us, her skin freshly scrubbed and glowing, a notebook clutched proudly in her hand.

"I remember about the debentures now," said Archie. "We did eat them. Horace told me so when I wanted them for new joists for the stable. You'll have to look at the stable, Jim, before we get horses again."

"We'll make a list," said Lucy. "We'll put down everything and the cost so we'll know exactly. In the factory we had project lists and progress reports and we always cheated on them and made it up next week."

After breakfast we walked out together to the stable. We had to get Allen to fetch some tools from the basement to pry open the door. A rusted hinge broke off in the process and one look at the interior made even Archie blink. Time, decay and the weight of snow on the slates had cracked the old roof wide open. We entered a ruin of rot and cobwebs. The little wicker pony cart sat serenely under a quarter-inch coat of dust, paint scaling from its aged red spokes.

"We would have used that after gas rationing," said Archie, "but it wasn't entirely practical; we had no pony and there's no place in town to keep one now that they've closed the livery. That cart should be reconditioned, Jim. In fact we'll have to recondition everything in here. You can sell something or get a loan from Hewitt."

That had been the prevailing policy for the previous twenty years. The Tuttlewises had sold something or got a loan from Hewitt. The security list and farm rolls, when I got them, were fiscal counterparts of the stable. There was a fistful of defaulted bonds. Receivership notices were neatly pinned to most of the stock certificates. The good farms had been mined without fertilizer, rotation or repairs. The marginal ones and undesirable tenants were built into the estate with umbilical cords of mortgage and debt.

In my office Archie had spoken lightly of salvage; a first appraisal ended my levity. Under current tax rates it would be impossible to recover the opulence they had known. With discipline and luck I might save the house and a reduced scale of living for them. The discipline, I knew, would be either easy or impossible. The luck turned on Archie's life. He was no longer insurable. The specter of inheritance taxes was always before me.

For me no more than for the Tuttlewises would Archie pay any attention to detail. When I had drawn a budget based on my first appraisal I did my best to make him go through it. He shook his head.

"I'll do without whatever you say but arithmetic, no. It's the dreariest of man's devices, Jim; permutations of ten symbols that always come back to digits in a ledger proving I'm wrong. The dullest book you can find offers twenty-six symbols and the ultimate reward of proving someone else was wrong."

"I want a budget," said Lucy. "Every couple I know has one. It will be exciting."

In a sense it may have been less than exciting; in another it was critical. And so it was that we began, in my office, her instruction in the ominous portents of the ten symbols. To my relief, she gave them, at least for a while, attentive and sober thought.

"This does mean no more horses, doesn't it, Jim?"

"Not for five years at the very least."

"All right. Daddy didn't really enjoy it, because of his leg. He just rode because he always had and he thought we should. But he's nearly five years from it now and he won't be able to resume after five more."

"With luck you might, some day, Lucy."

She was silent and then shook her head thoughtfully.

"We'd better cut clean, Jim. I can remember Daddy telling Artie and me about Cheval and how he named a culture. He'll never understand but about all that's left of chivalry is the horse's ass."

Then she looked at me again and I saw the old glinting merriment break through her new gravity.

"Why, Mr. James; I've shocked you. Our army was much too sheltered. You should have worked in the factory."

She had been amused by Miss Premm's office formality and increasingly, when we were alone, she would copy it to tease me. I don't know when I first began to notice it and enjoy it and want to hear again the unique blend of mockery and intimacy her lips always gave it.

She was by no means uniformly tractable. She had accepted the budget delightedly. It was a novelty; she liked the identification with the problems of young wives she knew. As we progressed to more serious reform, I met, head on, the latent stubbornness of her blood and nature.

"Jim! You can't think of selling Widgeon Lake!"

"Thinking's over; we're doing it, Lucy."

"Never! Daddy has shot there all his life."

"Lucy, on the tables, his life is three quarters over—"

"All the more reason for him to enjoy the rest of it. You can sell or mortgage or hypothecate something else."

"We're selling it to buy something else."

"What?"

"Income and reserve for inheritance taxes. It comes from this or out of you and your kids."

"We are *not* penalizing him for me or grandchildren he may never see. That's final, Jim."

"I'm sorry. Where do I send the records?"

"You burn them and never mention Widgeon Lake again."

"I mean all the estate records."

"You keep them right here, of course."

"Not unless I'm managing, Lucy."

She stared at me; her eyes widened.

"Are you threatening to quit us?"

"This is not a threat, Lucy. I either manage or quit."

She crimsoned and very becoming it was, too. I think that was the first time I ever noticed that her hands when she was disturbed always toyed with that little gold chain on her neck. When she spoke again uncertainty had crept into her defiance.

"Daddy wouldn't let you quit," she said.

"Then let's get to work. There'll be capital gains tax on this, of course, but with what's left—"

She was absent and abstracted through the rest of the afternoon. I had to repeat myself about things she would ordinarily have grasped at once. She kept darting looks at me from under those lovely cornsilk eyelashes. When the work was done she pushed the paper back on my desk and eyed me squarely.

"Jim, would you really have quit us?"

"Yes."

"I mean truly," she said. "It's over and we'll do it but weren't you bluffing a little?"

"No."

"Do you ever bluff, Jim?"

"No."

"Why not?"

"It's a tactic to get something for nothing; in the long run you don't get it."

"Do you always think for the long run?"

"I'm paid to try, Lucy."

"Oh, stop it. Work's over. I mean about everything."

"I don't have to think about everything."

"So I've noticed," she said dryly. "It's all in perfect compartments, isn't it: lists and rolls and dossiers and a master calendar full of racy dates with Uncle Hewitt at the bank? Everything is in perfect order, isn't it?"

"Not yet," I said. "But we're making progress."

"I'm glad to hear it," said Lucy and rose. Then as I was helping her into her coat she suddenly smiled.

"I didn't mean to be bitchy, Mr. James, but you really would have quit us, wouldn't you?"

"Yes."

"I'm glad," she said. "I'm glad you would. I'm going to tell Daddy the whole thing."

I I I

The downtown work was laborious and protracted but relatively simple in nature. It amounted to bringing harmony out of chaos in that realm of human affairs Archie so blithely dismissed as "digits in a ledger somewhere." As a practical matter this meant reversing a twenty-eight-year habit of spending three dollars for every one the estate took in.

The process taught me more than arithmetic. Hewitt had been voluble about Archie's need for a new man and warmly cordial at first. He was nettled when I took up with him the item of interest on Archie's bank debts.

"Damn it, Jim, he insisted on having the money. And he's a heavy stockholder here, or was."

It would be wrong to say that Hewitt and the Tuttlewises had cheated Archie. They had allowed his impetuosity to commit him to arrangements profitable for the bank. Then, between them, Hewitt and the Tuttlewises had selected most of the securities in the estate portfolio. They had balanced an ultraconservative position in overpriced bonds with the kind of stock that shows very high yield at the time of purchase. Taken as a whole, their record was a little better than Archie's unerring instinct for the catastrophic but it was far less than distinguished. For years they had been letting Archie eat what was good and making him loans against the dubious. They would never take their medicine on a mistake.

To Hewitt's unexpressed vexation I turned the whole list over to the town's solitary investment broker. Kevin Inglis was a patient Scotchman who had made an excellent record, for clients and for himself, with no assistance from cadmium reefs. The medicine he prescribed was bitter but our reduced foundations were orthodox.

Similarly it had been the habit of the Tuttlewises to discuss farm problems with tenants on Sunday afternoons if the roads were dry and the weather fair. They had farms of their own and, in two cases, desirable previous tenants of the Maynards' on them. I looked over what was left and drove up to the dean of the Maynard Institute at Prairie. Archie was still a trustee of the school, though he never went near it. The dean, who knew him, clucked sympathetically.

" 'The eye of the master maketh fat the ox,' Mr. Denton."

"Not this master," I said. "You've got to help us."

In the end he gave me a list of farm management firms and, lowering his voice a little, put a pencil mark by one of the names. I turned the farm problem over to them with consequences as promising for the future as they were painful at the time.

"My God, Jim! There were six covies on that place," said Archie.

"And twelve bushels to the acre, sir."

"All right, all right, spare me the arithmetic." Then his face brightened. "Maybe we can poach there. You know, I always envied poachers."

The insoluble nightmare was River House itself.

"The one horse shay lasted a hundred years," said Lucy. "That should give us another twenty-five."

At a price, it would. The place had been soundly built with unlimited nineteenth-century dollars. Every stick of it had begun to scream for union labor repairs with the residual trickle from twentieth-century taxes. There was a larger staff on pension than on the place. The four survivors were nearly as decrepit as the house and united solely in their determination to die with it. It was one point on which I allowed Archie and Lucy to overrule me.

"It's their house, too," they both said.

The arithmetic on pensions, and replacements, if we could have found them, favored the Maynards. The consequences did not.

"I was not instructed in the plumbing way, sir," said McClintic with morose pride. "I was always stables."

"I'm sure it's all very well about one stove if they want the soup cold, sir," said Douglass reproachfully. "But with Frieda so old downstairs and the drafts in the dumbwaiter . . ."

"Gas we already got upstairs," said Frieda furiously. "You wait; you'll find that Douglass dead of gas but not in my kitchen. Weicker always said coal; 'carry your own coal and wake up mornings,' he said."

"I'm not disputing college engineers," said Allen huffily. "But with the flues as they are, it's more coal or freeze the west wing pipes again . . ."

"Jim, you mustn't fuss with trifles; when you need something, buy it," said Archie.

"You're cute when you're cross," said Lucy. "If I give in about the greenhouse can we have the porch fixed?"

It all took me continually to River House. At the outset I had resolved not to become involved with the minutiae of the place. The minutiae of that place were a series of fuses, smoldering while you slept.

"Don't let me tear you from Blackstone," Lucy phoned cheerfully, "but we're having a wonderful fire in the roof. Will you come out for picnic lunch in the ruins?"

In the other houses of Wiasota people chased the squirrels out of the attic. Archie said they had been there as long as he had without ever short-circuiting the wires before. He couldn't see why his water pressure was any business of the insurers.

"They don't seem to comprehend that without a fire now and then there wouldn't be any insurance business," said Archie. "What's this nonsense about new pipes?"

"It's very sensible," said Lucy. "While we're all torn up we can have the baths retiled, can't we, Mr. James?"

"Excuse me," said Archie. "I've heard this before. I'm going to take a nap before Jim says we can't have beds."

He usually left us after lunch and that day Lucy resumed the attack over coffee in the library.

"Tiles wouldn't cost what we saved by not regraveling the drive. Come on, Jim; what's firstly, secondly and thirdly about that?"

"Firstly, you can do without. Secondly, we've got to do the drive anyway when we can afford it—"

"And thirdly," she mimicked solemnly, "every dollar of capital takes four of income to replace and the taxes will get us if we don't watch out and I can't have new tiles but you might at least stay and quarrel a little longer instead of rushing back to your office."

"I will if you order tiles," I promised her.

"Mr. James," she said, "this relation has all the disadvantages of a marriage."

That may have been the first time I acknowledged to myself an element of flirtation in her teasing. It haunted my lonely drive back to town. Women of her age must flirt if only for practice. I was the most available man through a span of time that left her poignantly isolated.

The boys of her age had married. She was already odd girl among happy couples. The demands of the house itself took up too much of her time. She had spoken to me of getting work in town. She put it on terms of trying to earn something for her keep; we both knew that what she wanted was a wider world. But seeking it would have left Archie alone in that mausoleum.

"He has no one left but me," she said.

It was true and it was also true that she had no one left of her own age. Consciously or not, part of her flirting with me was an instinct to rebuild tissue over the scar that had been Vinty. She was peculiarly vulnerable.

I told myself sternly that she didn't mean a word of it. I asked myself what I would have thought of a trustee who made it his first office to court the heiress. I told myself I was as silly as Mother and Miss Premm. I had no right even to think of such things until I had that estate solidly in order. I told myself that time would work it out.

Perhaps time would have, if we'd been left alone in it. The world does not leave you alone. Madge Randolph was our first intruder. As Hewitt's wife, Madge considered herself queen of our community and took her authority seriously. In youth she had been strident and assertive. Confidence and Hewitt's increasing eminence in town modified her manner. For years she had kept a narrowed, suspicious eye on Archie; his unwillingness to remarry had finally left Madge without a rival in her domination of social Torrent. But she had been a local golf and tennis champion; she remained a natural-born competitor.

When she and Hewitt went to Hawaii, the weather was better than other people found it there. When they went to Yellowstone, the geyser shot higher. Her Hepplewhites were older than most Hepplewhites. When Hewitt sought refuge from all this in discreet philandering, Madge waited it out with smoldering, silent dignity and Hewitt always came home.

She shared his passionate determination to hold on to youth. Their house had always swarmed with company of all ages. As Vinty and Gretchen grew up, the age lines of their parties merged. Madge always insisted that the younger folk they took up should call her Madge.

The war had hit the Randolphs cruelly. Even before Vinty was killed they had lost Gretchen by marriage to a nice youngster from Minneapolis. He had returned but in spite of her protestations and Hewitt's offers, Edgar had insisted on taking Gretchen to Minnesota with him. Madge and Hewitt were left with a deserted house.

Like the Maynards, they had not gone into formal mourning for Vinty. They dined quietly with friends but there had not been a party in their house since his death. People had begun to wonder if there ever would be again. Then one morning Madge called the office and asked me to dine there in the following week.

"Good," she said. "And I have a favor to ask. It's a bridge party and I'd like you to bring Lucy."

"I'd love to, but won't Archie?"

"We're not asking Archie or your mother, Jim. Lucy's got to make a start again, just as we do."

"Wouldn't she prefer someone her own age, Madge?"

"You're a very suitable age for her," said Madge firmly.

"If she'll accept, I'll be delighted."

"She'll accept," said Madge. "But she must think it's your idea. Please don't tell her I suggested this."

Up to then I had never asked Lucy out in the evening. She and Archie had dined at home with Mother and me. I had often taken out my skates on a late afternoon errand and spent an hour up the river with her before staying on for dinner. It didn't take my mother's chuckles to make me realize that this was a new step.

"Trust Madge," she said. "She'll have a quiet talk with Archie and manage the whole wedding."

"Mother! For heaven's sake!"

"No, dear. For Lucy's and yours. Considering Vinty, I think it's handsome of Madge, although she couldn't have kept her fingers out of it anyway. I hope she's very firm with you."

"You sound a little jealous of Madge."

"No need," Mother laughed. "Madge isn't very subtle but this won't take subtlety. You're exactly like your father, dear; he thought the law governed everything, too."

"Have you got the children named yet?"

"Lucy will do that," said Mother. "They'll be fine children and very troublesome."

Lucy and Archie were in the library together when I called for her. It was the first time since the war that I had seen her in an evening dress. As a youngster at the Country Club dances she had looked skinny. The strapless effect of what they were calling the new look showed a mature and handsome woman. I couldn't help being aware of the matchless bosom and full shoulders, of long straight legs under the wide skirt. Reflections of the firelight danced and flickered in her hair. I remember feeling annoyed that she had disfigured herself with lipstick. She didn't need it.

"Just time for a sidecar," said Archie happily. "You'd better have two. Hewitt used to make a decent drink. Now he's joined the ten-to-one Martini cult and looks pained when you speak of Ponce de Leon. I'm using a second lemon, Jim. We'll make it up by not going to Florida this winter."

With him we were always relaxed and at ease. As I threaded my way over the ruts in the long driveway I felt a sense of constraint. I was wondering how to conceal it when I heard its echo in her voice beside me.

"Jim, did Madge make you do this?"

"No one makes me go to parties."

"I mean, stop for me."

"I wanted moral support," I said. "Most of Hewitt's gang make me feel as young as you are."

"Jim," said Lucy, "don't ever try to lie in court. You don't have to work for us at night."

"I don't have to work for you at all, Lucy; it's fun."

"I'm glad it is; but I'm rather dreading this."

"We can leave early if you like."

"No, we can't; but never mind, if you don't hate it."

She didn't say another word until I had parked in Hewitt's circle and we walked up onto the porch. There she scrutinized me and her voice was suddenly merry again.

"Someone should have told you about wing collars ten years ago, Mr. James. But when you're not dragging that briefcase you are taller than I am, even in high heels."

The door opened on Hewitt, dapper and immaculate in a snowy shirt, pink carnation and turned-down collar. He extended both arms to Lucy.

"Lucy! You become more ravishing every day!"

"Good evening, Uncle Hewitt; watch out for my lipstick."

Though Madge Randolph could be bossy, that executive side had its advantages. She had planned that party with thoughtful care. Inside we found only old friends, Tom and Hattie Gilchrist, Marian and Kevin Inglis. Inevitably there was a bad moment; Lucy took it in stride with poise and self-possession.

The first thing that met our eyes in their parlor was the new portrait of Vinty over the piano. With the greetings behind her Lucy went straight up to it. Her scrutiny was level, her voice even.

"It's wonderful, Madge. I don't see how he did it."

"He's the best man in the country," said Madge. "But even so we didn't expect this just from photographs. He got the mouth, didn't he?"

"He got it all," said Lucy. "It's just right."

"My dear," said Hewitt. "You can have sherry or something sterner as you wish. Jim has no choice. I'm going to show him a Martini trick some of the boys in Chicago are using."

The instant he left us Madge took over again.

"We're having the last of the canvasbacks," she said. "And I've got to know exactly how long you like them. Did you get any canvasbacks this year, Jim?"

"I'm sorry to say I did not."

"Most people didn't," Madge beamed. "But Hewitt always does. These were December birds and fatter than the early ones; you'd better say eighteen minutes."

When she had gone, Tom was at our side, friendly and easy as always.

"I want to complain about the Maynard estate, Jim. You're neglecting its greatest asset."

"I thought I'd brought her to dinner."

"Nice for us but not productive," said Tom. "I want Lucy for our Society Editor; she'd be a natural for it."

"Not sufficiently educated," said Lucy. "I've just begun arithmetic, as Jim and Mr. Inglis will tell you."

"I'd like more such beginners," said Kevin.

"Total waste!" said Hattie Gilchrist. "I'm mad for Lucy to be Sybil when the Group does *What Every Woman Knows*. Unfortunately they're making me do Maggie but where could we find a femme fatale like Lucy?"

"Then you'll rehearse afternoons only," said Marian Inglis. "The hospital's a new place since we got Lucy. We're putting her in charge of Towel Inventory."

"The thing," said Hewitt as his deft hands flashed over the grog tray, "is bigger ice cubes. You get a larger aluminum gadget. I'll give you the address, Jim."

Then, as we all hesitated a second, he raised his glass in a general gesture; his eyes were on Lucy and me.

"Welcome all," said Hewitt. "Here's to the future."

We broke up about midnight after an innocuous evening of bridge and the farewells were warm.

"We want you soon again, both of you," said Madge.

"Sunday evening, then; we're counting on you two," said Hattie Gilchrist.

Driving back to River House Lucy was as silent in the car as she had been most of the way to dinner. Then when I opened the door for her and began to say good night she took me impulsively by the arm.

"Come in, please. Daddy's probably asleep and I want a drink."

Her usual habits were abstemious. She would always take a cocktail with company. She seldom took a second and I had never heard her say she wanted a drink. Archie had gone to bed. We stirred up the fire in the library and then she left me and brought a tray from the pantry.

She had been animated and responsive, without being exactly gay, through the party. Now she changed; she had rubbed off her lipstick in the pantry, and with it her festive mood. I tried to help her recapture it over our drink. It was gone. Our post-mortems of the bridge hands were perfunctory and became heavy. Then, abruptly, she spoke her mind.

"That was a bad corner, Jim. Thanks."

"Everyone has 'em, Lucy. You got yours a little young."

"That's over," she said. "That's why tonight was bad; don't you see?"

"I saw you showing a lot of guts."

"I wasn't, Jim. Not the way you think. That's why I wanted this drink. I knew what would happen and it did. Everyone in the room was taking care of poor grieving Lucy. They were sweet and that made it all the worse because I'm not. I felt like an impostor. Something happens to grief, Jim. When it's gone it's gone and you haven't got it any more, even though people expect it of you."

I offered some homily about time; she shook her head.

"It isn't time. Oh, God knows I was sorry for myself when it happened and for a long while, too. But it's gone now and the factory didn't take it, or time either. The more I think back on it the more I realize that there never could have been as much to it as we thought. Vinty was the sweetest boy who ever lived but all we really had together was childhood and sex."

I raised a hand in protest and she smiled wanly.

"Don't worry. I'm not going into gory details. In fact, there weren't any. That's the thing I mind most about it, not for myself but because it's the only real thing I could have done for him and we never did. All I really meant by sex was being aware of the compulsion and of propinquity and youth and, of course, the others around us. Some of them did and whether they married afterwards or not, those girls had given their men something before they left.

"I would have, too, if I could. We used to neck a little, in fact a lot, and we were sure we loved each other, oh, entirely. One night out on the raft we'd been swimming alone and we both wanted to and I urged him to go ahead and he took off my bathing suit and then he suddenly picked me up and threw me into the water and dived in after me and when we came up he said: 'We'd better cool off, Lucy; we've got a long life ahead of us.'"

"Lucy, please; you musn't tell me these things."

"I have to, Jim. I've never been able to tell anyone else, even Artie. You see, I never gave Vinty anything. I should have insisted and he would at least have had that but I didn't and after he was gone I felt like a stingy slut. Then gradually I stopped feeling anything.

"It was over and I could see 'Poor Lucy' in every face around me and I felt like a shallow hypocritical bitch. That's why it was a bad corner tonight. I knew Madge was giving that party to help me and she was even thoughtful enough to make you take me and everyone was thinking how brave I was but I wasn't. That's all over and done and gone."

She stopped and sat staring, pensive and dry-eyed, over her glass. I watched the reflections of the firelight in her eyes and hair and bit my tongue over a dozen platitudes and finally kept my mouth shut. What is there to say of someone else's bereavement? Impulsively she closed a hand over mine and her eyes were penitent.

"Sorry, Jim: this reminds me of those awful words on the citation they sent with Artie's medal: 'above and beyond the call of duty.' I won't do this to you again."

We rose together and put our glasses on the tray and then as I extended my hand she leaned over it and kissed me on the cheek.

"That's for tonight, Jim, and for never treating me like poor Lucy. I'm not."

I drove home with that faint fragrance on my cheek suffusing the turbulence of my thought. Taken one way, the conversation and kiss were unequivocal. I wanted so much to take it that way that I could not. Vinty had been dead for nearly three years. Her vitality was astir again but if she was no longer pathetic she was still more vulnerable than she knew. I had to torment myself not only with the question of whether she might have me but of why. Time, I thought, would settle that and perhaps it would have if the world ever left you time.

The world around us chose to accept Madge's party as a signal. There is no giddy whirl in the life of Torrent. Neither is there much for people to do in the evening except dine with each other. Increasingly my phone rang invitations; every one of them carried a corollary:

". . . and Jim, would you mind bringing Lucy?"

Mind? She and I made jokes about it.

"You're stuck with me for bridge again at Marian's, Jim."

"It's time we won back some of Kevin's commissions."

And so, in increasing intimacy, we wore away the winter and began drifting down the spring together, or so it seemed. In fact, you do not drift. We were borne, gently at first but with quickening velocity and momentum, on the pressures around us. We were seated together, paired for bridge, re-invited over farewells and in conversation until my ears echoed with: "Lucy and Jim . . . Lucy and Jim . . . Lucy and Jim."

It is hard to say exactly when the cumulative pressure began to intrude upon our pleasure. I found myself becoming self-conscious and wishing for a respite, until I had one. A single evening at home with Mother stretched my ears for the next phone call. The houses of old friends had become flat without Lucy. I knew that I wanted to take her out alone, to enjoy her without enduring a roomful of chattering people. But I was seeing her almost daily on business. Independent dates would be a significant, perhaps an irrevocable step. I told myself it was premature and cursed myself for caution and worked with an ear to the phone.

Late one afternoon I went out to River House with some papers for Archie to sign. It was Saturday and they could have waited till Monday or, for that matter, a month. But no one had asked Lucy and me out for dinner that night. We were in the raw span of spring between skating and swimming. She had not been to town for several days; the office was desolate and bleak.

They asked me to stay to dinner as they always did. It had become such a habit that I made myself decline. I accepted a drink and felt hollow and empty as she walked me to the door.

"Planning a good day's work tomorrow, Mr. James?"

"Just in the morning; it's Sunday, isn't it?"

"Good for you! Bet you still don't know which one."

I remembered that Easter was past. I had seen her in new clothes on my annual excursion to church with Mother. I shook my head.

"Opening day for walleyes," said Lucy, "and the ice is all out of the river. If I make lunch will you take me fishing?"

"I'd love to."

"Come about ten and we'll catch some of the lunch."

Shooting was the major passion of my life. Until that moment I had been an indifferent fisherman. I began to think.

"We'll have to plan a little. My boat's been dry all winter and so have yours and I have no license and . . ."

"Jim," she said, "you can plan things to death. Just be here about ten."

When I arrived next morning she was waiting in tight faded blue jeans and a singularly advantageous green sweater. It was new and it gave the impression of having shrunk. Her face was glowing and eager.

"No Archie?"

"It will be raw on the river; can't you stand me alone?"

Overhead it was bright and sunny; around us there was a sharp southeast breeze. In the distance we could see it roiling the river as we walked down to the boathouse. She skipped ahead of me impatiently through the rose gardens. Her hands were a little nervous on the lock of the door.

Then as we stepped inside I saw why. The day beds and wicker furniture had been pushed over against one wall. In the center of the big room was the medium canoe, still mounted on sawhorses and glistening with two new coats of green paint.

"You see," she said triumphantly, "I *can* plan. I embezzled the paint out of Household and got McClintic to help me carry it in here and did it myself this week. Come on, Mr. James, I'll bet you a tax receipt on first fish."

She had planned more than the canoe. A haversack full of lunch gear was waiting with the rods and tackle box. We got into storm jumpers and oilskin pants from the general boathouse wardrobe and then we put the canoe in the water and loaded in the gear and some cushions and a blanket and set off through the rough chop.

In the storm jumper she was shapeless as a man. Few men I have ever known could drive a paddle with her long easy stroke. It was raw on the water, as she had said, but with storm gear and the work of paddling we didn't mind. The splash wasn't high enough for hoods. She had hers turned way down. As we paddled I could see color freshening along the back of her neck and watch the wind flicking wisps of her hair across it.

There were other boats on the river, mostly with outboards. As we worked upstream one of them passed close, standing in a little to give us his wash.

"Get over, you bastard!" cried Lucy.

I can still remember his look as he saw that she was a woman and the way he sheered off and the impenitent tilt of her nose as she turned a laughing face back to me.

"How's that for fisherman's talk?"

Her planning had not included frogs or minnows. We worked the cut bank and rock cliffs on the north side with plugs and spinners, trolling with the current or paddling for each other in the back eddies, and got nothing for a couple of diligent hours.

"Hungry?" I asked her.

"Sure, but we came for fish," said Lucy.

We crossed over to some of the bars we both knew on the south side and worked them hard with no better luck. By then our blood was up. We paddled on up to the riffles off the shoal side of Leary's Island and broke out a fly rod with pork rind. I held the canoe into the riffle while she whipped both sides. In twenty minutes she had two, winter thin but nearly three pounds, firm and frantic and icy cold as I took them out of the net.

Then we worked around and beached on the lee shore of the island. We carried the gear in, through the willow clumps, until we found a little natural clearing, sheltered from wind and river and hot with the direct sun beating down through the leafless trees.

"I'll come back and help with the canoe," she said.

"It's all right."

"If we pull out of sight no one will bother you about your precious license."

"I'll do it while you make a fire," I said.

"Good; I'm famished but we came to fish."

I helped her gather some driftwood from the early freshets and then I walked back out to the shore and hid the canoe and filleted the fish. When I re-entered the clearing she had the grill set up over a skillful fire, compact enough to work without discomfort and artfully layered up out of pine and hardwood to make a uniform bed of coals.

She had taken off her storm gear and, seated as she was before the fire, no one would have taken her for a man. She had bacon going, a kettle started for tea and was giving a preliminary toasting to big diagonal chunks of French bread with cut cheese waiting near for the finishing touches.

Exertion had already taken most of the river's chill out of us. I'd brought up the cushions from the canoe and the blanket for Lucy. I fixed seats by the fire and then started the fillets. While I was working on them she turned her back so as to mask the haversack and fumbled in it and then I heard a familiar pop. When she turned back to me she was pouring a bottle of Archie's Pinot Blanc into tin cups.

"When I've squandered the estate can I get work as a squaw, Mr. James?"

"Can you make moccasins?"

"Not yet but I've got a fine big blanket; want some?"

"Thanks, I'm not really cold."

"I'd hate to be around when you are," said Lucy.

We sipped the wine until the fillets were done and then I pulled the grate off the fire and built it up a little and we stretched around it, upwind of the smoke, with the food and cups and bottle between our heads. While we ate, the wind died. The clearing was hot and still with only the occasional chatter of a bluejay and the muted whine of outboards on the river.

We had fished longer than we realized. It was nearly four when we had eaten but the sun through the leafless trees was almost summery. I took the gear down to the water and scoured it with sand and put it back in the haversack, except the cups, which I'd left out for the last of the tea.

When I got back to the clearing she had rearranged the blanket so that she was lying on top of it with her long legs extended and a little apart and her face turned up to the sun. For the moment I couldn't tell whether she was napping. Then as I came up to the fire she stirred and propped herself up on an elbow. I divided the last of the kettle between us, lit a pipe and sat down and looked regretfully at the sun.

"I'm sorry to say it's getting on, Lucy."

"'The world is too much with us, late and soon' . . . can you say the rest of it, Mr. James?"

"No. I can't even hear Triton for the outboards."

"The outboards don't know we're in here," said Lucy. "This is as primitive as you can get now. At least we're away from most of the world."

"I'd like to see Hattie's face if she heard you speak of her as the world."

"Relax," said Lucy. "No one has ever been on time to the Gilchrists'. This is no place to think of clocks; we're playing primitive, remember?"

"Complete with Pinot Blanc?"

"They had wine," said Lucy, "and everything else we've had except that pipe of yours."

"Does the smoke bother you?"

"Not the way you mean. What would Grandpa Primate have thought of you, sitting there with your eyes on your wristwatch and your face all locked up on a pipe?"

"I don't know about the watch; he missed a lot in tobacco."

"Apparently," said Lucy. "But he had compensations, including us, if you stop to think about it. Perhaps you think that served him right but I bet he had more fun than we'll find at the Gilchrists'."

"Will you explain this to Hattie?"

"She knows it," said Lucy. "Those are nice kids. It wasn't women who sold the race out for clocks, Mr. James."

"We both accepted the invitation."

"That's right." She sat up and smiled wryly. "And I guess the acoustics are wrong here for Pan as well as for Triton. But I did get you fishing without a license; that's something."

I knew I'd been overtense. I didn't realize how much so until involuntarily my hand flickered toward my shirt pocket. I checked the gesture as it started but she had seen it and her eyes went wide.

"Don't tell me you did get one!"

"I wasn't going to tell you but I did."

"You couldn't have! How?"

"Bud Huston opened his store for me after dinner last night. An attorney's an officer of the court, Lucy."

"Just what we needed," said Lucy. "I should have asked the rest of the court fishing, to chaperone us."

"Is there anything wrong with having a license?"

"Everything's wrong with it," she said. "It's exactly like a man. You spend your whole time complaining about the government and then

[108]

go and get down on your knees to it for permission to fish! And Bud Huston helps because he hates the government too and all men have to stand together! It's disgusting! I get along perfectly well with the government and don't mind it at all because when I want to fish without a license I fish without a license and I don't give a damn what the government or anyone else thinks!"

She sprang up and whipped up the blanket and her cushion and hurried off through the willows toward the canoe. I felt the pipestem break in my teeth and took it out and threw it into the fire and stood there for a second, wondering whether everything I'd ever been taught and accepted was frivolous. Then I sanded out the fire and took the rest of the stuff out to the canoe. She had it in the water. As I came up she spoke very stiffly without looking back at me.

"Get in or we'll be late to see Tom put on his chef's apron."

She paddled furiously all the way downstream without once turning her head back or speaking. The back of her neck was redder than it had been in the morning. The last of the breeze still flicked little wisps of hair across it. As we eased into the slip in the boathouse she banged the bow carelessly against a piling. We put the gear on the catwalk and racked the canoe without a word. Then we each took an armload of the stuff and went up the stairs, through the inner door into the main room of the boathouse.

There we hung up the storm gear and stretched the lines on drying spools and put the cushions and blanket back on one of the day beds in the same neutral silence. I picked up the haversack to carry to the house and held the door open for her. She started out through it and then stopped, very close to me on the threshold. Her anger was gone; her voice was troubled.

"Jim, I owe you an apology."

"Nonsense. I owe you thanks for a swell day."

"I'm glad if you thought so."

"Didn't you?"

"For a while."

"I'm sorry if I did anything wrong."

"You never did anything wrong in your life; that's the trouble. This was my job and I botched it again."

"You didn't botch anything; forget it."

"This," said Lucy, "was the flattest flop in the history of seduction. Didn't you even know I was making a pass at you?"

"Yes, I knew it."

Her eyes widened, not with anger now but with a furtive curiosity, through which I could imagine I saw the tiniest flicker of fear.

"Well, then, what's wrong with me?"

"Nothing. You're a very desirable woman."

"Am I really?"

"Of course you are. Don't punch so hard."

"Then you tell me how. Haven't other girls made passes at you?"

"All people make passes at times, Lucy."

"Did they work, when other girls made them at you?"

"What do you want, a case history?"

"You have had other girls, haven't you, Jim?"

"Yes."

"Were you in love with them?"

"No."

"Well, what did they have that I haven't?"

"It doesn't work that way, Lucy."

Pique was replacing that little flicker of fear in her face; the curiosity remained. She waved a hand around the room.

"Because I have too much of everything else?"

"No. The other girls and I never gave a damn what became of each other; it was just animal fun."

"Isn't every girl an animal?"

"Sure, except to the guy who takes her seriously."

"What's the difference how you take her?"

"I don't take anything seriously until I earn it, Lucy."

"Jim, you take everything too seriously."

Her pique was gone, her eyes gay and companionable again. We went outside and I locked the door. Then as we started up the path she took my arm. Her voice was nearly penitent.

"Jim, I loved the fishing. Will you take me again?"

Chapter Six

HATTIE GILCHRIST had been the first to call us "you two" and of all our circle of friends Hattie was the most relentless. It irked her that Madge Randolph had asked us out together first. Hattie and Madge had long since patched a tacit truce over the intimacy which the limits of our town forced upon them. Madge was our dowager, Hattie our intellectual force. Neither of these customary postures survived their collision at matchmaking.

Three nice children and a devoted husband could not begin to use up Hattie's energies. She had remodeled and rebuilt the old Gilchrist house in successive stages from colonial to modern ranch around the patio. In the intervals she had drunk yogurt and learned to meditate while standing on her head, or at least to gasp to a roomful of admirers that she was meditating.

Hattie had been psychoanalyzed. She had shattered, reformed, abandoned and recaptured our Little Theater Group. She had formed a Practical Atheists Circle which lasted for three meetings, led a mission to Washington on behalf of the Navajos and mortified old Tobias by begging at the door of Hewitt's bank for a Negro accused of rape in Georgia.

Hattie had lustrous black hair worn in severe bangs, bold dark eyes, a high color and a tense, emaciated look that concealed her natural force until she spoke. Then you could never be quite sure whether you were conversing with Peter Pan or Lady Macbeth.

Over the years I had known her affectionately in all these guises. After she and Tom became clients I had learned to respect the hard substratum of common sense under her restlessness. She could be as remorseless in rejection as she was enthusiastic in experiment. When it became evident that her project for that year was to expedite a match between Lucy and me, I tried to remember the brevity of some of her other fads. The difference was that matchmaking is not a fad.

Tom and Hattie were both hospitable and loved to fill their comfortable house. Their especial pleasure was what had come to be called the Gilchrists' Sunday Nights. At these Tom in chef's hat and apron presided over barbecue and juleps or bean pot and toddys. Afterwards there was beer and bridge or word games, unless Hattie chose to read aloud from Chaucer with the original sound values. I had always enjoyed their parties and that spring Lucy and I became regulars.

The transparency of Hattie's purposes was amusing at first. We might as well have been labeled: Fragile, Handle with Care. People would wait until we had separated in the general company and then accost Lucy with elaborate casualness.

"How nice to see you, dear. Did Archie bring you or may we drive you home?"

"Thanks. Jim Denton brought me."

"Why, the lucky dog! Good for him."

I got variations of the same theme of arch surprise and then resounding approval.

"She's a wonderful girl, Jim," they all said.

For a few Sundays everything was so scrupulously impersonal that I could imagine Hattie saying on the phone to other guests: "Whatever we do we mustn't rush them." I could not imagine her following her own advice very long and Hattie didn't. She greeted us at the door one evening a little more briskly than usual.

"So good of you to come. Lucy, dear, you must not come near the kitchen in that divine dress. You help Tom with the sauce and I'm going to appropriate Jim for the garlic bread."

You usually worked for your dinner there but previously tasks had been haphazard and informal. I followed her into the kitchen with foreboding. There to my relief I found Tommy and Janet finishing their supper. I did my best to keep them; you couldn't beat Hattie at her own game.

"Time!" she said firmly. "Finish your ice cream upstairs. Mr. Denton and I have to do the garlic bread."

"You did it all afternoon," said Janet.

"Mr. Denton wants to see my gun," said Tommy.

"Then he has to see my dolls," said Janet.

"He doesn't want any silly dolls. He's going to show me how to shoot skeet; he promised Daddy."

"Off with you both while we work," said Hattie.

"Then why did you just say 'Thank God the work's done for once'?" asked Janet.

"So we could do it again—without you," said Hattie.

They departed with their ice cream and she laughed disarmingly.

"Someday, Jim, I'll learn that subtlety ends in the delivery room. You go to sleep a person and wake up a policeman."

"They're good kids, Hattie."

"They're fine," said Hattie. "But the purpose of all these deplorable lies and maneuvers is to talk about you."

"Your purpose," I said. "You talk."

"Jim, it doesn't matter at all about Lucy's refusing to do Sybil; the thing is to get her out of herself."

"I thought you wanted to talk about me."

"I am," she said. "It's fun, watching that armor crack."

"My armor is my innocence, Hattie."

"Stop it," said Hattie. "We both know better and I'm very glad you didn't marry either of them. I admit I was mad at the time. Now I realize it was providential. The whole town weeps for Artie and Vinty and puts their names on a statue but the real casualty of it is poor Lucy, practically relegated to suttee!"

"And no garlic bread, unless we get to work."

"I'm working now," said Hattie. "There isn't another suitable man in town. Torrent expects you to do your duty."

"As expounded by you?"

"Jim," she said, "independence doesn't work. You can't beat the world, dear. The only real good you can do the human race is in bed. You'll have wonderful children and they'll have a wonderful time repeating all your mistakes."

"Won't you arrange their lives, too?"

"Jim," she said happily, "you wouldn't be mad if you didn't agree."

We finally got to work and carried the bread in to where Lucy was watching Tom roll beefsteak around in a tray of his special sauce. Tom was a happy man in cap and apron. Even then he liked the scratch of the hair shirt.

". . . you can call this lunchtime patriotism corny," he was telling her. "But Jim ought to start with County Council this year . . ."

He saw us and broke off self-consciously. "Just in time. We've got the future so well settled we might as well start worrying about dinner."

"He's been telling me," said Lucy, "that man doesn't live by garlic bread alone and you should be in politics, Jim."

"We just put the future to bed," I said, "and it looks good to me; he's about ready for skeet, Tom."

"You see," said Tom. "Shooting skeet while Rome burns. . . . Why, Madge! How pretty you look! Good evening, Hewitt."

They had come in together from the driveway, Madge a little ahead, her eyes tense and anxious to pick up whatever she might have missed. Hewitt had on one of the new flowered sports shirts he had brought back from Honolulu that spring. His flannels had knifelike creases leading down to shiny tufts on black loafers.

"Politics already, Thomas? If management retains any prerogatives at all in this century of the common man, I'll settle for an immediate Martini."

"So nice to see you and Lucy, Jim," said Madge. "Hewitt and I were saying on the way over, we want you two and the Gilchrists, of course, for Saturday night at the club."

As I drove Lucy home afterwards we went through the usual postmortems and then her voice quickened a little.

"Are you going to speak on Tom's lunch panel?"

"Not for anything."

"Why not?"

"There's enough hot air in Torrent's present for three futures."

"Did you ever think of going into politics, Jim?"

"Yes. I thought: 'No.'"

"I'm glad," she said. "I can't imagine you kissing babies. But Tom says you have great knowledgeability. What, by the way, does that mean?"

"I'm too ignoranceable to know."

She laughed. "They are pretentious but they're good and kind and sweet, too. If only they weren't so . . . Oh God, Jim, where is the line between being impolite and being possessed?"

I I

She telephoned one effervescent May morning with the light note that I had learned to distinguish from her natural merriment.

"Do you know what date this is, Mr. James?"

"What have I missed, your birthday?"

"I'm through with those, too many already. This is the six-month anniversary of your tyranny over us. Daddy thinks we ought to do the arithmetic, just informally."

"He's right, Lucy. I'll bring the books out."

"Actually he's busy with pergola posts. He wants me to come in and do it."

I had pressed an accounting on them every month since taking over the estate. Archie still refused to look at digits in a ledger and would pay no more than fleeting attention to oral summaries. Lucy had enjoyed the new toys for a few months and then lapsed into a similar indifference. The main outlines were fixed in her skull. She had no taste for the day-to-day struggle.

Everything except their household bills was cleared and handled through our office. She had urged me to take on the household budget. I had refused for the solitary motive of keeping it in her mind. Meat and sugar and the servants' payroll were realities to her. I rubbed her nose in them as a tactic to make her relate them to the bank debt and the tax structure.

"We're doing without everything possible so why worry about the unavoidable?" she asked.

With the major problems I was making respectable, albeit slow, progress. The jettisoning of the junk I had taken over had produced an appalling reduction in the hollow totals the Tuttlewises had delivered me. It had also produced a promising infusion of new revenue that enabled me to whittle methodically at the debts. The house still stretched insatiable tentacles for every dollar in sight but its worst secrets were known to me now. With concentration on essentials only and with continuing luck on Archie's life, I could begin to hope for restoration of a solvent balance.

Lucy arrived in the afternoon, bringing springtime into the office in a flowered print that widened Miss Premm's approving eyes.

"It's beautiful, Miss Maynard," she said.

"Thank you, Miss Premm. Will you remind Jim of that when the bill comes in?"

"I won't need to remind him; he's seen the dress."

"How many years does this set the new roof back, Lucy?" I asked.

"You see?" She turned triumphantly to Miss Premm. "We don't even need a roof till winter but he wants me naked all summer paying for it."

"I'll get the files, Mr. James," said Miss Premm hastily. Lucy looked after her with amusement.

"Miss Premm thinks I'm an abandoned hussy."

"Miss Premm is very observant."

"I'm glad someone is; I was getting ready to tear it and scream, just for attention. What would she have done?"

"She'd bring her notebook and ask whether to take deposition for defense on rape charges or a direct petition to have you committed."

"It's a man's world," said Lucy. "That's what's wrong with it. We should be swimming in this weather."

That day she was more attentive to details than she had been since the first days of her instruction. Her questions were sensible; her manner thoughtful. As we came to the end of it she was pleased and complimentary.

"That's wonderful, Jim."

"No. But it's progress."

"No one can ever say we're millionaires, can they?"

"They certainly cannot."

"Will we ever be again, if all your little amortizing schemes work out?"

"Not possibly, under present tax schedules, Lucy."

"Good," she said. "I hope they keep the taxes up. Gretchen and I used to talk about it and she said no one likes millionaires. She had a hell of a time because Edgar was skittish about appearances, even in the war. Uncle Hewitt was being pompous about it, too, and talked to them about communities of interest. Then when it got serious Uncle Hewitt looked into it and found that Edgar's father was a millionaire himself in Minneapolis. So then he said that Edgar was a very fine boy with a wonderful future if he got through the war and he would never object to him. Just as if Gretchen had given a damn whether he objected or not! Her trouble was with Edgar but that did clear the air about the money."

"And now they're living happily ever after?"

"They're very happy," said Lucy, "and not about money, either. She's got away from Uncle Hewitt and Madge and she's going to have another baby this fall. She says it's all right if you're both millionaires or if neither of you are but a hell of a lot more people aren't. You ought to put our decline in the paper and then I could go around whistling at sailors, if I could find sailors."

"Edgar wasn't a sailor," I said.

"Same principle," said Lucy. "He was just another PFC in the U.S.O. Club until Gretchen drew a bead on him. Only now the club is closed and I'm too old for soldiers. But you have extended my striking range, even if you did sell Widgeon Lake to those disgusting men from Chicago."

"They weren't disgusting and we got a very good price. I want you to see what became of it."

"I don't want to," said Lucy. "It's too sad. Daddy and Artie loved it so and sometimes in September when it was still warm they took me for teal and I never want to see it again."

"This view won't be painful," I said.

I fished among the securities into which Kevin had converted Widgeon Lake and handed her a certificate. She took it, interested at once to find it tangible before her eyes, and studied it with thoughtful scrutiny.

"How fascinating. What does Colossus do, Jim?"

The whims of corporate finance had chosen to ornament that particular certificate with the conventional etching of the Colossus of Rhodes peering down with like benevolence upon the vessels between his mighty legs and the name of the stockholder.

"Nowadays he manufactures facial tissues," I said.

"My God!" said Lucy. "Show me the rest of our etchings, Mr. James. Have we an Aphrodite presiding over a mattress factory?"

"No, but here's a beautiful Ceres."

I shoved it across the desk and her face lit up.

"Indeed she is, with no bra and lovely cornucopias, too. What's she doing this fine spring day?"

"Small loans and short-term commercial paper."

Lucy snorted and pushed the certificates back across the desk. Then she arose slowly and stretched herself into a silhouette that Ceres might have envied.

"The flutes of Arcady are very faint in here, Mr. James: how about that swim?"

"I've got work to do, Lucy, thanks just the same."

"Didn't I just tell you we don't need more?"

"This isn't for you; it's for me."

"Oh. Making yourself some etchings?"

"Of a kind."

"Well, I wish you a deskful of paper nymphs if you really prefer them to a live one."

"You can't eat your cake and have it too," I said.

"Very sound," said Lucy, "if you want stale cake."

Our jocularity was stretching precariously thin. Whether it deceived her or not, I was no longer kidding myself. I wanted to marry her.

As a practical matter I had, at the time, little more than good intentions to offer her. Another six months would show solid progress in my own affairs. They would leave the Maynard estate in a condition from which I could retire if she wouldn't have me. And they would mean for her the difference between a considered choice and a reflexive response to her loneliness.

When Sunday came around again I drove out as usual to pick her up and take her to the Gilchrists'. An early heat wave had opened the verandah for the first time that year. I found her and Archie out there together, waiting for the first drink which, by custom, we now always had with Archie before going off for the evening.

Lucy's eyes were aglint with mischievous satisfaction a more experienced man would have spotted at once. It took me a few minutes to realize that she was wearing another new dress, a powder blue of some feathery summer substance that should have made its designer proud. Once I would have remarked on it as soon as I noticed it. We had reached the time when I was chary of personal remarks. Archie and I spoke of other things while he busied himself over the sidecars. From the corners of my eyes I watched indignation welling up in her.

"Do you ever see anything but proxy notices?"

"I do indeed," I said. "That's a very professional-looking job on those pergola posts, Archie."

"Daddy, could we sue Jim for negligence?"

"Not sure," said Archie. "Can you plead both sides of a case, Jim?"

"Sure, and judge it too. What's the problem?"

"The problem," said Lucy, "is that I've turned over half the town for spring clothes and you applaud cedar posts."

"Stout fellow," said Archie. "*De minimis non curat lex.*"

"Trifles hell," said Lucy. "Wait till you see the bills. This was only copied Fath. Tomorrow I'm going to take those posts back and get an original. Learned Counsel will notice the figure on that."

She was vexed all the way to the party, silent and withdrawn. There the dress made a great stir. Tom, with a husband's training, saw it at once and burst into flowery congratulations. The other women flocked for an admiring clinic. The whole room was listening when Marian Inglis summarized:

"It's divine, Lucy. Did Jim help you pick it out?"

"Bloody likely," said Lucy. "Blackstone here wouldn't notice Lady Godiva in a ponytail."

Admiration had mollified her a little but not with me. She avoided me the rest of the evening, insisting upon helping herself to beef and buffet. Then she seated herself between Leonard and Margaret Tuttlewise and interrogated Leonard so flatteringly about farm values that Margaret became nervous and took him home at ten o'clock.

Hattie clucked and fussed, pretending not to notice and scurrying around the rest of the party like a puppy in the paint. Her eyes kept going back to Lucy and to me. Just before the Tuttlewises left she made an excuse to take Tom into the house. When I arose to leave she took me aside before I could speak.

"Tom has to see you after the others go; it's important, Jim."

The Gregorys were the last to leave. Hattie closed the door on them with an audible sigh and then turned back to us, her face aglow with anticipation. Tom had become very silent. I remembered how in the old days live decoys always shut up when the calling was done and the shooting was about to start.

"Tell them, dear," said Hattie brightly. "It's your idea and we won't take no for an answer."

Committed, Tom managed a convincing enthusiasm. He told us that he had to go to New York for a printers' convention in the following week. He had been dreading it until it had suddenly occurred to him that with the right company the trip would be a romp.

"Our first real binge since the war," said Hattie. "And we want you two. We'll be proper chaperones and very discreet. Now don't tell us you can't."

She babbled on, trying to overwhelm us before we could reply. A sheik and a rabbi would be addressing a subconvention of the Single World Movement. Hattie Carnegie would be having an invitational showing. Tom knew a man who could get us tickets to *Oklahoma*. One of Hattie's cousins was co-chairwoman of a Shostakovich festival. You could still get fresh cherrystones even if May had no *r* in it.

"And the Yankees will be at home," said Tom dutifully.

"And Tom wants Jim to choose a twenty-gauge for Tommy," said Hattie.

I had a vision of Tom and me explaining to Bud Huston that we had bought a shotgun in New York. Torrent does not work that way and no one knew it better than Hattie. Lucy had been silent through this. Her eyes had widened, however, and the pique of the earlier evening was not in her reply.

"Sounds wonderful, Hattie. I'd love to if Jim would."

I still think that alone I would have accepted at once. We were not alone; we were up against that determination of Hattie's.

"I'll have to look at my desk," I said.

I was the one who rode tense, silent and unresponsive on the way back to River House that night. At the door Lucy put a hand on my arm again.

"Please come in. I want to talk about New York."

Archie had gone to bed. We went into the library, where for the first time that year there was no fire to stir up. It was still warm with the day's sun and the mild spring night.

Lucy went out to get us a drink and I stood there, listening to the ticking of the hall clock through the open door and the hooting of an owl down by the river and smelling the honeysuckle wafted in through the screened windows. She came back and set the tray down and came over to me and put a drink in my hand. Her voice was grave and rather low.

"All I wanted to say about New York is—it's sweet of them but you don't have to if you don't want to."

"Lucy, I'd love to, if I can."

"Would you really?"

"Of course I would."

She looked at me, still gravely; her voice was tense and a little hurt but without any shade of reproach.

"Then why didn't you accept at once, as I did?"

"My time isn't entirely my own."

"Jim, did you never in your whole life do anything on impulse?"

The word itself ripped it. At that moment I was consciously struggling with an impulse to grab her and kiss her and I knew it for exactly what it was. I could feel the same impulse stirring in her. The whole spring had been maneuvering us inexorably to this point. Hattie herself was only a minor, accidental instrument of a combustion that had done its work. It had moved us up, face to tense face, and then stepped back, confident and smirking as it left us to inevitable impulse. If Lucy hadn't spoken the word, I'm sure it would have happened. The very syllables revived in me the old delusions of self-control and responsibility. I took a long step back and tried to smile.

"Most of a lawyer's life is correcting impulses, Lucy."

She turned away abruptly and settled into a chair and matched my own forced smile.

"I hadn't thought of it that way," she said. "I guess I haven't thought much of your life at all. It's so funny; you know everything about ours and we scarcely know a thing about yours."

"Most of it is as dull as it looks."

"Nothing is the way it looks," she said somberly. "Are you going to be a judge like your father?"

"That's for others to say, years from now."

"They will," she said. "You love the law, don't you, Jim?"

"I guess so. It's imperfect but so are people. We've just had a taste of living without it. Ten years ago we were taught it was the only difference between us and animals; now I think you could say ashes."

"Jim," she said, "it's all right about New York."

"I'm sorry, Lucy. I didn't mean to be stuffy. I'll let you know as soon as I can."

"You have," she said. "But it's all right and that's all I was trying to say."

She rose abruptly and left her drink unfinished and hurried out into the hall. I heard her footsteps quick-paced and resolute on the stairs. I sat very still, listening to the frogs and the owl and the whisper of the river and the ticking of the old clock in the hall until it had sounded two more melancholy laments for the quarter hours gone and I knew Lucy wasn't coming back either.

At home I lay awake most of the night. Three times in the morning I reached for the phone to tell Lucy I would go and three times I pulled my hand back. At eleven, when I knew she would be out on the place with Archie, I called the house and left a message with Douglass that I would be unable to attend the party with the Gilchrists.

The rest of the week I reasoned the inside of my skull raw with self-justification and stayed away from River House. It was pure irony that presently offered a vestige of justification to my pigheadedness. That was the week Rocky Slade went to River House with Mr. Franklin's offer. When Archie summoned me, I told myself it was a good thing I was on the job instead of in New York.

It was neither good nor bad; the mischief was done. I would have failed to make Archie sell it anyway and he would have had his coronary anyway. Even if we had gone to New York, Rocky would have brought the offer sooner or later and she would have asked him out to River House to swim. The trouble was not in New York. It was in me. It was what barbed the needle in her subsequent teasing:

". . . It's all your fault."

Chapter Seven

ONE effect of Archie's heart attack was to relieve the personal tension between Lucy and me. If anything, we saw each other oftener than before. Now it was by day for either explicit business or joint efforts to ameliorate the tedium of his convalescence. For several weeks no one asked us out together in the evening. No one asked Lucy anywhere.

She would not have gone, if people had, but it produced an intensification of Archie's somber "Nature abhors a vacuum, Jim." The vacuum in its turn had already begun to produce Rocky Slade.

At first I was scarcely aware of it. It wouldn't be accurate to say the illness had increased my work on the estate. I was already doing nine tenths of it. After Archie's attack I no longer bothered him about anything. The details didn't change much. All my long-range planning had to be revised against the probability of immediate inheritance taxes. My own business was picking up steadily. I needed it as an offset for the drag of the estate, against which I had always insisted on a scale of charges deferred to long-range accomplishment. I needed it for myself and for the day on which I would offer Lucy more than impulse.

In consequence I began to add regular night work to an increasing schedule. That, in its turn, kept me from realizing how often Rocky was going to River House. After he began his active campaign for the council he was usually working or speaking in the evenings. More and more frequently he went out there in the afternoon to swim with her while Archie was napping. Before his formal nomination he had begun lingering for an occasional dinner there.

When Rocky had asked me to get him a place on Tom's panel I had thought it a spontaneous fancy. It was a carefully timed step he had begun to premeditate before he ever went to River House. My first realization of that came from Lucy herself.

Once Archie was established in convalescence at home I began systematic visits, usually at lunchtime. At first he was confined to his room. There Lucy and I would eat with him from trays, doing our best to amuse him and enjoying the summer freshness over river and valley through the big windows.

Normally I departed even before his obligatory nap. One day Lucy insisted on detaining me in the library. I was fearing fresh tidings from Jamison's morning visit when she opened an entirely new subject.

"Jim, has Rocky any real future in Torrent?"

"Why not?"

"Don't hedge with me. I'm serious."

"I'm not hedging," I lied. "Why wouldn't he have?"

"Never, in that grubby little office."

That was true. I didn't think she knew why it was true.

"The town's full of offices," I said.

"Would you take him into yours, if he studied law?"

"No."

"There," she said. "That's the whole thing."

"What whole thing, Lucy?"

"You're not fair to him," she said. "Nobody is. Look at Daddy and me not selling the house when it meant so much to him."

"Did he say that was unfair to him?"

"Of course not! He was very understanding. He's very realistic and objective about everything, Jim."

"What else is he realistic and objective about?"

"Our whole social structure, if you want to know. This town has always underrated Rocky."

"If true, that's the foundation of a fine future."

She either didn't notice or willfully ignored my irony. She went on eagerly, earnestly.

"Jim, would Rocky have a future in politics?"

"Probably."

"I knew it!" she said. "That's why we've got to help him."

"Help him do what?"

"Politics," said Lucy. "He's reluctant because underneath he's really very shy. He hates the baby-kissing side of it as much as you do. But he's thought the whole thing through a lot farther than you have because he's been in a position where he had to think about it. He's got some wonderful ideas, really frightening ones when you stop to think about it."

"What are they, Lucy?"

The American contempt for politics, Rocky had told her, rested not on moral superiority but on accidents, on a kind of luck that was running out. We differed from the economic and social cannibalism of Europe only in time. Once we had been lucky enough to apply a selectively vigorous bloodstream to the greatest natural resources ever blundered into by man. We had been so prodigiously wealthy in land, water, timber, ore, fertility and petroleum that there had been more than enough to go around for everyone. Wealth had beckoned to enterprise from every horizon. The best brains and energies had found unlimited outlet in simple acquisition. There was always enough.

"Like Grandpa stealing all our land," said Lucy.

"Did Rocky tell you that?" I demanded.

"Not exactly, of course."

"It isn't true inexactly. Your grandfather paid an agreed price to some poor but dishonest homesteaders who got the land free or very cheaply from the state and thought they were fleecing Hewitt's father out of options on it. You'd better tell Rocky to knock off misquotations of *Das Kapital* and try reading Darwin some night."

"You're not fair to him," she said. "You might at least hear the rest of this."

"I heard the rest of this in kindergarten," I said. "But go on."

America, said Rocky, had been glad to turn over politics to any scum that wanted it because Americans remembered that in Europe politics were just a device to redivide existing wealth. Here, there was enough new natural wealth to reward superior energy anywhere. It had been fine while it worked but those days were over, according to Rocky.

Our own community, he said, was a perfect microcosm of the country or, for that matter, of the world. All the land and natural resources had been pre-empted and were nailed down. Even the good jobs now passed only by nepotism.

Rocky didn't mind this for himself, he insisted, because he had learned at his father's knees that there was more to life than grubbing for money. In the long run the only satisfaction was service to your fellow man. But it was that very thing that had made him think twice about it. When he looked around at his fellow men he saw that all the avenues were closed from the top. He saw seven million veterans returning from the wars to realize they'd been giving their life blood to keep Hewitt Randolph in bridle paths.

"Those bridle paths," I said, "are abandoned wagon lanes on private property. Hewitt has given time and thought and probably money to keep the county from buying them at exorbitant prices from him and you and the others out here. He did it to prevent Democratic administrations from paving them with silver foil and Republican administrations from repaving them with gold foil and passing on the tax bill to these poor veterans you're bleeding about."

"You always think about details," she said. "You don't see the big picture."

The big picture worried Rocky. He looked around him and saw the pressures of discontent building up irresistibly under closed outlets for talent and he had to wonder where that force was going. He had to face the fact that we must either have better statesmanship than we'd ever had or the worst explosion in the history of the world. The other veterans like himself had been brought up to believe that all men were created free and equal but all they had to do was look around for themselves, even in Torrent, to see it wasn't so. The potentiality of it frightened Rocky.

"It frightens me, too," I said. I had just bamboozled Tom into putting Rocky on his speaking panel. I could hear the echo of some of Tom's more juvenile fancies in all of this but it wouldn't fool even Freddy Eastman. If Rocky spouted this kind of economic baby talk to the Chamber of Commerce we'd have him on relief the rest of our lives.

"Then you agree, if it frightens you," said Lucy triumphantly.

"Not with one word of it, Miss Maynard. And you either should have ducked Smith altogether or stayed longer."

"Don't call me Miss Maynard," she said. "You're as backward as Daddy and Uncle Hewitt and all the other silverspoons we know. You know all men are created free and equal."

"No two men in history were ever equal, Lucy; even in dropkicking. And no man who eats has ever been free and I've got to get back to town and buckle down to resisting the statesmanship we already have."

"Go on," she said. "Go get us another Colossus of the facial tissues and leave the country to any scum that wants it."

"Cheer up," I said. "He hasn't got it yet."

"You distort everything, Jim, just like Daddy. He won't even listen about Rocky; he says it hurts him to laugh so hard. But it may interest you to know that some very knowledgeable men take these things seriously. Tom Gilchrist has asked Rocky to speak on his panel."

I I

Before Dr. Jamison pronounced him out of danger Archie insisted on giving a dinner party. He arranged it by phone without consulting either Lucy or me. To our belated protests he replied blandly that he was bored with a steady diet of our company. In fact he was already concerned with the recurring appearances of Rocky in the vacuum.

Archie was following Rocky's campaign closely by newspaper and radio. He had begun with a perverse delight at the discomfiture of Hewitt and his other neighbors. He affected this vein long after his perception acknowledged Lucy's increasing absorption in both campaign and Rocky. Archie intended the party as a hint that Lucy was again available for invitation from her normal friends.

We could not countermand it. With Jamison's help we limited it to the Gilchrists, Randolphs and ourselves and an understanding that we leave soon after dinner.

We gathered on the verandah for cocktails in the summer gloaming, punctual and guarded in deference to Archie's condition. The others knew as well as we that he should not be excited. After the first greetings this produced a muted insipidity. The rest of us might have managed indefinitely with the weather, garden, swallows, fireflies and river.

Madge Randolph was born believing that rules are for other people. She was equally convinced of proprietary right in Lucy.

"Haven't I seen you two swimming a lot lately?"

"You've seen me," said Lucy. "Jim prefers Blackstone on hot afternoons."

"I was sure we saw another figure through the trees."

"You saw a fine one," said Lucy. "Rocky Slade's."

"Rocky swimming here?" Hewitt feigned incredulity. "Is he after your vote, Lucy?"

She flushed and Archie saw her annoyance.

"Foresight," he said. "He's enjoying the place before he bulldozes it. Will your den make a filling station, Hewitt?"

Hewitt glowered and Tom's face clouded with contrition.

"I've spoken to Rocky about that hatred angle," he said. "He says himself it's just campaign talk. You know what politics are."

"We're learning," said Archie. "Or perhaps we're recalling and your gladiator is learning, Tom. The circuses are fine. Can we count on free bread when our gardens have become the imperial highways of Slade the First?"

"Joke if you like," said Hewitt. "The man in the street is taking this seriously."

"So's the girl on the verandah," said Lucy. "It's time we woke up. Gabriel's probably played encores we never heard out here."

"You'll hear the tumbrils," said Hewitt.

"Hewitt!" snapped Hattie. "Was your mother frightened by a liberal?"

"Mortally," said Hewitt. "She understood it always winds up as liberality with our possessions. What's his line with you, Lucy?"

"A happy synthesis," said Lucy, "of politics and sex."

Madge winced as Lucy had intended her to do and then chuckled nervously. Hewitt always left himself a line of retreat into levity. His smile held it; his voice probed on.

"Lucy, you've hit on our salvation. I'd forgotten that Achilles might have a heel as well as being one. Are you prepared to print both sides of this holy crusade, Thomas?"

"Always," said Tom a little sharply.

"How about a front page picture of this champion of the downtrodden sunning himself beside Lucy on Archie's dock? I'll donate a cooler of champagne for a prop."

"You will not," said Lucy and then she caught herself and smiled wickedly. "He's miles ahead of you, Uncle Hewitt. He won't even let me help with clerical work for the campaign. When I asked him to dinner tonight he said all he needed was to be caught playing footie with the River Set."

"You asked that . . . that demagogue to dinner?" asked Madge.

"Smart," said Hewitt firmly. "Very smart, dear. We'll trust you to tame him for us, Lucy."

"For you indeed," said Lucy. "When he's Rex et Imperator of Torrent County I'll be chief concubine."

We laughed together but her color was high and Hewitt's eyes were thoughtful. Through dinner we talked of other things. We sent Archie to bed from the table. Then, when Douglass brought the coffee service into the library, Lucy spoke up firmly.

"I don't mean to rush you but as your hostess I have planned a diversion that begins at nine. We're all going to hear Rocky speak at the South Side School."

Madge stared until she realized Lucy was in earnest.

"Thank you, dear. It's much too late."

"He's always a little late," said Lucy. "Technique."

Hewitt looked at his watch.

"He's probably just stopping to put a fallen bird back in its nest. May I pause en route for a bomb, Lucy?"

"We're not going near that South Side School," said Madge. "Lucy, dear, you're carrying this joke too far."

"I'm not joking," said Lucy.

In the end Hewitt and Madge firmly declined to go. The Gilchrists drove Lucy and me. Tom was delighted and rather grateful to Lucy.

The amusement that had greeted his support of Rocky was becoming rancorous in the town. Hattie had defended both Tom and Rocky vociferously at first. Her enthusiasm had begun to wane. Opposition might have kept it aflame; she had a woman's sensitivity to the coolness they had begun to encounter. She could still needle Hewitt but she had looked troubled through our earlier conversation.

The South Side is as near as Torrent comes to having a slum. Lack of heavy industry and congestion have spared us the darker metropolitan horrors. By the time the war brought new factories, our underprivileged were driving their own cars from housing projects and trailer parks. The area is, however, one of low rents and small houses merging imperceptibly into miniature farms and open country.

Immemorially the South Side has been short on plumbing and paving. It has been long on vigor, fertility and independence. Of late years the Democrats, assessing the first two of these assets judiciously, traded it a gleaming new school for the third, to the lasting anguish of Republican statesmen and contractors alike.

The school has every piece of mechanical equipment purveyed by Democratic firms for a hundred miles around. It has also the biggest gymnasium in the city. This is used not only to refresh its students from a curriculum that runs to citizenship and typewriting but as a community dance hall and forum. The grateful South Siders understood their instruction; our outwitted Republicans had practically written the district off until Rocky's campaign.

Rocky was the first Republican in a decade who was conceded any chance to crack the South Side. His athletic record was cherished there. His attacks on power, profit and private interests were its familiar political diet. And on the South Side, as everywhere else, he had the incalculable benefit of Winifred's militant support.

Winifred had been on our ostensibly nonpolitical school board when that school was built. More importantly, she was still on it. She was still president of the Torrent Parent-Teachers Association. Theoretically that was nonpolitical, too. Winifred made an asset of that handicap. She had astutely avoided partisan commitment during her long club life. She could speak with a straight face of Rocky's candidacy as a boon to "all of Torrent."

She could also, in private, remind teachers of their need for a friend, "above petty politics," on the council. She could remind mothers that the South Side Woman's Club was a stanch element in the All-Torrent Clubwomen, an ally in its insistence on a decent future for Torrent's children. No woman in the city wished to be counted in opposition to that.

Winifred herself was speaking from the platform as we slid into seats in the rear of the gym. The meeting had been adroitly represented as a spontaneous public service of the Parent-Teachers Association to give Torrent the truth of the campaign and "every civic-minded citizen of the South Side a chance to shake the hand that beat Notre Dame."

"Corny but smart," said Tom. "Not a dime for promotion. The party saves dough and gets the illusion of a crusade."

There were perhaps a hundred and fifty people in the room, yawning a little over Winifred but respectful before the solitary American flag on the platform and the disarming presence of the school principal and the president of the local P.T.A. chapter. The absence of bunting, placards and clamor was reassuring. The audience was doing its duty and would presently shake hands with Rocky.

". . . and so," Winifred went on, "if this were just the ordinary Republican-Democratic wrangle I wouldn't be here and you wouldn't either. I think we all have too much sense of humor for that! And I *know* we've all heard enough political promises to last us a long, long time. When the party asked my boy to serve his community I will tell you, in confidence, he was a little skeptical himself. He came home to his father and me and he said:

" 'This isn't like winning a football game, or even a war. If I ask those people to elect me, how do I know I can really serve them?'

"His father just looked at him and said: 'Have you forgotten that God will help you, Roscoe?'

"He had not forgotten. He was wondering in all humility whether he was the proper instrument for this service. We had to remind him that God helps those who help themselves. Could we doubt that He would help those who sacrifice to help others?

" 'You may be young,' I said, 'but serve, you must! Look at the way our people have been served. Look at our friends and fellow citizens on the South Side. When have our politicians bothered to pave their streets for them? When have they had a share in Torrent's park program? When has one single voice suggested that they have as much right to a freeway as all those noisy merchants with their big stores and high prices?'

"That's what our politics have meant. That's what they will mean, to you, until Torrent has a councilman who will give it action instead of talk!"

She stopped, to polite, if less than explosive applause. Then, instead of relinquishing the rostrum, she stood there, bowing between anxious looks toward the wings. As the applause petered out into curious craning of necks, she spoke again with expert simulation of embarrassment.

"You're wonderfully kind," she said. "I'm beginning to be embarrassed because I know you didn't come here to hear me. I'm sure Roscoe is on his way . . . Oh! There he is!"

Rocky hurried out from the side, hair rumpled, coat a little askew and rather shabby. He looked harassed and contrite as he smiled wanly at the house and then, making straight for Winifred, kissed her warmly. She returned his kiss and stood half smiling beside him until the outburst of clapping had died down a little.

"Ladies and gentlemen and Mother . . . my apologies," he began, when she cut him off.

"Rocky, you're late and you'd better have a good alibi. I was just about to tell these kind people that you were late the morning you were born . . . but they don't know how well you were worth waiting for!"

This produced an explosion of applause and laughter. Winifred blew Rocky another kiss and seated herself between principal and P.T.A. president. Rocky raised his hand for silence and smiled his rueful boyish smile.

"Don't know whether to risk an alibi after that one, folks," he said. "But for what it's worth, that darned old jalopy of mine couldn't take the bumps on South Street and quit cold about three blocks from here. Lucky I was brought up to walk."

He stopped and spread begrimed hands to sympathetic chuckles.

"Kind of hard to tell whether I need a new car or you people need new streets. Reminds me of the old saying: 'It may not be a crime to be poor but it sure can be inconvenient.' Well, folks, if our troubles were just inconveniences like we all put up with in the war, they wouldn't be worth worrying about. We'd know we were all in it together for the good of the country and each other.

"But I didn't come here tonight to talk about conveniences. In fact, you people out here haven't been given enough of them to talk about. I came here to speak about crime. I came here to ask you to help me fight crime—the same old crime of privileged people playing power politics with your safety, your future, your rights. . . ."

Tom caught my eye and frowned apologetically. Then, as we both saw the house quicken and lean forward, he half shrugged. The rest of it was the same speech, the only speech Rocky ever gave.

We slipped out unnoticed in the tumult of applause that followed. Tom was still troubled and rueful. Hattie was very silent. Lucy's eyes were shining. She spoke a little defiantly as soon as we were settled in the car.

"All right! But what did you or I or Uncle Hewitt ever do for those people?"

"We let them alone," I said.

Hewitt, as I tried to explain, had done much more. He had been unable to save them the triple prices they were paying for that gymnasium. He had defended them, backstage, from both Republican and Democratic road contractors. He gave continuing hard work to the County Hospital, he gave generously in both money and time to our Community Health Service. Through both council and city supervisors he kept a vigilant eye on our Fire and Police Departments and the sheriff's office. He fought underwriters as implacably as assessors and politicians to keep our tax structure sound. He was proud of the fact that the bank never made a nickel out of the city. If a solvent community benefited him, it benefited everyone else.

"Just what Rocky says," she retorted. "Millions for property values, not a cent for human values."

"What's the human value of hatred, Lucy?"

"They love him," she said. "They'd die for him."

"They may at that, paying taxes on his free reforms."

"Jim," said Tom, "you're an unreconstructed Tory. Why in hell shouldn't free people vote themselves a freeway if they want it?"

"He wasn't asking them to vote a freeway. He knows that's all settled, or will be, in the legislature. He was asking them to play Robin Hood: This freeway stolen for you from power and privilege by courtesy of Rocky Slade. Vote again, folks, and I'll steal you more."

"Jim, you have to ham it up and demagogue a little in politics. What are you gonna do?"

"I'm going to vote against him," I said.

"And I'm going to be a repeater, in disguises," said Lucy.

We returned her early to Archie but as we went back out to our cars in the driveway Hattie and Tom insisted on my going over to their house for a nightcap. When I demurred, Hattie jumped into my car.

"Go ahead, Tom, while I speak to this idiot."

We weren't out of the lane before she got to work.

"Jim, this is serious."

"Tom was the one who started him, Hattie."

"Tom didn't start him swimming with Lucy. How long has this been going on?"

"I don't know."

"That's great," said Hattie. "That's just what we need. Our great tax authority doesn't know how long that torso has been stealing his girl."

"She isn't my girl."

"Jim," said Hattie, "she's just as proud and pigheaded as you are but she's over her depth now. It's compulsive for a girl like that to flirt but Rocky won't flirt. I don't mean that I think he has horns and a tail the way you and Hewitt seem to think. What's really dangerous about him is that sometimes the damned fool is sincere within his own frame of reference. I'm sure he's sincere about Lucy in his own way but his own way, Jim, is totally amoral."

"Is that why you're backing him for office?"

"That's Tom's idea and just politics anyway. This is serious."

I I I

Rocky's victory in the election should have given me further reflections. But its immediate consequence was that for several weeks Rocky practically disappeared from daytime Torrent. I knew he was spending most of his time at Prairie, trying to promote Torrent's claims to a freeway. What I didn't know was that he was doing it with money Hewitt had given him and building himself solidly into state politics in the process.

I should have caught the news when Hewitt asked me to second him for the Torrent Club. The whole thing, however, was deceptively consistent with Hewitt's usual policy.

"We can't ignore that plurality, Jim; I'm thinking ahead, for the bank."

Hewitt's sponsorship alone would have ensured Rocky's election to the Torrent Club. Its character was commercial, its doors were open to nearly anyone with the dues and Rocky's grandfather had been a member. Most of the membership ranged upwards from a decade older than Rocky. Hewitt told me he thought it proper for Rocky to be seconded by someone closer to his own age group.

His admission to the Country Club was as normal. Our Country Club did have a few rather silly social pretensions. It also had a chronic deficit and a generous dues policy for young memberships. Again, the Parmenters had been members. It was one of Winifred's grievances against life that she could not belong. The restriction was neither social nor financial. The Reverend's congregation might have considered it worldly.

In high school days Rocky had gone regularly to its Saturday night dances. The rules were unwritten and simple. Anyone might be asked to one of the various dinner parties that always preceded dances. Sons or daughters of members could take dates there alone. It was tacitly understood that after school days, nonmembers went only as guests of formal parties.

Lucy and I had gone there together several times to parties during the spring. I had thought of asking her to the dances and then thought again. To begin that habit was to continue it. To continue it amounted to a public declaration of courtship.

After the election she and I had lapsed into a guarded truce. I saw her often on business and still stayed for lunch or dinner with her and Archie frequently. I avoided being alone with her. At first she teased me about my habitual excuse of night work. Slowly she accepted it in silence.

One morning in midsummer Madge called me with a note of urgency in her casual tones. She and Hewitt were planning a small dinner at the Country Club for the coming Saturday. She hoped I would bring Lucy.

"But call her this morning, will you, Jim?"

On the phone Lucy was as cordial as ever but rather gayer. Her merriment had a note of complacency.

"I'm so sorry, Jim. Rocky's taking me that night."

When I called Madge to report I could tell, even through the telephone connection, the way her eyes were contracting.

"Exactly what I feared," she said. "That's why I called you first. He's not taking her to any party of ours. I told Hewitt it was insanity to put him in the club at all."

When Saturday night came Lucy and Rocky made their first appearance at the club, dining together at a table for two. Afterward, to the whispers of the whole room, they danced together for most of the evening. I cut in on her once but we had only a moment before Leonard Tuttlewise claimed her. As I returned to the stag line Rocky came up to me.

"Jim," he said, "that's worth all the fancy clothes and fuss of being here."

"What is?"

"Seeing Leonard Tuttlewise get something away from you. Come on down to the grill and I'll buy you a drink."

"Thanks, Rocky. I've had about all I need."

"This isn't for need," said Rocky. "This is pleasure. I owe you one for helping me into the Torrent Club."

I followed him down to the grill, where members hide from their wives on these occasions. Old Lowell had been tending bar there when Rocky and I were in knee breeches but Rocky made a fuss with him over brands of bourbon.

"Here's for your trouble and help, Jim," he said.

"No trouble and as for help, I voted against you, Rocky."

He laughed forgivingly. "Jim, don't ever change. You make a perfect guinea pig. But just for the record, what was your beef?"

"You could have won without all that cheap demagoguing, Rocky."

"Maybe," he said. "But in politics there isn't any could have, Jim. There's just did."

"Well, now that you have, I hope you'll grow up."

"I wouldn't dare," said Rocky, "until the voters grow up. Boy! Mr. Denton and I will have two more of the club specials."

Upstairs the tongues were still wagging about Rocky and Lucy when the party broke up. A faint drizzle was falling and a dozen women gathered on the front steps waiting for the men to bring the cars. The Randolphs had driven me out and so I was waiting beside Madge when Lucy came over to say good night to her. We chatted together inconsequentially and then we all saw that Cadillac whirl up to the steps with a swish of gravel. Rocky jumped out and took his time helping Lucy into it. The car was not new but it had been shined until in the half-light it glittered. Rocky protracted his attentions to Lucy at its door until everyone on the porch had an eyeful and the cars behind his were honking impatiently.

"Where on earth did he get that?" demanded Madge.

"I don't know."

The competitor in her looked at it angrily. Then her face softened. For just a moment on that swarming porch I found myself with a very different woman from the Madge I had always known.

"Jim, that makes me very sad," she said.

I knew she was thinking of Vinty; I kept my mouth shut and she went on, oblivious of the people around us.

"It's not just Vinty. I love her very dearly for herself."

"She loves you, Madge."

"I hope so," said Madge. "And I do hope this isn't snobbery, Jim. I know we all came down out of the same tree. But she has character and taste; he'll never have anything but energy."

Hewitt's arrival spared us further talk. His had been the car behind Rocky's; he bustled us into it with marked irritation and it broke her mood. She reverted to the Madge we all knew.

"I did hurry, Hewitt. Did you see who was ahead of you?"

"See it!" exclaimed Hewitt. "I damned near let my clutch slip and make an end of this nonsense."

"It's your own fault," said Madge. "You put him up there. And if he can get a Cadillac I don't see why you can't get one for Gretchen!"

Hewitt glared at her and then suddenly began to laugh.

"For your information," he said, "I was trying to get that one. You'd better plant your anatomy a little more firmly before he gets this one out from under us."

"Hewitt! If you thought a little more about Lucy and less about the bank . . ."

"Now you're quoting him," said Hewitt. "What was it, Jim: 'human values instead of property values'?"

Next day the phones of Torrent sizzled. As it was Sunday I didn't have to face Miss Premm, but Mother was waiting for me at the break-fast table with the society section of the paper spread wide.

"Did you know about this?" she asked.

"Yes."

"Couldn't you have done something about it, dear?"

"We're meeting with seconds as soon as I've had coffee."

She put her glasses on the table and looked at me patiently.

"Jim, do you want this to be a joking matter?"

"What would I do if I didn't?"

"You might remember," she said, "that modesty can be presumptuous too, dear; she doesn't look at things the way you do. And those Slades are all devious."

In some things Rocky was devious. In that courtship he was, after the election, unequivocally open. Lucy told me later about that first date. She was still a little astounded and she was still pleased.

Rocky never asked her out until his membership in the Country Club was official. Within an hour of learning that he had telephoned and invited her to the dance. She liked being asked. She couldn't help remembering his refusal to dine at River House and some of his confidences throughout the campaign.

"Won't people see us together in daylight?" she asked a little dryly.

"I want them to, now," said Rocky.

He requested her particularly to be ready by seven o'clock. She was a little concerned about leaving Archie for the evening. She prepared things for her and Rocky to have a cocktail with him on the verandah before they set out. Rocky went out there to make his manners to Archie but he refused the cocktail with his eye on his wristwatch.

"I can buy us one at the club now," he said.

They left Archie and went out through the darkened hall to the front door and then out into the early summer twilight. She had felt an excitement in him that she could not understand in the house. As she stepped out the door she saw that Cadillac.

"Rocky! Where on earth did you get that?"

"Looks right, in this drive, doesn't it?"

"It would be beautiful anywhere but . . ."

"But what?"

"I guess I'm just surprised." She tried to cover.

"Get in," said Rocky, "and make it more beautiful while I tell you about it."

She thought she had covered her near-question with compliments. Rocky drove beside her, silent until she had praised it enthusiastically. Then he turned to her quizzically.

"Now what about that but?"

"'But'?"

"'But can you afford it,' wasn't it?"

"Yes," she said, "it was."

"I can't," said Rocky. "That's what makes it fun, that and a lot of things."

"What things?"

He told her happily of the deal Ed Delany had given him and of Hewitt's frustration. She laughed with relish.

"Uncle Hewitt's really sweet," she said, "but I'm always glad to see someone push him around for a change."

"Uncle Hewitt," mimicked Rocky, "is sore as hell but he'll get over it. And Ed will sell a lot of these buggies when I get him that freeway."

"I bet he will," said Lucy. "I never thought of that."

"Even that isn't the real point," said Rocky. "I spent ten years chiseling rides for double dates with kids whose families had cars. I'm not crying about it, either. I always figured I'd get this just like I'm going to get everything else I want."

"You will, Rocky," she said. "I'm sure you will."

"Want to know what comes next?"

"Of course."

It was still only early twilight and they were driving along the main road to the club with cars full of other people in the habitual Saturday night procession. When Lucy said "Of course," Rocky steered over to the side of the road, stopped the car, pulled her over to him and kissed her hard.

"It was the first time since Vinty," she told me. "I thought of Vinty and then of what I was doing and I liked it but I didn't really kiss him back; not that time."

When Rocky realized that she was submitting without either response or struggle, he let her go and moved her quietly back to her side of the seat. Then he examined his face in the car mirror for lipstick, wiped it off with a handkerchief, took out a pocket comb and began combing his hair. She said nothing and presently he had to speak.

"You said you wanted to know."

"All right," she said. "Let's go to the club."

"Okay," said Rocky. "But you're going to marry me."

That startled her. She decided to deal with it at once.

"No," she said. "I'm not. Really I'm not, Rocky."

He scrutinized her while he put his comb away carefully. Then she saw his eyes sweep the interior of the car; his hand made a little possessive gesture.

"So it's second hand," he said. "But I'm not. You're the first dame I ever decided to marry."

"It was perfectly melting," she told me. "He was half asking me to marry that damned car but it was more than that. There was a confidence in him you could feel in your marrow."

She had temporized and spoken of friendship. He started the car and drove on, snorting.

"Friendship my ass! That's impossible for us."

"Why?" she demanded.

"Because of the way I feel."

"My feelings have nothing to do with it then?"

"I'll make you feel this way, too. Wait and see."

Part of her could laugh; part was aware of something she was not certain of controlling; she tried to evade it in jest.

"A month ago you wouldn't be seen in public with me. Now look at this car and your asking to marry me. What will your precious voters think of that?"

"Voters don't think," said Rocky. "Voters feel."

"What will they feel?"

"They'll feel I'm an operator now and it's okay 'cause they helped to make me one."

"It was strange," she told me. "He could be so timid and tentative about some things but even under that you could feel strength; perhaps that's what the voters felt."

When they reached the club she made a mistake. She told him just to drive out to the parking lot where young couples go to neck during the dance. Then she remembered the implication of going to the parking lot instead of being delivered to the door on arrival. The earlier stages of courtship always paused there for a last kiss before going in. Rocky shook his head firmly.

"I'm taking you to the door," he said.

There, as he did on departure, he managed to cause a minor traffic jam, creating an audience on purpose to see him helping Lucy out of the car. She tried to hurry to the ladies' entrance. He detained her on the steps, elaborating a plan to meet in the lounge and combing his hair while the other cars lined up behind his.

"All right," she said, "all right. You're blocking traffic, Rocky."

"I'm paid up," said Rocky. "Let 'em wait."

"Rocky, will you do something for me?"

"Natch."

"Don't comb your hair like that in public."

"What's wrong with it?"

"Never mind," she said. "Just don't do it."

He broke the comb in half and threw the pieces into the driveway.

"Okay. I can teach you things too, Lucy."

Chapter Eight

AFTER she had told me in so many words that she was not going to marry Rocky, I found it all the easier to ignore the advice and gossip with which I was being bombarded. Rocky was still roaring around the state in his Cadillac, giving his freeway presentation wherever he could find an audience and helping to make audiences where he couldn't find them. A lot of Wiasota wanted to shake the hand that had beaten Notre Dame.

When he was at home he continued to swim at River House in the afternoons. He returned every Saturday night to take her to the Country Club dances, which intensified speculation for the rest of the summer. I was still convinced that it meant nothing when Archie asked me out to dine alone with him on one of those Saturdays.

Rocky had swum and changed his clothes there that day. He was more at home in the club now. Lucy had been able to insist that they linger for a first drink with Archie and me before setting out. I found them on the verandah together, Archie in an old blazer and flannels, Rocky resplendent in his new white dinner jacket with a maroon cummerbund.

"Where do you think our councilor has been?" demanded Lucy.

"Kissing babies," I said.

"Not this week," Rocky grinned. "This week it was grandfathers."

He told us exultantly. Out of a clear sky Dennis Flynn had summoned him to Prairie. Word of the popularity of Rocky's presentation had moved upward rapidly from the county seats. Dennis had thought it would be a wonderful thing for all of Wiasota if some of the party's truest friends had a look at it in Washington.

"I don't kid myself," said Rocky. "The presentation is not that caliber. It had to mean he thought I was. He was showing me the promised land, real fatherly."

At the time I should have remembered that Dennis had always been more renowned for frugality than for fatherliness to County

Councilors. Rocky did not tell us that they had made the trip on the funds supplied by Hewitt. He had regarded it as an investment and he had got his money's worth. He bubbled over to us about the other details.

He had taken time out to visit the standard shrines, the Capitol, a limited tour of the White House, the Lincoln and Jefferson Memorials and a long session in one of the top offices in the F.B.I.

". . . they're smart," said Rocky, "you talk to them an hour before you realize that you're the only one talking. They got a real lather on about this communism; I told 'em it might be fine there but it wasn't worth a vote here."

They had dined at Hall's and Harvey's: "You can get a better steak in Torrent but you see big wheels there." And in private rooms with Dennis's cronies in the Shoreham and Wardman Park, Rocky had given amended versions of his presentation before selected groups of Congressmen, minor Republican appointees who had survived the Democratic era and some impressive brass in the Republican national organization.

". . . the only real smart choice I ever made was parties, Jim," he said. "The Democrats are coming apart at the seams and every Republican I met was a hundred and twelve years old."

"How did they like your soak-the-rich angle?"

"You may have a point there," he grinned. "Dennis had made me tone it down a lot but even so they all quacked. Said it might offend some big party dough in the East. I told them I'd worry about that after it got me East."

With old Herman Brodbeck, the lingering relic of Wiasota's former Republicanism, they had had sessions which Rocky pronounced worth the price of the whole trip.

"He talked the old pious guff about service," said Rocky. "But you learn things, just keeping your eyes open in that Senate Office Building. In his anteroom there were six standard-sized filing cases marked 'Veterans.' And half the country still thinks he's an old fool."

"Weren't you afraid the Democrats would steal your freeway?" asked Archie dryly.

"Not a chance," said Rocky. "We won't get a federal dime out of this Congress; didn't expect to. But every Republican we met knows we're gonna sweep the state with it this fall. When we talked they listened."

He was brimming over with what Lucy had called the confidence you could feel in your marrow. He had been to the promised land; his manner more than any word told us he knew it would be his. You could laugh at the details and feel the tingle of that vitality while you were laughing.

They went off presently, leaving Archie and me alone on the verandah. Fond as I was of him I found it flat to be sitting there looking at the chair Lucy had just left.

Through dinner Archie was absent and preoccupied. The lingering presence of Douglass limited conversation. I arose from an excellent meal with a sense of emptiness and apathy for the chess ahead. When Douglass left us with coffee and brandy, however, I asked Archie if he'd like me to put out the set. He shook his head impatiently.

"Jim, Roscoe is courting Lucy."

"Looks like it, sir."

"I didn't even suspect," said Archie, "until he insisted on showing me that preposterous automobile."

"It isn't preposterous to him, Archie."

"You sound like her. She calls it pathetic."

"She has a lot of penetration."

"All women have, until they need it," said Archie. "Objectively, you might call him pitiable. His life has been a quagmire of humbug. Maybe it takes one parasite to smell another but I've been a candid one. This boy is the triumph of willful hypocrisy.

"Most people understand that survival and the golden rule are antithetical and adjust as they can. Roscoe still thinks he can have both. He was taught to pray for sacrifice and service and success in the same breath. He was taught that all men are created equal and his grandfather was a Parmenter. He was hired by the official repository of this state's culture and ethics to win amateur football championships. He was taught not to covet but to cultivate kids with cars. He was taught not to kill and drafted into the army. Come to think of it, the Sixth Commandment is probably the only one he's left intact. The army drafted him to save democracy and made him a master sergeant to coach football.

"He's been taught that the meek will inherit the earth, if they vote right. He has been taught to love God, abjure Mammon and get on in the world, to pray to the Trinity and worship the new subtitles on the three-headed golden calf: Success, Democracy and Romance."

"It takes two to make a romance, Archie."

"Madge says I should take her traveling," said Archie. "As if she were a debutante with a case on a groom. But Madge isn't entirely a fool. What do you think, Jim?"

"Ridiculous."

"I agree. I spent my life running away from things that always caught up with me. But how can I stop this?"

"If she wants him, you can't."

"Lawyers!" said Archie. "You're all alike."

It stung. I retorted before I thought.

"This is not the work I undertook."

"Forgive me," said Archie. "Anything you need a lawyer for is your own fault. But faults are so damned cumulative, Jim. Could you find a discreet way to let Roscoe know how much of Father's property I've lost?"

"He probably knows. This is not mercenary, sir."

"I should have tried harder and lost it all," said Archie. "Money is as futile as I am."

There was little to say. I thought of his wife and of Artie and of Hewitt's industrious conformity and of Vinty.

"You're up against biology, Archie," I said.

"It isn't that simple," said Archie. "If it were I'd already have the back room in a cave full of that ape's children, unless they'd eaten me when the hunting was thin. Our troubles have come from trying to modify biology with ethics and taste and your goddamned law. We've traded simple forces for a remorseless conspiracy. That's what she's up against."

"I don't follow you, sir."

"The conspiracy," said Archie, "is love. We're trying to accommodate all of human thought and activity to love. It pervades our folklore and literature, it cloys our entertainment, it's the mainspring of Hewitt's precious economy. Take any book off the nearest shelf. Look, if you can stand it, at the newsstands. If you've a really strong stomach, turn on the radio for two minutes. Love, love, love! Love in the White House, love in the tabloids, love in the quiz contests, love in cars, kitchens, bathrooms, breakfast food and underclothing. It probably started with the fatal change from hunting and fighting to trade. We live for trade and trade lives on love.

"All her life Lucy has been under continuous assault through all five senses, for love. Hair curlers, toothpaste, piano lessons, dancing school, permanents, nightgowns and budgets—for love. You begin with seven or eight pounds of foolproof animal. You spend twenty years defending her flesh from microbes and her brain from mortals until you achieve the triumph of a healthy, educated woman. A twenty-second look around her converts that into incarnate terror, into fear beyond primitive superstition—no love. Then she comes down the stairs to talk about selling a house and there is Roscoe."

"She still has a free choice, sir."

"As between men, she might," said Archie. "Against the conspiracy there is no choice. Love doesn't even rhyme with approve."

He sighed and shook his head and gathered himself.

"Forgive me, Jim. I'm afraid it's not your problem, or even mine now. We might as well play chess."

He limped about the setting up of the board and poured us some more brandy. The clock whirred and ticked and lamented in the hall. I felt as old and tired and defeated as Archie. Then, abruptly, he chuckled and reached into his pocket.

"This *is* your business," he said. "I squandered estate principal for this."

He tossed a shiny new key across the table.

"Boathouse," he said. "Jamison won't let me row this year so I shall depend on you for ducks. My boat and Artie's are yours. I'll send the pickup for your own if you prefer but I want you to shoot from here from now on."

I thanked him and we talked of happier things.

"I can shoot doves anyway," said Archie. "We'll expect you for lunch and dinner on opening day."

"I was hoping to be asked," I said.

"Ordered," said Archie. "We'll have Lucy anyway, if not your father and Artie."

Then his face shadowed again.

"Jim, should I ask that halfback?"

"That's up to you, sir."

"He never has shot here," said Archie. "Does he shoot at all?"

"I doubt it. He always spent the autumns at football."

"Good," said Archie. "Maybe he won't come but I'm afraid I'd better ask him. You can't beat love but the quickest way to lose is to oppose it."

I I

At the end of August Lucy went to spend a week with Gretchen in Minnesota.

"Might have known Madge would have her way about travel," said Archie dryly, but I think both of us were grateful to Madge. County fairs had opened and Rocky was away increasingly, exploiting their natural audiences and intensifying his indirect assistance to candidates for the legislative elections in October.

In consequence I saw neither Lucy nor Rocky for several days until she returned to help Archie and me open the dove season. It came in early September that year. I took my gun and a bag of gear in the car and after a morning at the office drove out to River House.

Grandfather Denton had quarreled with Simeon about everything except shooting. They often did that together, betting on birds and bags in the days when there were no limits. Archie had shot with them as a boy. Later he had often invited Father and me to shoot with him and, as they grew up, Lucy and Artie had shot with us.

Archie had added skeet towers to the trap Simeon always maintained on the bank above the river. Both the twins had had the benefit of expert teaching and adequate practice. Most of our duck shooting came in weather too arduous for Lucy. Doving, in our tranquil early Septembers, was easy and convivial. When she kept her mind on it she was an accomplished wing shot.

She and Archie made an odd contrast when I came into the library. For shooting on the river or at Widgeon Lake or afield around the state, Archie always wore the conventional brown duck. On some of his own places, for upland shooting, he still affected a Burberry tweed relic of his grouse shooting days in Scotland. Lucy was in tennis shoes, the blue jeans of our fishing trip and another tight green sweater.

"I've even got a license, Jim," she said, displaying the little metal tag.

"You don't need it on our own place," said Archie.

"You'd be surprised where girls need licenses nowadays," said Lucy.

I thought the week away had done her good. She was eager and cheerful and relaxed with us.

"This is only sherry, Jim," said Archie. "They won't fly till three o'clock and we'll have it all burned out of us by then. Lucy, fetch another glass, will you? This cork is going to make a mess."

When she left the room he winked at me happily.

"I did ask him," he said. "He's kissing babies. Asked Hewitt, too, and he has a meeting. This is our day, Jim."

She returned with another glass. He poured slowly for all of us, scrutinized his glass against the light from the window and then raised it solemnly.

"Your father, Jim. I'll miss him today."

"And Artie, sir," I said.

We were shooting less than a mile from the house but most of it was uphill and on Jamison's insistence we drove Archie to the field. It was a forty-acre patch of corn on what they called the home place, adjoining the estate itself along the northwest boundary. Our farm manager had been scandalized about planting corn so high on the moraine. It was one of the old customs I had conceded as a kind of *quid pro quo* for Archie's sorrowful acquiescence in the sale of Widgeon Lake.

The crop itself had been hogged without plucking from the stalk. Shocks lay trampled and strewn in every direction. Under them the field was aglint with missed kernels, gleaming gold through the green and brown of ripening foxtail grass. We left the car in the woods above it and walked slowly down through it toward the Osage orange hedge line which commemorated one of Simeon's early experiments.

We were high enough on the moraine for a twenty-mile view of the valley across the river from us. Red tractors and harvest machinery moved through it like toys in the distance. To the southeast we could see the spires of the town's taller buildings and the dark mass spread out around them.

Midafternoon had brought the faintest suggestion of haze, softening the light into a shade of saffron. It was warm enough for the lightest of jackets but we didn't need the autumnal flame of maples in the woods to remind us that we were close to frost. The breeze was light with a foretaste of chill; the booming of earlier guns along the valley echoed with a rounded resonance.

We had all shot the field in other years. The only real variations in it were for wind or freakish concentrations of grain. Archie had been watching it with field glasses for a week and had made two studious afternoon reconnaissances. We went part way down through the corn and then over toward the hedge line so as to have the sun at our backs and the low trees for partial horizon cover.

"Most of them crossed about here yesterday," said Archie. "We'll put Lucy here and you and I . . ."

"You will not," said Lucy. "You shoot between us."

"Nonsense," said Archie. "Host takes the thin end and bets you a bottle apiece for first bird and first limit."

"You shoot between us," said Lucy. "If you stir to pick up a bird, Jim and I quit shooting."

He protested in vain. Separately each of us had spoken to Jamison about this and we overruled Archie together. We left him comfortably seated with enough cornstalks to break the more grotesque outlines of that Burberry. Then we separated, moving out to about seventy yards either side of him. Archie's heart was not what it had been; his eyes were. I was still scratching up some cornstalk cover for myself when I heard his low call:

"South, Lucy."

My angle of vision let me pick up the bird before she did. It arrowed out of the treetops east of us and would cross within her range. I watched the transitions of its flight, hurtling dark and blocky as I first saw it and then changing with the light to a flashing long-tailed meteor, gray and silver. It crossed the hedge line, high and already a little spooky from the remembered sound of guns reverberating through the valley.

She had never learned to shoot sitting; she could compensate in agility. She came up slowly, her gun rising with her in fluid motion until it locked into her shoulder and her whole body started tracking it from the ankles up. You could tell she was on it by the arc of the muzzle alone. As it puffed I looked up and the sound of the gun reached me just as the shot took the bird.

In one second it was a glinting horizontal trajectory. Then it checked with a silvery puff of feathers, somersaulted over and over slowly and fell, in the long even tangent of the clean air kill, almost at her feet.

"The bottle will be Chanel Cinq," she called and stepped forward to pick up and then froze in her tracks as she did.

"Over you, Daddy . . . high . . . HIGH."

She needn't have called. Archie sat immobile until a pair cleared his sight line over the hedge and then began to swing with them, tracking as expertly from the waist alone as Lucy had done from her ankles. We saw the double puffs and heard the evenly spaced reports and watched them thud down as momentum carried them far behind him.

"I'll get 'em," she called. "Oh. North, Jim, NORTH."

We made it last until dusk, stretching our limits after the first excitement by taking turns and watching and kidding each other about the misses. The trampled corn and grass made a troublesome drop. We triangulated for each other and picked up as soon as we killed and in the end we got every bird we hit, spreading them to cool as we continued.

Then I brought the car down into the field to spare Archie the walk. The day when you just delivered birds to willing hands in a swarming kitchen was past, but doves are the easiest of game to handle. I put them by the car and ran a preliminary swipe through the gun barrels while they were still warm. Lucy was already at work on another ritual.

While Archie and I turned the birds inside out, leaving all but the breasts for foxes and coons, she got out the big Thermos. She and Archie had made the traditional brew of iced tea and rum that morning. We stood together sipping from cups as we did the birds and watching the heavier mist from the river burn the crimson out of the sun until it vanished into a blue and starry twilight. Lucy was flushed from sun and exertion; the last light on her hair and in her eyes was something I shall not forget.

"This was the first thing I thought of in the hospital," said Archie. "I wanted one more day like this."

"I always forget between seasons," said Lucy. "You can't remember anything as good as this."

"Shooting," said Archie, "is the only thing I've ever done that rids me entirely of Archie Maynard."

"We've got the war to make up for, too," said Lucy. "Now that we've got shells and time. When will you come again, Jim?"

"Tomorrow," said Archie. "This field will stand another day and we'll lose 'em to the first heavy frost."

"Oh, damn!" said Lucy. "I promised to go to a football game with Rocky."

"Good God!" said Archie. "Football lasts all fall and this won't. Bring him shooting."

"He won't," said Lucy. "He won't do anything he can't do well."

"How does he propose to learn?"

"He doesn't," she said, "and this is important to him. It's just the South Side Athletic Association but they practically made it a Rocky Slade Club in the election and he's promised to referee for them tomorrow. Oh, damn it all! I'd much rather beat you two out of some more bottles."

"Your choice," said Archie curtly. Our mood was gone. We had all been rid of ourselves all afternoon. Rocky was with us in the silent car as we drove back to the house.

After doving we usually changed in the boathouse. Now we were saving fuel on that until freeze-up demanded pipe protection. That night I took my time in the drafty bath of the upstairs guest room. When we gathered again in the library Archie was more cheerful. He had broken out a bottle of Simeon's Haut Brion in honor of the birds.

We made a happy, companionable dinner over extended post-mortems of the shoot. We remembered other shoots with Artie and my father and we spoke of them almost as if they would be with us again later in the season. For a time we nearly managed the illusion that they might be. Then as Archie rose to divide the last of the bottle we could see that he was fatigued. He held it to the light and shook his head slowly.

"It's going, Jim," he said. "There are only two more of these and we'd better do them this season. Time gets everything."

"It gets you to bed, too," said Lucy. "I bet you and Jim have been carousing over that chessboard till all hours while I was away. Off you go or Jim won't shoot with you tomorrow."

"All right," he said. "Cigars are on the table for you, Jim."

We saw him to the foot of the stairs and went into the library and put on another log and chatted of commonplaces until Douglass creaked in with coffee and brandy and left us alone. As the door closed behind her Lucy shook her head.

"Jim, I'm sorry about tomorrow."

"We'll miss you."

"I'll miss you. But Rocky wants to marry me."

"Tomorrow?"

"He would." She half smiled and then her voice was somber. "Jim, am I just being a teasing bitch?"

"How would I know? Have you teased him?"

"Not the way I did you that first time we went fishing. I don't know whether it's because I wouldn't dare or just don't want to. He feels that way but I don't, or not enough. There's so much more to it than sex. It's humiliating to be always available, to have Hattie and Marian making dates for me, to have Madge foisting me off on Gretchen. She was nice about it but it just rubbed the whole thing in.

"When you visit a working marriage you may not want the sex but you can't help wanting the babies and planning a dinner for someone besides Daddy and having your own man to complain of the coffee and be cross at breakfast and then call up and send flowers.

"That quaint old Miss Maynard is getting too damned efficient about the laundry inventory at the hospital and understanding your bookkeeping and taking the power mower in the truck for repairs. Even the girls I know stop or change the conversation whenever I enter a room; it's all birth control or babies and I'm not in the union.

"All the men we know are freezing up about Rocky's politics. He says we're all stuffed shirts trying to crawl back into the past. Perhaps poor Daddy is ineffectual but he does love me and he can't bear Rocky. What do you think, Jim?"

"Your father's not marrying him, Lucy."

"You're a big help! That's just what Rocky says."

"He's right about something anyway."

"I don't want to marry him and I don't want to lose him for a beau either. Perhaps I am a teasing bitch but I've only kissed him back two or three times. It seems to mean so much to him and it never stirred me the way it's supposed to, or not enough. He says it will be all right when we're married but I think you should feel a little more that way first, don't you?"

"Your business, Lucy."

"You don't have to be so damned neutral; part of it's yours, too."

"What part?"

"Jim, if I did marry him we'd always be friends, just like this anyhow, wouldn't we?"

"I hope so."

"What do you mean, 'hope so'?"

"Men like to choose their own lawyers, Lucy."

"Then women can, too. You'll always be mine."

"As long as I can help you."

"That is always," she said. "You always do, except about this and it isn't really your fault. Oh, God, Jim, if he were just a little more . . . a little more convincing."

Chapter Nine

MY first year with the estate would end that November. Long before we reached it I knew there was fear as well as obstinacy in my determination to wait for that date to propose to her. Part of me could whisper that I was gambling, for the first time in my life, with the most important thing I had ever found. The rest of me could insist that nothing worth while is decided by a gamble. The year's work had won a kind of independence for them as well as me. Anyone could follow the patterns I had set. With help from Kevin and the farm manager Lucy could do everything I was doing, if Archie would not.

The stock-market break in September had given some of my arithmetical projections a nasty knock. We had never speculated. The Maynards still owned what I had acquiesced in buying for them. Kevin and I both had confidence in its recovery and in its long-range potential, if Archie's heart allowed us the long range. In the meanwhile it looked as if I had squeezed blood as well as water out of the estate. Archie, of course, was delighted with the market break.

"It always broke when I bought, too, Jim: I've had the pleasure of telling Roscoe we're seriously hurt."

"You're only hurt on paper, sir."

"Oh." His face fell. "Now when I was doing it I was always hurt for keeps. But Roscoe won't know that."

He would not have cared if he had. Lucy and I both knew that Rocky wanted to marry her for herself and part of me was very glad he did. She had needed a determined beau to exorcise the ghost of Vinty. She had had one and in November she was going to have another and freedom of choice between them.

Madge and Hewitt had always maintained a line between bank and home. Downtown Hewitt kept a well-polished fingernail in every significant pie in the community. He could be distant for policy or easily familiar with scores of men who called him Hewitt and would never cross his threshold.

Madge wrote their personal invitations with a choosy hand. They crossed age lines for more reasons than the Randolphs' desire to keep up with youth. The number of contemporaries they received was limited; they preferred extending their acquaintance downward through generations.

They had been married in October and from this, over the years, had evolved the institution of the Randolphs' Halloween party. It had begun as a simple annual dinner for their intimates. With the maturing of their children it had expanded to include another generation.

Somewhere along the line it had outgrown their parlor and had been transferred to the main pavilion and hayloft of their big barn, changing its character with the move. Long before the war Hewitt had found some talented rural fiddles, guitars, an accordion and a square-dance caller. The first experiment was an overwhelming success; thereafter guests were required to wear overalls, which many had to borrow for the occasion.

During the war these parties had been discontinued. That fall there was conjecture about whether, considering Vinty and Gretchen's residence in Minnesota, they would ever be resumed. As the time approached, people wondered. One morning early in the month I found Madge's invitation on the breakfast table, from which I was shortly summoned to the telephone.

"Jim," she said, "will you call Lucy immediately?"

It was impossible to refuse without making too much of it. I called Lucy with memories and foreboding. Even before I had said my say I could hear her chuckling.

"Madge gets up early, doesn't she?"

"I wouldn't know. Our postman does. How about it?"

"I wondered if they'd ask Rocky. Now I know."

"Would he grudge you one evening with an old friend?"

"That's not the point," said Lucy. "Will you do something for me?"

"Sure."

"Tell Madge I didn't have a date with Rocky until you called, but now I do."

"Lucy, you're imagining things."

"I'm remembering things," said Lucy, "and you should, too; can you remember the rest of it, Mr. James?"

"What rest?"

"You must never try to lie in court. I'll see you at the party."

I reported a suitably amended version of this to Madge, who was normally fastidious in speech.

"Damn!" she said. "Damn him; that cunning, cunning brute. Her date is with Roscoe, of course?"

"That's what she said."

"That crafty brute! He knows perfectly well we can't *not* have Lucy."

For once circumstances were not fair to Rocky. I could scarcely tell Madge so. If Lucy was going to force him on her party that was her business and theirs. Before the campaign Madge wouldn't have thought twice about asking Rocky or anyone else for whom Lucy might have requested an invitation. The antipathy he was now meeting in some parts of the town was more than a tribute to his exertions. It was a confirmation of his strategy. Every informed man in Torrent had laughed at Rocky's first pretensions to influencing the freeway.

Despite all the noise he had made he was influencing it then no more than he had done in Freddy Eastman's office. But the noise had done its work. Many of the people who affected to ridicule him were now blaming him angrily for it. Hewitt might still know better. Madge and most of the guests she would invite had swallowed the propaganda they condemned.

The party fell on a night to make the blood surge. Indian summer had lain drowsy and languid over us all day. Sunset showed the dark silver cloud bar of a cold front moving in from the northwest. After dinner I drove out the Ridge Road. The air was tonic with the promise of heavy frost, seasoned with the pungency of burning leaves and, as I reached higher ground, the clean astringency of the pines. Leaves skittered restlessly across the road. Moonlight was patchy with shadows from scurrying cloud and naked branches. The long hoot of the eight forty-nine coming up from the lowlands was a mournful requiem for the declining year.

Hewitt had been unable to resist some incongruous embellishments of his rural scene. The first of these was the town's solitary marquee, imported for the occasion from Ezra Beloin's funeral parlor to grace the main entrance of the barn. You passed through it from the wild autumnal melancholy of the night to brightness and hilarity.

The big pavilion shone with festoons of Christmas-tree lights, Japanese lanterns and candles in pumpkins and gourds. Fresh straw made a golden floor. Arranged corn shocks hid the utilitarian outlines of the stalls.

Downstairs old Lowell from the Country Club presided over a dress parade of bottles and mixing gear set up on sawhorse tables. Upstairs in the loft Stewart from the Torrent Club stirred and poured over its counterpart. Already caterers were setting tables for supper in the box stalls and some of the guests were dancing in the straw around them. Time had modified the overall requirement a little. The men wore red deer vests or gaudy lumberjack shirts. The women were bright in stoles and flaming blouses, gypsy shawls and earrings.

Dust from the loft above mingled with the discreetly prevailing animal and straw odors and the fainter tinging of tobacco, cosmetics and good liquor. The shuffling and stamping overhead muted the music; it hung faint, evocative and heady in the air. Older couples were arriving steadily. Occasionally younger ones would come down from the loft muttering improbable explanations about handbags or coats as they scurried back out through the marquee to darkness and parked cars.

At the bar Lowell told me that Madge and Hewitt were busy with a set in the loft. Square dancing was something I always left to others. I had a drink with Kevin and Marian Inglis, who were of a similar mind. Then we heard the end of the set and I went up to the loft to make my manners. When general dancing was resumed I asked Madge, who for years had declined to dance with anyone but Hewitt, and then began with Hattie Gilchrist.

Hattie and I had patched an uneasy truce over our differences about my duty to Torrent. She greeted me with a glaring, "You're alone, I suppose," and then allowed herself to be diverted briefly into her newest enthusiasm.

"I'm positive it was Bacon," she said, "but it's just like the other great ideas, Jim. The philosophical significance of it is enormous, the Baconians are so grubby and pedantic it might just as well have been Shakespeare."

She sighed and began to scold me about the State Department and China until the entrance of Rocky and Lucy brought her back to Torrent very fast.

"Look at him," she said. "New overalls yet and bowing and fawning over Madge as if she wanted him here."

"She asked him, Hattie."

"Jim," she said, "I know why you're letting this happen but that will never make me like it."

"You know a lot that I don't, Hattie."

"I know a lot you don't face," she said. "You're thinking about appearances. He's thinking about her and he has sex an old bag like me can feel across the street. You'd damned well better get busy."

"Since you're running my life what's the next step?"

"The next step," said Hattie, "is to drag her by that gorgeous hair to the nearest justice of the peace. After that if you're still in doubt, Aunt Hattie will send you a book in a plain wrapper."

When I got a chance to cut in on Lucy I found her gay at first with a hint of mischief in her animation.

"Did Madge make you dance with me too, Mr. James?"

"No. Hewitt's giving me a dollar for extra duty with wallflowers."

"Cut me in," said Lucy, "and I'll keep you in a career."

"I wouldn't trust you; people tell me you're considering marriage."

"I've heard the same rumor," said Lucy, "but I don't believe all I hear."

"I had this from a fairly reliable girl, Lucy."

The gaiety went out of her then, fading slowly.

"She's not reliable, Jim. And it's going to make a hell of a lot of trouble."

"What kind?"

"The worst; the only kind, really."

"Nonsense; what trouble could he make?"

"Trouble," said Lucy, "is what you do to other people."

"Don't be a damned fool; you've done a lot for him."

"That's what I told myself, especially at first. It wasn't quite honest but there was that element in it, like breaking a colt, even if you're going to sell it. I guess all girls have to manage someone and I did do some things for him like, well, like this. He was crazy to be invited here.

"He even hinted about it and I wouldn't bite until Madge took it into her head that she had to get me a date as usual. But that wasn't honest to him and in his own way he has been with me and now I've got to tell him that I'm not going to marry him. I've always told him that but I've got to make it stick this time and it's going to hurt him."

Henry Perkins cut in on us then. I relinquished Lucy with a relief I had not known for weeks. For the first time I admitted to myself that I had been as smug and stuffy as Hattie said. What I didn't realize was how scared I had been.

In different ways Lucy and I had both been resisting the community around us. In different ways we had both learned that it does not work. There is no independence and she knew it, too. My year was not up and I had a meeting at the bank at ten the next morning and I was going to go straight from my breakfast table to River House and stay there until she promised to marry me and the bank and all the rest of the world could go to hell.

Relief gave me a new perspective on Rocky himself. Consciously or not I had been jealous of him. Now I could look at him again with objectivity and even a stirring of the pity that had first touched Lucy. Hattie's outburst about his arrival had been unfair. He was not arrogant; he was unsure of his welcome.

The competitor in Madge could lose small skirmishes gracefully. Tonight she had broken her rule of years to accept Rocky's invitation to dance. They were whirling around the floor as lightly as if they'd been dancing together all their lives.

You could see the restoration of his confidence under Madge's determined cordiality. Rocky had always danced well. Hewitt never permitted popular music at these parties but as a concession to the war he allowed some of its by-products. They were waltzing Matilda with light-footed grace. Rocky had begun by holding her away from him with an exaggerated formality. Before they were through he had closed up nearly cheek to cheek with her and was hailing every other couple in the room over her shoulder.

I had joined Hewitt and some of the other stags before Stewart at the upstairs bar when the music ended and Rocky returned Madge to Hewitt with an almost proprietary air of triumph.

"It was delightful, Rocky," she said.

"May I look forward to another?" he asked her.

"Not tonight; this was a year's quota at my age."

"Then I'll look forward to another year," said Rocky.

If he had left it there it would have been all right. Madge was pleased with herself for being forgiving and that had momentarily pleased her with Rocky. That competitive instinct in him had to keep punching even after he'd won.

"Thanks, again," he said, "and I'd like to tell you this is one hell of a party, Hewitt."

Perhaps none of us then knew that in the private relation he was already calling his host Hewitt. It would have been a small thing to a bigger man. We all felt the temperature fall as Hewitt paused, a little too long.

"Thank you; I'm glad you approve of us, Roscoe."

Rocky flushed and started to reply. Then you could see him bite down on his jaw. He made a half bow to them both and walked off toward Lucy, his ears crimsoning as he went.

"Hewitt!" said Madge. "We *did* ask him."

"You did, damn it," said Hewitt, and then looked at the rest of us. "I'm afraid I owe you gents an apology."

He knew as well as we did that he owed Rocky the apology. Lucy had forced him on the party. It was Hewitt who had put him in a position to be forced. He could not face that any more than he would face the crisis when it came.

The rest of the evening he did offer indirect conciliation, making conspicuous efforts to be jovial and familiar with Rocky at bar and stag line. The damage was done, or rather, it was begun and gaining momentum. Rocky avoided him, dancing almost continuously and strolling away from the groups in which Hewitt would try to engage him in general chat.

Supper was always served in the box stalls and main pavilion about twelve-thirty. People grouped as they chose when the time came. I wanted to keep away from Rocky and Lucy for the rest of the evening. In the general drift of the crowd I found myself seated with the Gilchrists, Jane and Henry Perkins and Hewitt and Madge. We had an agreeable half hour over the bouillon, scrambled eggs and champagne before the dancing was resumed and the Perkinses excused themselves. I was rising to go home when Rocky and Lucy came over to our table.

They explained that they were going to slip away after the next dance and wanted to say good night without disturbing the rest of the party. Hewitt insisted on their having a stirrup cup with us. He still had a bad conscience about that earlier curtness. He made a great point of going off for a cold bottle of champagne and serving it to us himself. The attention reassured Rocky. He had come to the table still resentful and diffident. He drank sparingly; it was the cordiality more than the wine which made him try to get in one last punch.

"I'm real grateful to you folks for asking me," he said.

"We're delighted that you enjoyed it," said Madge.

"I sure did, Mrs. Randolph. Anything I can ever do for you people, just ask me."

"Hewitt says you're doing a great deal for all of Torrent."

"Oh, that," Rocky deprecated with a shrug. "I meant I'd like to do something personal for you two."

"Don't be too reckless," said Hewitt. "We might ask you for some of those choice football seats you distinguished alumni always get."

For Hewitt, it wasn't bad. Rocky knew Hewitt didn't go to a State game once in five years. He understood the conciliation in this, and the opportunity. They had risen during his last words. Now he took Lucy by the arm and pushed her gently down, seating himself in the other vacated chair and seeming to expand before our eyes.

"Mr. Randolph," he said, "you just had the idea of the century. I been trying to get Lucy up to State for a game all fall. If you folks, I mean every one of you at this table, would be gracious enough to come along with us I can set our whole gang on the fifty-yard line Saturday. It's only Iowa but they should be hot this week," he went on, warming to it. "I can drive the whole bunch of you there in two hours flat. Afterwards—" he suddenly spread a thumb and forefinger a couple of inches and brandished them before us—"I know a steak joint where I'll get you a steak that thick, so tender you can cut it with a fork, and I'll have you all home earlier than this. How about it?"

Madge spoke immediately with smiling finality.

"Thank you, Roscoe. It's very kind of you but Hewitt and I will not be free."

Rocky flushed but kept quiet. Tom spoke, too quickly.

"Sounds wonderful, Rocky—"

"But unfortunately, we're not free either," Hattie interrupted firmly. "Thanks just the same, Rocky."

Rocky made himself smile.

"Party's shrinking but the offer still goes, Jim."

Of them all mine was the only valid excuse. I was leaving on Friday, by long prearrangement, to shoot with friends upstate. It sounded lame and hollow as I said so. Rocky and Lucy rose together, both blushing. After another round of good-bys they went straight out through the marquee instead of upstairs for the last dance they had mentioned.

"Oh, dear," said Madge, "I feel as if I'd slapped him and yet . . ."

"Honestly," said Hattie. "Give Rocky Slade an inch and you're pregnant! The nerve of calling us his gang—"

"Damn it, Hattie," said Tom, "we put him into politics and he's our friend and you might at least have thought of Lucy."

"I was thinking of Lucy," said Hattie. "The sooner she realizes that all that disgusting hate talk of his has alienated every thinking person in town, the better off she's going to be."

On the way home I tried to feel sorry for Rocky and then dropped it. Compassion was hypocritical humbug. I was not sorry for him. I was wildly exhilarated with what Lucy had told me.

It was coming on to storm and my spirit by some unfathomable inversion rose on the turbulence of the lowering pressure. I had lived too long in the insipid high of balanced restraints. I didn't know whether Lucy would have me or not. I knew I was going to keep after her until she did.

I went to bed and lay sleepless. I could hear the wind lashing at the windows with rain and sleet and gusts of snow. My excitement was chasing itself around in circles as I waited for the morning.

When my watch said three-thirty I couldn't stay in bed any longer.

[157]

I went to the window and saw the storm still rising and made up my mind. I'd go out to River House and take my boat up the river until it was breakfast time and then go into the house and have it out with her. My duck gun and gear and boat were already in their boathouse. I could shave and clean up there when I came off the river.

I left a note for Mother and took the key Archie had given me and a Thermos bottle and set off through the gale. It was blowing harder than before and now the gusts were all snow. It would make a fine shoot and seemed a good omen. I'd have some birds to take them.

In a hash house in town I had the Thermos filled and ordered a breakfast I was too excited to eat and then drove back out along the ridge route. Through the bare trees I could faintly see lights still burning in Hewitt's barn as I passed it. I could laugh to think of how despondent I had been on my way out there a few hours earlier.

I drove down the Maynards' lane and then, with an eye to the snow, forked away from the main door and drove down to the barn and left my car in the lee of it. Then I cut across the lawn till I struck the path through the rose gardens and made my way down that, approaching the boathouse by its upper front door.

The wind was stiffening from the west into a noisy gale. As I reached the door I could hear the waves slapping at the dock and pilings and along the little beach upstream. I knew there would be a heavy chop until I got across into the lee. I remember planning to put on storm gear and a jumper.

Then I unlocked the door and shut it behind me fast to keep the gale out. My hand groped along the west wall a second until it found the light switch and flicked it on. The first thing my blinded eyes made out in the sudden glare was Lucy and Rocky in one of the day beds.

How long the light remained on, I cannot say, For a matter of seconds I was too stunned to flick the switch again. I remember noticing their clothes across one of the wicker chairs, just before the Thermos bottle slid out of my arm and broke with a crash on the floor.

They raised up together, half out of the blanket, and sat there frozen as I. We simply stared at each other. Then Lucy began to laugh, a high nervous laugh, close to hysteria.

"What the hell?" began Rocky.

"It's only Jim, going shooting." She laughed again, her voice rising.

"Cover yourself!" said Rocky and began to fumble the blanket around her. She kept on laughing.

"You're not decent!" he said.

"Jim's used to it," she said. "You ought to see the girls on stock certificates."

My wits and reflexes returned. I switched off the light and slammed the door behind me and started back up the path to my car. I hadn't gone fifty yards when I heard the padding of feet behind me. Rocky's hand clutched my shoulder hard.

"Jim . . . come back, please. We want to talk to you."

He had on nothing but his hastily donned overalls. I remember noticing how he shivered in the raw wind. When I started to protest the grip on my shoulder tightened. If I hadn't gone back he would have dragged me.

When we re-entered the boathouse Lucy had put on the lights and some of her clothes. She was sitting on the edge of the day bed, barefoot in overalls and sweater, solemnly trying to pour the remnant of coffee from the smashed Thermos into a tumbler.

"You needn't have broken this," she said. "But with luck I'll salvage enough for . . . well, let's call it a loving cup."

"Lucy," said Rocky. "We've got to explain to Jim."

He glared at her and at me and then went over to the chair and began pulling a lumberjack shirt over his shivering torso, his eyes fixed on us.

"Jim's a big boy," said Lucy. "He knows all about animal fun."

Rocky looked at her again, annoyed at the laughter in her voice. He buttoned some of the buttons on the shirt and faced me defiantly.

"I want you to know," he said, "that this is the first time and we don't mind your knowing because Lucy is going to marry me."

"I am not," said Lucy. She put down the coffee and stopped laughing. "I told you I wasn't, Rocky."

"Yes you are." He turned, almost as if he were appealing to me. "I promise you, Jim, she is."

"Leave Jim out of this," said Lucy. "You'd better go, Jim, or you'll miss first light. Don't mind us. You can change in the dressing room, but you'd better go."

"Just one thing first," said Rocky. "We *are* going to get married."

"We are *not*," said Lucy. "But we needn't drag Jim into that. Please go, Jim. I've got to get back to the house before Daddy wakes."

For the next couple of hours I scarcely knew what I was doing. I changed my clothes mechanically in one of the dressing rooms. When I went back out through the main room to the boat level they were gone. The blankets were neatly folded on the day bed again.

The next thing I fully realized was that I was set up and ready to shoot on Leary's Point. The sky was full of new mallards. They had come in on the storm and were sweeping back and forth across an angry dawn, milling around the quieter reaches of the river to study the feed possibilities before deciding whether to stay or ride the storm on south.

The swish of wings dropping into my decoys and the flutter and hammer as they climbed out brought me back slowly to a consciousness I had lost. I discovered that I'd set decoys and masked my boat out of pure instinct, without even knowing I'd done it. I was waiting very still, already cold in the biting air, almost unaware of where I was.

I sat so for quite a while longer, heedless of the birds around me and my increasing chill. Then I began to curse myself for everything I was. I began to remember in vivid detail how she had looked with that autumn hair streaming down over her bare white shoulders and breasts. I remembered the high note of her first laughter and tried to recall forgotten information about hysteria.

The solid fact that loomed through everything was the firmness in her voice as she had said, two different times, that she was not going to marry him. The more I revived the more I clung to that. It was all I had. My watch showed that it was still too early to go to the house. My whole body was beginning to shiver.

That morning I missed a lot of easy birds at first. Then I settled down and killed half a dozen between long looks at my watch. As soon as I thought it was time I picked up my decoys and rowed on down the river. The storm had begun to blow itself out as the birds had known it would. The sky was still full of them reconnoitering the new country now for a longer stay. But I had calculated to the minute the time it would take me to clean up in the boathouse and go on up to the house without arousing undue curiosity in Archie.

In the dressing room there was a penciled note on my toilet case. "Please come up to the house when you come in." They had left the boathouse before me. The note meant either that she had come back to it after Rocky left or she was already awake and had come down before breakfast.

Douglass greeted the ducks and me at the kitchen door with an unloving eye. It softened a little when I explained that I'd have the ducks done in town and only wanted her to keep them cold while I went into the house.

"We've put a place for you, sir. Miss Lucy saw your car from the window. Of course we've only store eggs."

It was one of her endless oblique reproaches for the new economies. I wondered whether she knew how far we had all come from the old days.

In the dining room I found Lucy and Archie breakfasting together in a tranquillity which assured me that he, at least, knew nothing. She was scrubbed, shining and scented in a blue negligee, pouring coffee as I entered. She greeted me casually, as if we had not seen each other for a week.

"Saw your car," she said. "You must be ready for some coffee. How was your shoot?"

The ducks got us safely through breakfast. Her eyes mocked me at Archie's mystification over my rather absent-minded post-mortems.

"Why did you quit without a limit on this wind?"

"You know Mr. James," said Lucy blandly. "Probably afraid some client would get into trouble the minute he turned his back."

"Serve him right," said Archie. "A client who gets into trouble in duck season deserves what he gets."

"Maybe you've got something," said Lucy.

After we had eaten, Archie asked me into the library for another round of coffee.

"Thank you, sir, but I came for a word with Lucy."

"Of course," he said. "You two use the library. I'm going upstairs to watch the river through the glasses."

When we were alone I handed Lucy her note. She dropped it into the fire and watched it flare and flicker and vanish. Then she turned to me. Her fingers were beginning to play with the little gold chain on her neck. Her voice was firm.

"There's something you should know about this morning."

"I don't want to know any more about it."

"You have to. That's why I left the note."

"Lucy, will you marry me?"

She took a long step back from me. Her face began to lose color. As the skin paled her eyes brightened. Her voice was suddenly angry.

"What is this, a rescue mission?"

"I told you. I want to marry you."

"You don't even love me."

"I do. I always have."

"You chose a hell of a time to find it out."

"Will you marry me, now?"

"Like this? Of course not! I found out some things myself last night!"

[161]

"I don't give a damn about last night."

"I do," she said, "and you're going to hear it, too. Last night was all my fault, every bit of it. Madge and Hattie needn't have been quite so nasty but I had forced him on to the party. He wanted so terribly to—to belong. When we got into the car he asked me to elope with him right then. I refused, of course, and he said:

"'This means never, doesn't it?'

"I had to tell him it did, right on top of the way they'd treated him. It made him very bitter. He said we were all living in the same dream world. Whenever we met life face to face we turned up our noses and wouldn't play any more. He said I was the worst of all because I'd mixed sex in it, just using him for a summer beau to make you jealous.

"It was true enough to hurt, because it was hurting him. I tried to tell him I'd promised nothing. I began by wanting to help him and he wouldn't even let me work in his damned campaign. He said he didn't want women working for him. What he wanted in a woman was for her to be a woman and I was only a spoiled child, playing kissing games with a man's feelings.

"I have kissed him back a few times but only because he wanted me to. I hadn't felt much at the time and I'd told him so then and I told him so again last night. He said I never would feel much until I got over being a stingy, self-centered slut.

"I suddenly remembered Vinty and I almost cried and then I began to get too mad to cry. Rocky said I could go on cheating all my life, playing peasant in make-believe overalls and keeping my fancy pants buttoned up against life itself, until some day I'd find out who it was I'd really cheated. I said I supposed he meant myself and he said:

"'I do. If you don't believe it, I'll show you.'

"I asked him if he really thought that was all there was between people. He said of course it was and only cowards like me and all the rest of us ever pretended there was anything else.

"I said if he really believed that we'd go right straight down to the boathouse then and there and go to bed and settle that for keeps and be quits and I wouldn't marry him afterwards, either.

"He said I'd see, once I quit being a spoiled brat and let a man teach me that I was a woman. So we did exactly that in perfectly cold blood on my part, except that I was mad. And I didn't see anything at all, either. I think it's the most overrated experience there is.

"He didn't really care anything about me or even himself. He was just trying to prove something that didn't have anything to do with love at all. Then he fell asleep and I was just lying there, feeling disgusted, when you came in."

"Lucy! None of this matters—".

"Doesn't it? For all I know, I may be pregnant!"

"I don't care."

"Oh, you don't!" She was close to tears then and angrier than I had ever seen her. "How magnanimous! How perfectly correct, to stoop to the fallen woman—"

"Shut up! I told you I love you and I do."

"You never told me," she said. "You never gave a word or sign! You were always so self-sufficient! You never thought about anything but appearances. He, at least, knew I was a woman and wanted me and took me!"

She turned suddenly, choking, and ran for the door. I ran after her but she got through it and up the stairs three paces ahead of me. I heard her bedroom door slam and the lock turn in it just as I threw myself against it.

For several seconds I stood there hammering on the door and calling her name, unaware of anything else. Then I realized that she was not going to open it and I stepped back and saw Archie, still in his dressing gown, with field glasses in his hand, blinking at me from the door of his own room.

"May I ask what you want?" he inquired.

"I want to marry Lucy," I said and banged the door again. Archie gaped and then he put the field glasses under one arm and hurried forward, hand extended.

"Good God!" he said. "I've done *one* thing right."

"It isn't," I said, still banging the door. "She won't have me."

"Nonsense," said Archie. "Of course she will. Women always get the vapors about marrying, Jim. Let's go get some brandy."

"I don't want brandy," I said. "I want Lucy."

He gaped at me again, his eyes twinkling a little but warmer than I had ever seen them. Then with a force I had never known in him he stepped over and took my arm and stopped it. He spoke affectionately and patiently as if I were a child in a tantrum.

"Jim, it's all right. In fact it's wonderful. Just get yourself together. Women are always like this. Her mother behaved the same way until —until the twins were well along. Then she gave in and we had a wonderful marriage. It's just some notion they have about independence. It takes them longer than us to learn that there isn't any. Lucy will get over this along with her vapors and marry you and scold you for taking so long to make her do it. In the meantime we'd better have some brandy. I haven't been so pleased since I got married."

Now I know that I should have got an axe and broken in the door and made her marry me that morning. Instead I let Archie lead me down to the library. I didn't believe his reassurances. He didn't know what I had seen; it was impossible for me to tell him. He was so confident and happy that I felt an ingrate for refusing to drink brandy with him. I couldn't have done it without choking. I took a sheet of paper from the library desk and wrote on it that I wanted to marry her and always would and asked Archie to give it to her when he could.

In town I canceled my upstate shooting date and lived by the telephone for three days. The afternoon of the third one Archie came into the office looking pale and tired and simply handed me a note.

"I'm sorry," it read, "for all the foolish things I said. I want you to know that I'm going to marry Rocky. I don't like what I've been and done and I'm going to try to think of something besides Lucy."

I put it down on the top of the desk and thanked him for bringing it and we looked at each other in silence for a while.

"Jim," he said, "I guess I'll always be wrong."

"That makes two of us, Archie."

"I've got to ask you something," he said. "I've considered this very carefully. I want you to keep on with the property."

"Does she?"

"I wouldn't request it otherwise. She does."

"There isn't much to do now but routine, Archie."

"Jim," he said, "there will be. She's going to need your judgment more than ever, now."

"All right, as long as she wants it," I said.

"Thanks, Jim," he said, "thanks and goddamn it all."

Two days later Tom printed Archie's formal announcement of the engagement. It said, among other things, that owing to the pressure of Mr. Slade's well-known activities at Prairie, the marriage would not take place until early in the new year.

For many weeks after that I saw her only in the presence of Archie and rarely then. Archie and I never discussed it again until Rocky's money troubles began to come out. I was never sure, until she warned me in my office, that Archie did not know what I had known about her and Rocky.

Now in his own way, Rocky was warning me that investigation of him might lead to public exposure of that. Philosophically, I couldn't imagine Archie's independence of spirit caring about any gossip. But life had already brought him to the empty limits of philosophy. Lucy was all he had left. We would be dealing with the impact of scandal on a crippled heart. As Rocky and I stared at each other across my desk I wondered if he could hear her voice still ringing in my head: "It's all your fault."

PART III

Chapter Ten

"ROCKY," I said, "why should your private affairs come out?"

"Jim, they're after me. They'll use anything."

"Where did they get this information?"

"She spent a night with me at the Prairie Plaza this week. I give you my word, Jim, I had no idea I was being watched. But Brady of the Prairie *Times* knows it."

"Rocky, the Prairie *Times* hates Dennis Flynn. Why should it help him get rid of you?"

"It's the old story, Jim; strange bedfellows. The pack eats the weakest wolf first."

"You told me Flynn wants this hushed up."

He checked his irritation again. There was still fear in him; you could almost see the chemistry of it generating defiance; his voice was measured and thoughtful.

"Flynn wants most of all to be rid of me. Naturally he doesn't want a scandal in the party. He may think it's worth it to ditch me publicly before that Senate seat opens up. But he isn't going to do it, if I have to spell every word of this out to Archie himself."

"What good would that do you?"

"He'd help me, if he knew," said Rocky, stubbornly. "All you damned amateurs are alike. Your old man would have sent a beggar to jail for stealing bread and so would you. Archie would sit up all night spouting Gibbon and ethics at you until his own daughter's involved. Then he'd remember the code very fast."

"Rocky! This is romantic nonsense!"

"It's the kind he lives by," said Rocky, "but I have to live, too, Jim. My whole political life is at stake."

"Are you trying to blackmail me?"

"Hell no," he said wearily. "I don't want Lucy involved. But it's out of my control now, Jim. It would be my duty to tell Archie that she may be unless you get off your high horse and help me."

Miss Premm put her head in the door and beckoned me. I excused myself and went outside. In the hall she told me that Hewitt insisted I should come to the bank at once. When I stepped back into the office I had an unexpected glimpse of Rocky. His elbows were on his knees, his head in his hands, his brow was wrinkled all the way up to that receding hairline. He had been alone and he was genuinely scared. I told him of Hewitt's message and he smiled wanly.

"Nothing as scared as a scared banker."

"I'm scared myself, Rocky."

"Jim," he said, "I didn't plan it this way. Things get out of your hands. You were always loyal to me, Jim."

"I'm going to talk this over with Hewitt," I said. "And then I'll go see Archie."

"I'm lunching there," he said. "I'm counting on you, Jim."

I I

It was snowing hard as I walked up the street to the Maynard National Bank. Shop windows were blurred, the pedestrians hurrying along with hands clutching up their collars looked lonely and isolated. Cars crept slowly, their drivers peering tensely out through the little windshield-wiper arcs at a world they no longer dominated. Their horns were muted and plaintive.

For three generations the bank Simeon founded had been the geographical as well as the fiscal heart of Torrent. As nearly as matters it is Hewitt's bank now and it is still supreme in the affairs of southern Wiasota. You walk up Assiniboine Street through the older part of town, passing a melancholy reminder of decay and ephemera, rundown shoe stores, a noxious blast of stale popcorn and candy from the bustling dime store doors, McGregor's perpetual luggage sales, the garish window cards of a chain drugstore, the starving gentility of Ewart's bookshop, then you step across Hewitt's threshold into a granite strength and solidity.

Newer buildings shadow the old high windows now. The one significant change, to electric lights, was modified to preserve the dim reassurances of marble, oak, latticed grillwork and massive green safes.

From the wall above the depositors' desks a life-sized portrait of Simeon still glares impartially at customers, at the tellers behind the main counter and at the lesser officers, bunched to public view in the little enclosure outside the swinging wooden gate to the corner office.

It was Hewitt's boast that that gate swung open for anyone in Wiasota. It was Miss Temple's pride to gauge to the minute, without help from the foot buzzer, when her entrance with a note, or, in delicate cases, a telegraph paper should terminate interviews. That morning she was clearly primed for me; she scarcely bothered to rise as she nodded me toward the door behind the gate.

The corner office had been discreetly modernized. Simeon's rolltop and straight wooden chairs had long since been replaced with oak, leather and glass of a subdued elegance. Every stick of furniture had been cut to compensate for Hewitt's slight deficiency of stature. Whether from chairs or leather settee, you found yourself looking slightly upward to the alert figure at the bare-topped desk.

The dark paneling, sooty windows and ornate drop light still suggested the solidity of the past. Newer glass-fronted bookcases housed a small orthodox library of finance. Their tops made a platform for uniform silver picture frames enclosing Madge in evening dress, Gretchen in riding habit and Vinty in uniform.

Beside Hewitt's chair a little table housed an intercom with closed wooden doors. A Thermos set and matching humidors covered another corner table. Hewitt jumped from his chair as I entered and came around to the door for a warm handshake.

"Hope I didn't break into your morning, Jim."

He made a fuss of seating me before the desk and then flicked his intercom.

"No interruptions, Miss Temple. Now: how's that for setting the stage, Jim?"

"Not bad. Shall I lock the door?"

"No, it won't open. But before we slug, here's one more softening touch."

He opened a drawer of his desk and tossed me a small box. Inside it was a beautiful pipe of clear, straight grain with a heavy silver band around the stem joint. As I admired it he walked around to the humidors and pressed tobacco upon me.

"Too bad you know I don't use 'em," he grinned. "But I really did ask for this one for you. Guy I know in the Chicago National has 'em hand made. Am I scaring you?"

"I'm already scared, Hewitt. You slug first."

Hewitt can play poker with anyone. That morning his buoyancy was genuine as the complacency of his half smile.

"Jim," he said, "relax and enjoy that pipe. Dennis Flynn called me again this morning. He said in so many words that he wants Rocky cleaned up at any cost. How do you like those apples?"

"I'd like to know more about the cost."

"Quit kidding me," said Hewitt. "We're on the same side, young fellow. Any cost is the freeway where we want it and a very neat trim in that parvenu's sails. The mills of the gods grind slowly, Jim—and I hope you're enjoying that pipe."

"Hewitt, did you rig this to fight the freeway?"

The smile faded out of his face until it was bleak and guarded.

"What makes you think I rigged anything?"

"Rocky told me you gave him that money."

"Rocky told you that?"

"This morning."

He shook his head and half shrugged with an air of pained disappointment. Then he turned on the poker smile.

"I'm glad he did. Now we know what that bastard's promise is worth."

"What did you promise him?"

"Jim," said Hewitt evenly, "I don't like that tone."

"I don't like any of this, Hewitt."

He studied me patiently for a few seconds and then shrugged again a little ruefully.

"The world is full of things neither of us like, Jim. I disliked telling you less than the whole story last night. Discretion has its own embarrassments. All of us who were in this had agreed to keep it confidential. Since Rocky has chosen to dishonor his side of it, I think it's perfectly proper now for me to tell you the rest of it.

"I started what we called the Rocky Slade Fund. You remember how we all laughed at him until we counted that plurality. Then I had to start thinking, not only for the bank but for the whole community. It wasn't a case of if you can't whip 'em, join 'em. I didn't want to join him. I wanted to disarm him. A man with nothing to lose is always dangerous, Jim. We held a very informal little meeting and decided that Rocky needed something to lose."

"Who is 'we,' Hewitt?"

"There were eleven besides me," said Hewitt. "I'm not going to name names. You know and respect every one of them. You sit on our board with some of them."

"Is Archie one?"

"He is not," said Hewitt. "The rest of us were disappointed in him. I put it to him personally. Archie told me to go home and read up on the Praetorian Guard."

"Were all the others vulnerable to the freeway?"

"Some were. Some are your close neighbors, miles from it. I told you this was for the whole community."

"What did you make Rocky promise for your dough?"

It is hard to irritate Hewitt when he's on his guard. He let me think my question had done it at once; I couldn't be sure.

"Jim, do you think I'm an idiot, fishing for a state freeway through a county councilman who won't vote on it? For your information, that water has been fished with bigger bait than Rocky ever saw. The fish wouldn't rise, either. Until this morning, Flynn has sworn he was helpless between Park and Highway Commissions. Now with this Senate seat coming up, he seems to have found some help. This part is pure accident, Jim, but it's playing into our hands better than we could have planned it. I needn't remind you that Archie will benefit."

"Are you positive that Flynn wants this hushed up?"

"I just told you. He said 'at any cost.'"

"Hewitt, did you tip off the Prairie *Times* to investigate Rocky?"

This time his gape was genuine; so was the indignation that followed it.

"Do you think I'm insane?"

"Did you tip them off, Hewitt?"

"I certainly did not."

"Did any of the other philanthropists involved?"

"I am not enjoying these sarcasms, Jim."

"Would you enjoy indictment for bribing a public official?"

"We're miles ahead of you," said Hewitt. "That was carefully considered. There is no bribery. Rocky won't even vote."

"Any way you twist it you've had a public servant on a private payroll."

"Expense money," said Hewitt. "A gift. Happens every day."

"It's being investigated today. Did you reveal it?"

"I did not; what the hell are you driving at?"

"Someone did. I want to know who it was."

"I told you last night," said Hewitt. "It's the Prairie *Times*. Harry Caldwell's an embittered radical. He even used to support the New Deal; now he hates everyone."

"When did you start giving Rocky this money?"

"Jim," he said, "I didn't ask you over here to play the demon cross-examiner."

"Hewitt, you've asked for a public cross-examination that would make this sound like a love sonnet. When did you start giving Rocky money? Was it all after the election?"

"Of course. He wasn't dangerous until then."

"And when did you stop giving it to him?"

"When he became engaged to Lucy," said Hewitt. "You know how I feel about that but it happened. The engagement itself accomplished all we'd been trying to do. It gave him a hell of a lot to lose. Some of our little group were sore about Archie's not being in it anyway; they didn't feel like subsidizing his son-in-law."

"So as soon as his interest in the freeway seemed to coincide with yours, you cut him off with nothing to lose?"

"Jim, you're being very obtuse. The freeway had nothing to do with it. He'd used it for a springboard. I used it a little for camouflage with him. I was perfectly willing to let him think that's what we were afraid of."

"What were you afraid of, Hewitt?"

"I've told you; we knew Rocky was corruptible."

"So you decided to corrupt him?"

Hewitt was thoroughly angry now. He knew it and he was trying to control it. He fought it back under an effort at chilly hauteur.

"Jim, when you're older you may understand the difference between creating a thief and controlling one. We didn't make Rocky what he is or make those damned voters what they are."

"You corrupted him, Hewitt. Why? Why did you have to play God with him?"

He glared at me a second more, reddening from his gray hair to his collar line, and then his face hardened into a final defiance. He pointed a shaking hand behind my head.

"I'll tell you why," he said. "I did it for Vinty and for America, too. And I'll tell any jury in the country so."

It poured out of him then in a torrent of anger that fed on itself and on the convictions boiling under it.

"You're too young to know, Jim. For ten years I sat on my tail in here and submitted to total perversion of our government. I swallowed the lies, the broken promises, the manufactured emergencies, the falsified budgets, the secret diplomacy, the systematic inflaming of hatred and envy and fear. Sure, I bellyached—and did nothing. I was afraid. I was afraid of persecution, of tax troubles, of alienating the whole new class of depositor we were getting. So I sat still in here and groused in the Torrent Club and kept my neck in until one fine morning I found my country at war and my boy in uniform.

"In a few months I got that telegram. I didn't have a boy any more. He was killed, defending what we'd let this country become; what I'd let it become. Maybe it couldn't have been changed but I'll never know. I didn't have the guts to try in time. I was scared of my own government.

"The war was scarcely over when it began again, in my back yard. Here was Rocky Slade in our own streets, crying the same old envy and hatred and fear: 'Soak the rich! Freeway for the poor! Decadent reaction! Power and Privilege! Run it through their rose gardens!'"

He paused and wiped his forehead with a handkerchief.

"Hewitt, for God's sake," I said. "The New Deal didn't invent chicanery."

"Hitler didn't invent lies, either," said Hewitt. "But look where they took him and the world. 'The evil that men do lives after them,' Jim. Do you suppose I was naïve enough to think Rocky could affect that freeway, or gullible enough to think he cared about it? Never! What I heard in his hot air was an echo and fair warning. I could hear Rocky's voice, next time, closing solvent banks to produce a political panic. I could hear him using those same promises to unite gangsters and unions and reliefers into another holy crusade for another fifteen years of total tyranny until we needed more total wars to insure total submission.

"Rocky was even smart enough to change the label. He knows people are tired of pulling the Democratic lever. But he knows they'll never tire of hatred and fear and envy and promises of something for nothing.

"To fight him frontally was to play right into his hands. You've got to fight that kind of fire with fire. You cannot corrupt a politician, Jim; the words are a contradiction. The best you can do is control him. That's why I did this."

He stopped suddenly and used the handkerchief again on his eyes. He was crying openly now, with rage and his own grief. I knew now it would be useless to speak further and I knew why. I still had to try. I tried to speak gently.

"Hewitt," I said, "I agree with a lot of what you said; the fact remains that the country approved of it four times."

"Vinty didn't!" said Hewitt. "Vinty never got a chance to vote. They killed him."

He mopped his eyes again, balled the handkerchief with decision, rammed it into his pocket and squared off.

"Sorry, Jim," he said. "You asked me. Let's get to work."

"On what?"

"The loan from Archie," said Hewitt.

"Hewitt, we cannot falsify a loan."

"What's wrong with Archie lending his son-in-law money?"

"Rocky says you want a retroactive date on it."

"That's a detail; precautionary cover."

"Would you deny under oath that you gave Rocky money?"

"Are you seriously asking if I'd perjure myself?"

"Yes."

"I would not."

"Then why ask Archie to do it for you?"

On the desk his fist kneaded up slowly until white showed in the knuckles, but he was in control of himself again now. I had seen him cry. It was not going to happen again. His voice was even and a little cold.

"Jim, I wish you'd stop shaking my faith in your judgment. There won't be any perjury because there won't be any more questions. The loan stops them. I simply phone Harry Caldwell and tell him to call off his dogs because it's Archie's money, and it will be."

"On a loan dated today, Hewitt."

"Jim," he said, "you're missing the whole point."

"I hope not."

"Archie would be justified, in a matter of this gravity, in consulting older counsel."

"I'm going to tell him so."

"Jim," said Hewitt slowly, "we all respect your scruples. It can be dangerous to think you're the only honest man alive. The weight and substance of this community are involved in this. Your friends are in it. Your father sat in that chair once and said to me, on another matter: 'Hewitt, a gentleman is when it hurts.'"

"He didn't falsify records, Hewitt."

"You have a moral duty to clients," said Hewitt. "A scandal stigmatizes Archie and Lucy. Can't you think of that as well as your own neck?"

"I'm trying to, Hewitt."

"You'd better try harder," said Hewitt. "It would be sad for all of us to lose confidence in your judgment."

We were staring at each other when Miss Temple knocked gently and then put her head into the doorway behind me.

"Miss Premm insists on speaking to Mr. Denton on line two."

Hewitt flicked a switch on the little table and pushed the phone across the desk to me without a word.

"Mr. Denton," said Miss Premm, "a Mr. Brady of the Prairie *Times* tells me he is about to run an editorial you should read at once in the interest of clients. He's here now and says he'll have to see you within the hour."

"I'll be there in ten minutes. And, Miss Premm, does he know where I am now?"

"Not from me," said Miss Premm icily. It was the first time since I'd

[174]

been in practice that I'd given a damn whether anyone in the state knew where I was. I explained the call to Hewitt.

"Why are you going to see him?"

"I've still got a lot to learn about this, Hewitt."

"Will you come back here afterwards?"

"Not unless I learn something new. I'm going out to tell Archie what you want and I'm going to advise him against a false date, Hewitt."

He looked at me very steadily.

"Think it over before you do that. There comes a time when everyone has to stand up and be counted. It's here, Jim; you're either for us or against us."

I I I

"Mr. Denton," said Ed Brady, "I hope you realize that none of this is personal."

He had sprung up when I came into the anteroom and followed me through it so closely that I scarcely had a look at him. His eyes had narrowed as I opened the door of my office; his quick scrutiny revealed disappointment at finding it empty.

As I moved to my desk he seated himself before it with easy, familiar confidence. I looked into bland eyes and a round, disarming face. High forehead and scanty hair gave a suggestion of infantile innocence. The heavy spectacle marks along his ears seemed incongruous.

Brady's dress was not so much Bohemian as consciously careless. Rumpled shirt, sports coat, unpressed slacks and unshined shoes proclaimed a contempt for convention. He had been a powerful man with a big appetite; he was going to fat and enjoying the process. His merry, knowing twinkle seemed to hint of a fund of good limericks. Brady had been told that he had a great personality and he believed it.

"What's on your mind, Mr. Brady?"

"Ed," he said firmly. "If it makes it easier I'll call you Jim."

"What's on your mind, Ed?"

"When they gave me this story," said Ed, "I couldn't see much in it. I'm here because you're the only guy in town who can confirm that in three words."

He waited, presumably for the three words. I waited, too. He smiled again and made his eyes twinkle amiably.

"Come on, Jim," he said. "Pros don't kid each other."

"You haven't told me your story."

"Can't we save each other's time?"

"My secretary said you wanted to talk to me."

"Okay." His tone was gently reproachful. "We do it the hard way. Will you read it?"

"Sure."

He pulled a sheaf of folded copy paper from his coat and tossed it across the desk.

"A story should explain itself," he said. "This is in case you make me smoke him out on the editorial page."

I began to read, conscious as I did of the unwavering penetration in those twinkling eyes.

Public Service and Private Ethics

Lobbying is nothing new in Wiasota. The wise provisions of the Statutes of '38 and '45 requiring registration of persons, purposes and expenditures were designed to regulate rather than to abolish a practice with some claims to Constitutional validity.

Contravention of those laws, accomplished legally or not, does affect the public interest. The people of Wiasota have a right to public explanation of private pressure upon their representatives.

Our proposed Freeway has produced political pressure on the Legislature and the Park and Highway Commissions. It has produced candid lobbying from interested communities and industries. Evidence now in the hands of the Prairie TIMES strongly suggests another kind of pressure which should be thoroughly ventilated.

A councilman in one of the interested counties was elected last June on a platform in which his personal poverty was as loudly proclaimed as his pledge to bring the Freeway through his county.

Since then his efforts to that end have been conspicuous throughout the state. Less conspicuous, until recently, have been his expenditures in this interest. The Prairie TIMES now has a demonstrable record of these, aggregating over eleven thousand dollars. The Treasurer of his county reports that not a public dime was provided for this purpose. No responsible civic organization acknowledges any contribution to this effort. The salary paid the councilman since election totals less than fifteen hundred dollars.

The nine thousand-odd dollars over and above any visible revenue that this man has spent is only the known part. One thinks of icebergs. As an elected public official this councilman is exempt from registration as a lobbyist. As a public servant he can scarcely plead exemption from the practical question of whose money he has been spending and why. Prairie TIMES readers will share their paper's hope for a voluntary explanation of this financial virtuosity.

"I've read it," I said and handed it back to him. Brady folded the copy and pocketed it without changing a muscle of that fixed and twinkling smile.

"Jim, aren't you afraid of saying too much?"

"No."

"Did the Maynards give Rocky this money?"

"You're asking the wrong man."

"No." He shook his head patiently. "Rocky won't say. Old Maynard threatened to shoot me for asking. That's their business. This story is ours, if it is a story. Frankly, it wouldn't take much to make me think it isn't. At best it's just low-grade scandal on about the mayor-in-the-whore-house scale. Might sell an edition down here but I can't see it for page sixteen. At worst it's a libel trap or publicity stunt that could backfire Rocky into the U. S. Senate. My paper doesn't want him there. Kind of puts a leg man in the middle, Jim."

"Occupational hazard, isn't it, Ed?"

"You can say that again," Ed Brady sighed. "Rock was buying me drinks in Prairie before this ever came up. Here I am beating my brains out to wreck him for a paper that gives me a calendar every Christmas. Rocky's got a hell of a future, potentially, Jim. He tells me you're one of his closest friends and God knows I don't want to see him destroyed."

"Who wants to destroy him, Ed?"

"I don't make policy," said Ed Brady. "'Dig into Rocky Slade' says the boss and I dug and so far it's all too easy. But Rocky won't say it's Maynard dough and old Gay Nineties wanted to shoot me for asking. He wouldn't be quite so upstage if he knew that fancy daughter of his had been shacking up with Rocky at Prairie."

"You're speaking of a client of mine," I said.

"Relax," said Ed Brady cheerfully, "nothing personal in this. What's it to me if some corn-fed princess wants to beat the wedding bells? There's lots of angles to this, Jim. Rocky could be cleaned up very fast. Half the public men in America are taking private money. If he *is* the Maynards' boy, this story could stop right here. Why should a lot of people get hurt?"

"When do you need an answer, Ed?"

"I might stall 'em till this afternoon."

"I'll see if Mr. Maynard wants to make a statement."

"Fine," said Ed Brady. "I thought we could understand each other. Remind him there's nothing personal in this, Jim; just politics."

Chapter Eleven

THE storm had abated as I turned into the lane to River House. The snowfall had been heavier out there than in town. The lane was already marked with the coming and going of the morning tires. Then, as I reached the clearing, I could see the whole valley glistening in primal innocence. A rising wind was scouring the long silver scar of the river, opening drifts and patching over the clear reaches Lucy and I had skated the previous evening.

All over the valley snow had tufted corn shocks, fence lines and fields themselves into one uniform texture. The woods along the ridge brooded with dark, secretive stoicism; leafless branches writhed and shivered.

As my eyes picked up the house I saw it with a distorted perspective. Freakish patches of snow in the withered ivy created a broken, crazy-quilt irregularity, evocative and ominous. For a second I could not place it. Then the jagged angles of stone and gaping white became, for a second, the ruins of older houses I had seen, bomb-gutted and spectral, in London and across the Continent.

The illusion passed as I placed it. The memories did not. Three of Simeon's chimneys still puffed a brave defiance at the winter morning; under its camouflage the ugly rectangularity of the old house was unshaken.

I decided I was getting jumpy. It was nearly two years since I had heard the sirens and the guns, the screeching and the high thin whine, the thuds and lightning cracks or the rumbling muffled detonations that blossomed into charry, astringent dust. Nothing could have been remoter from the shining wintry peace before my eyes, until my mind came back full cycle to Ed Brady. The cordite, thermite and napalm were just politics, too.

"We've set a place for you, Mr. Denton," said Douglass. "If Miss Lucy and Mr. Slade get back with marketing. I see the delivery truck got into Mr. Randolph's very easily."

Douglass was remembering other days, too. She missed the cozy midmorning snacks and gossip with delivery boys.

In the library, bright with reviving sun now dazzling the windows, I told Archie what I could. The pattern that had seemed to begin so accidentally at my father's dinner table was now a web of many strands. Everywhere you touched Rocky Slade you found yourself lying a little. Lucy's personal affairs were inseparable from the information I owed Archie. I omitted all mention of them, confining myself to facts.

He heard me with his usual patient attention, nodding now and then but saying nothing until I had told him what I thought I could. His first remarks were salt in my uneasy secrecy.

"I wanted to tell you about Hewitt's fund," he said. "Hewitt said you were too ingenuous to understand. Apparently he now considers you disingenuous enough to get him off the hook."

"Hewitt can take care of himself," I said shortly.

Archie shook his head. "No, he never could. That's part of the trouble. The fault is mine, Jim."

"Yours . . . how?"

"It's always your own fault," said Archie.

"I can't agree on this, sir."

"You don't have to," said Archie. "Would just the loan without the false date cover this, Jim?"

"I doubt it, sir; it's gone too far now."

"Could Brady be bribed?"

"Yes sir, but his paper can't."

"So it's falsify or face the music?"

"Rocky started the music, sir. You can offer him an honest loan."

"That only clears my skirts," said Archie. "And he didn't start this. I did."

"I don't follow you, Archie."

"Hewitt is only running that damned bank because I'm not, Jim. I always ran away—schools, Europe, the war, San Sebastián and back to this library. I was always hiding, behind Father or Horace or Hewitt or Gibbon or you. I never killed anyone, except in the war, but I never wanted to be my brother's keeper or even my own. I wanted to live without strife and you can't. You've heard me ridicule Roscoe's education but his instinct is sounder than mine. Philosophy means search for truth, Jim. Truth is life and I didn't search; I hid behind a little money and a lot of inertia.

"Father used to say: 'Two conditions, Archer; progress or retrogression.' I didn't believe it; I didn't want either. The army, as you should

[179]

know, puts the same idea more lucidly: 'Kill or be killed.' It caught me at just the right age for drums and slogans and action. I thought for a while it solved everything. I learned that the drums are hollow, the slogans spurious and most of action is wasteful or vicious or both.

"I went to San Sebastián and wondered whether to come home and remake the world or lie on the beach and let it go to hell. Father had had strong views on the aristocrat as a repository of ethics, as a bulwark between corrupt church and state and vulnerable humanity. He always said democracy was an unworkable myth and he'd bought enough legislators to know. The proceeds bought me a young man's fun with the aristocracy of Europe but that doesn't work either. It adds up to happy balls and bellies for a few for a while and then the same old trench. Your generation called them foxholes but I doubt if they smelled any sweeter than ours.

"I couldn't see how to remake a world that doesn't want to change. We've spent two thousand years rejecting the Golden Rule and proving that the Decalogue doesn't fit man as he is. Action always winds up as aggression; compassion always becomes compulsion. Your precious law rests on homicide; ethics are a rationalization of advantage. It seemed to me the one thing no one had tried was letting his fellow man alone. But you can't even do that.

"I had to teach Lucy and Artie the standard conformities with a straight face. I could laugh at Hewitt but he was earning my bread at the bank and shaping our community on the school board. I was not. I thought it was enough to try to be honest and mind my own business. So Roscoe has become my business and I'm afraid he's about to rid me of the last delusion of honor."

"Archie! You're not going to falsify it?"

"Regretfully, I am," said Archie. "You go around a wide bush to self-preservation. Lucy's mine, Jim. I made her what she is. I owe her the last protection I can give. The family came before the tribe or nation. The country can still reject Roscoe if it wants to. I've got to think for her."

"Are you sure you're thinking straight?"

"I'm not sure of anything, except what I'm going to do. It involves a painful preliminary detail. I'm firing you, Jim."

"Firing me?"

"As of now. Hewitt and I can fix the papers."

"All right. I'm fired. Let's have a drink."

He had been very tense toward the end of his harangue. I could see him loosen up a little as he blinked.

"Before noon? This isn't like you, Jim."

"I'm tired of being like me. Get us some brandy."

He blinked again and limped out to the pantry without a word. I went over by the window and stood there looking out at the river and the valley and the snow. I wondered how long it was since I had felt this way and then I realized that I never had. I had never felt better in my life. All the brandy in the house wouldn't affect what I was going to do. Archie returned with the things on a tray and looked at his wristwatch.

"We won't have time for a sidecar, I'm afraid."

"We've lots of time, but this could be our last one and I'd like it straight."

"Jim," he said, "I wanted to speak about that. We can still play chess and shoot, can't we?"

"Let's do one thing at a time, Archie."

He poured a couple of stiff ones. We touched glasses without a word more and knocked them back straight. He sighed and looked at the empty glass and we stood there a minute perfectly silent while I watched it working into him. You could never tell much from his eyes. Presently I thought I could detect a general muscular relaxation. I knew it was on its way, even if I wasn't seeing it.

"Jim," he said, "this was kind of you but you'd better go now."

"I'll go when I've told them," I said.

"Told them what?"

"That you're firing me to clear my skirts while you do something crooked for them."

"Something legal," said Archie dryly. "Not that it matters; we make our own rules as we make our own gods, Jim. Mine haven't worked for her and this is my business."

"No, it isn't, Archie. This is public business."

"The public that elected him?"

"It's the only one we've got, Archie. It's the one we are. We began as cannibals. The very fact that this *might* make a scandal is enough. It's all we've got and it's taken us several thousand years to get here. Perhaps people still want their officials on two payrolls. But if it's worth lying about it's worth trying the truth."

"These are lofty and rather optimistic abstractions," said Archie. "I have to think of Lucy."

"That doesn't mean thinking for her."

"Jim, it's not your problem."

"Sure it is. I'm part of the public, Archie, and I've lied to myself and a lot of other people about Rocky and now it's everybody's problem. Let's have another."

He stared at me and started to speak and then he turned back to the tray and poured us another pair of stiff ones. His color was good, his hands steady. His face was set and enigmatic.

"There must be some other way," he said.

"We've tried the other ways, Archie."

"Why, Mr. James!" said Lucy from the door. "Brandy before lunch on a work day?"

I I

She had come in, flushed with the cold and bareheaded as always, her hair piled high and gleaming above the turned-up collar of her coat. Rocky came in behind her, towering briefly above her in the dark frame of the doorway and then striding straight to Archie.

"Nice of you to have me to lunch," he said. "I hope Jim is staying with us."

"Lunch will be late," said Lucy. "We carried the heavy things in but Douglass and Frieda are quarreling about the rest and they'll both punish us so I'm glad you're having a drink but it isn't like you, Jim."

"Join us, kitten?" asked Archie.

"No, but you might offer Rocky some."

"Thanks," said Rocky. "I've got serious work this afternoon, even if you two haven't."

"It's done," I said. "That's what we're celebrating."

Lucy had thrown off her coat and gone to the mirror to give her hair a push. At the word she came to us inquisitively.

"Celebrating what, Jim?"

"Your father's going to make Rocky a loan," I said.

"Oh that," she said and then turned to Rocky. "You see? I told you Jim would settle it."

Archie said nothing. He stood quietly with his eyes on his glass, the picture of modesty embarrassed by its own generosity. Rocky glanced at him and then extended his hand to me.

"Jim, you always come through," he said.

"You're thanking the wrong man, Rocky."

He caught himself and turned swiftly to Archie.

"I didn't want to bother you, sir," he said. "Lucy told me that Jim always does everything mechanical for us anyway. But I am more grateful than I can tell you. I only wish I could find some way of making you let me take Jim to Washington when we go. I could use him there."

"Jim doesn't like Washington," said Lucy.

[182]

"Hard to blame him for that," Rocky grinned. "But you're right. We need him here. Lucy and I have already talked about that, sir, and after—" he checked himself hard—"after our marriage it will be a big comfort to know that he's here on the job with you."

"I won't be," I said. "Archie just fired me."

I think Rocky understood at once, perhaps not Archie's motive because he would never understand that. But his quick instinct smelled trouble. You could see him responding with practiced resilience, the fading smile, the quizzical look stalling for time, the slight readjustment of balance on his long legs. It was Lucy who either didn't understand or would not yet face it. She looked searchingly at both of us and at the glasses on the tray; her quick smile was a little forced.

"What nonsense is this, Jim?"

"It's true," said Archie. "I've fired him."

"Daddy, do you feel all right?"

"I feel fine," said Archie. "I never felt better."

"Then I'm unfiring him, right now," said Lucy. "I never heard of anything so silly." Then you could see her mind catching up to it. "Why did you fire him, Daddy?"

"We disagreed," said Archie.

"Then I disagree with both of you," said Lucy. "And I want to know why."

"Lucy," said Rocky. "I don't think we should interfere in this."

"I am interfering," said Lucy. "Why did you disagree and fire him, Daddy?"

Archie and I looked at each other in silence. I waited but he did not speak.

"This loan," I said, "is crooked. Your father fired me to keep me from being involved in it."

"Is this true, Daddy?"

"It's a matter of judgment, dear," said Archie.

"It's a matter of simple loyalty," said Rocky. "The loan is legal and Jim knows it."

"Jim," she said, "why is the loan crooked?"

"The loan isn't. But Rocky wants a false date on it and that is."

She turned to Rocky very quietly.

"You never told me this," she said. "Why do you want a false date on it?"

Archie eased himself slowly into a chair. She flashed him a look of concern. He smiled reassurance but did not speak and she turned slowly back to Rocky. Her hand started for the little chain on her neck and then it stopped and remained at her side.

[183]

Rocky made as persuasive an explanation as words could effect. Her eyes widened a little when he told her of Hewitt's complicity but she checked her tongue and listened silently until he came to the end of it.

"How perfectly disgusting of Uncle Hewitt!" she said.

"Politics, dear." Rocky shrugged. "You can't trust anyone."

"You told me the money was for speculation," said Lucy.

"Politics is speculation," said Rocky. "This is our whole future, Lucy."

"But we'd have to pretend that we lent this to you before—before we were even engaged?"

"Before lots of things," said Rocky very slowly. "It's just a detail to keep the public out of our personal business."

"How flattering!" said Lucy. "Item: one fiancée, bought and paid for by said agreed date as witnessed and attested!"

Rocky could see the anger in her. He spoke very gently.

"You're missing the whole point, Lucy."

"I'm not missing that one," said Lucy. "And I don't like it, either."

"Would you like having our affairs, all our personal affairs, spread out in that damned paper?"

Involuntarily she glanced at Archie and we could see reluctance in her glance and hear indecision replacing the anger in her voice.

"Of course not," she said.

"All right," said Rocky. "This is just politics, dear. I didn't make 'em the way they are. We stole this country from the Indians and then your grandfather stole it from Civil War veterans and now we're still stealing it from each other with lobbies and pressure groups and we always have.

"Maybe someday I can make it better and I hope I can. But you can't do anything without power and that's what politics are. You have to win first. People like you and Jim can sit around in comfortable houses admiring your navels and worshiping the past and keeping your lily-white hands out of the slime around you. I've had to get down in it and fight and what I was really fighting for was all of you."

"Did you tip off the Prairie *Times* for us, too, Rocky?" I asked.

For a second I thought he was going to hit me. Then I realized that if Rocky were going to hit you there wouldn't be any second. He had come a long way from the football field. You could see the reflex start in his arm and you could see his brain check it and remind him that you didn't learn things by punching people. You could not afford emotion in politics.

"Did Brady tell you that?" he asked quietly.

"No. You told me, Rocky."

"I never told you any such thing, Jim."

"You told me yesterday afternoon you were fresh out of an issue. This is your issue, isn't it?"

He studied me for a second and then nodded.

"Head of the class for you," he said. "I did tip them off about the money. But it isn't quite as simple as you think. Hewitt had already ditched me. Archie wouldn't help me and Flynn was getting ready to ditch me. He still thinks he is. Not one of you was really loyal to me and I knew you wouldn't be until you had something to lose, too. You're wrong about just one thing, Jim. All I meant to start was a political scandal. I never tipped them off to anything personal. Unfortunately they've found out some things I never meant 'em to know. But they do know 'em, Jim, and if you've got any loyalty to the Maynards you'll tell them that they've got a hell of a lot to lose by an investigation, too."

Then for the first time Archie spoke.

"I should prefer to hear that from you, Roscoe," he said.

"I don't think you would, sir," said Rocky. "I never threw a pass I couldn't cover yet. I can still cover this one either way. I'm trying to do it the easy way, for you people."

"Rocky, you'd better shut up," said Lucy.

"On the contrary," said Archie. "I should like to know exactly what we have to lose."

"You asked for it," said Rocky. "It could come out that Lucy and I have been sleeping together."

"Rocky! You didn't have to tell Daddy that!"

"I knew it, kitten," said Archie. "What of it?"

She gaped and looked at him reproachfully.

"You might at least have scolded me," she said.

"It's not important, to me anyway," said Archie. "It's Roscoe who seems to be measuring us all by a vestigial membrane."

"I never meant it that way, sir," said Rocky. "I was giving you a chance to be loyal to your own daughter."

"Loyalty isn't lies," said Lucy.

Her hands worked together for a moment but it was not in distress. She was stripping off her engagement ring. She handed it to Rocky.

"I'm sorry, Rocky," she said. "You can say whatever you want to about me, but I'm through."

He looked at her for a second and then at Archie and me. Then he took the ring without a word and walked out the door. None of us said anything. As we heard the front door slam, Archie got up from

[185]

the chair slowly and started for the brandy tray. He had begun to smile and his smile was widening as he reached for the decanter.

Then we both saw it hit him. He gave a kind of gasp and, before I could catch him, fell heavily to the floor. As we turned him over he was still gasping and choking. Between spasms his eyes were trying to reassure Lucy. They were tender and very proud.

Chapter Twelve

WE scarcely needed Dr. Jamison's opinion. He came at once, bringing his office nurse, and emerged from the bedroom to which I had carried Archie, shaking his head.

"Lucy, this is terminal. We might stretch it a few days in the hospital; we might lose him getting there."

"He'd want it to be here, Arby," she said.

By midafternoon the upstairs was a miniature hospital, complete with oxygen gear and starchy nurses flatfooting softly through the halls. Lucy begrudged even their presence. Left to herself she would have sat at the bedside until the end. With Jamison's help, I was able to spare her some of that. Her devotion was as futile as our other arrangements. Archie was no longer with us. Through most of the time he was drugged beyond any possibility of regaining consciousness. In those intervals there was nothing for us to do but wait in the library, together.

It was so that we missed most of the ensuing commotion or rather absorbed it at second hand. Almost every ring of phone or doorbell thrust another facet of it upon us. The upstairs had barely been reorganized when Willis Beck's truck delivered an addition to the wedding presents in the west parlor. I had signed for it and was carrying it through the hall as she appeared on the stairs.

"I've got to do something about that, Jim."

"Not now, Lucy."

"Immediately," she said. "I don't want to injure Rocky but it's over. Will you call Tom?"

I called Tom. He had always been fond of Archie. We talked candidly and he accepted my responsibility for printing in Archie's name the announcement that the engagement had been broken by mutual consent. When we had that settled I could hear his sigh over the phone.

"Hate to bring it up, Jim, but I guess this answers the other question, doesn't it?"

"They never gave him a dime, Tom. Any news on it?"

"Some; all bad, I'm afraid. Our man phoned an hour ago from Prairie. The Prairie *Times* will report corruption tomorrow. They've evidently got a solid story from somewhere."

"Where will you stand on it, Tom?"

"The law's good enough for me, Jim: innocent until proved guilty. But it sounds messy."

I phoned Hewitt and he brought Madge as soon as they could get there. It was hard to comprehend the change in his gait and voice. He was far more shaken than the man who had cried to me in rage and grief that morning. He had known that this day was waiting for us. It found him broken and confused.

"I never minded his tongue," he kept saying. "I never minded the way he talked."

I had insisted that Lucy stay upstairs during their call. Madge made a feeble effort to persuade me to send Lucy to their house. We both knew she would not have gone. When Madge had accepted that she simply cried. I think she and Hewitt aged ten years that afternoon.

When he had put Madge in the car he seemed to gather himself a little and led me back into the house. He closed the door and then we stepped into the clammy west parlor, where we stood together with the chill and the wedding presents.

"Jim," he said, "none of this matters much now but after you left I had a long talk with Horace Tuttlewise. Maybe it's enough to say that my confidence in your judgment is stronger than ever."

"Thanks, Hewitt."

"It takes something like this—" and he lifted his tired eyes toward the upper floor—"to show you how foolish it is to get excited over trifles."

I said nothing; he gathered himself a little more. An edge of defiance came back into his stricken voice.

"There's going to be a stink," said Hewitt. "But when I take the long view I can stand a red face for getting that bastard out of public life."

As the news about Archie spread around town it precipitated a flood of calls and messages. Command of phone and doorbell was the price of sparing Lucy those. For several days I left the house only once. She came down for meals with me and at odd times to join my vigil in the library. It was through those hours that she told me the things I could not otherwise have known.

It was Archie who had insisted on a long engagement. They both knew he was still hoping that time would disenchant her. Rocky knew it, too. He acquiesced grudgingly and used his concession on that point for leverage in his financial talk with Archie. Lucy had not been present during that. Rocky had told her it was masculine business; he wanted to stand on his own feet. The men's mutual disappointment at the end of it was evident. Rocky had tried to dissemble his chagrin.

"I guess he loves you, too," he had said.

Archie had been equally tight-lipped.

"He knows he's not marrying a fortune," was all he would say.

It was a point of continuing, silent embarrassment. To Lucy money trouble still meant leaving the stables closed. To Archie it would always be digits in a ledger. Neither of them ever understood how ephemeral Rocky's surface prosperity was. He had brought her an expensive ring from Prairie, to the lasting outrage of our local jeweler. He continued to drive the Cadillac, to travel and to spend freely when they went out together. Whether from pride or scruple he had never told her of Hewitt's subsidy. She had no inkling that the engagement ended that.

In other ways she had worked hard to help him. It amused her that once they were engaged she heard no more of his scruple against having women work for him. He expected her to share, with his mother and sisters, the unending private drudgery that supports every public figure. She was delighted and eager to help with brain as well as fingers. She had read out the library on practical politics. She had written to the National Committees of both parties, had received and tried to assimilate stacks of instruction and advice. She had drawn plans for literature distribution teams, for baby sitters for election, for canvassing by phone, for the approved techniques of precinct, district and county work.

"Ours is a hell of a precinct, too," she said. "The best I could promise him was Douglass, Frieda, Allen, McClintic and me. I always had to keep Daddy in the doubtful column."

He was very pleased by her first efforts. Then as they inevitably led to hard questions he became irritated by her expanding curiosity.

"The mechanical parts looked easy enough," she said. "But when you broke down the instructions on the neighborly call, you realized it was a barefaced request for strangers to like and trust you. There's no reason why they should until you begin promising them something and everyone wants to be promised something different. At times I thought of it as glorified begging. Then I remembered that maybe Artie and Vinty were politics, too, and I ought to be proud to be begging for what was right—if I could just have been surer about what was right."

Rocky had been delighted when she started files and scrapbooks on his speeches. He was annoyed when she asked him why it was always the same speech.

"It's all those goops understand," he said shortly.

"Wouldn't it be worth asking, at one of your meetings, what they want instead of just telling them they want a freeway?"

"Dear," he said, "lists and leg work and neighborly chat are just working-level stuff. It leads nowhere. You spend your life ringing doorbells and setting up folding chairs and wind up as County Clerk in Republican years."

"Then how *do* you get anywhere?" she asked.

"With a break," said Rocky. "A big break like that freeway except that I've used it up. Don't fret your head about charming sewing circles or memorizing the state constitution. There are always lonely fools and pedants around a party organization to do the chores. A candidate has to smell out the big breaks or make them."

She wanted to help him socially. She realized that dinner invitations to their own circle of friends were not enough. She made systematic lists of their acquaintances, beginning from earliest years in public school. Patient cultivation of those could broaden the base of his solidarity through every stratum of the town. He shook his head at the suggestion.

"We've outgrown them," he said. "It would embarrass all of us; they'll vote for me anyway."

She urged him to bring his widening political acquaintance throughout the state to River House for a drink or casual meals.

"No. They're still minor league and we'd never get rid of them. We'll save this for the big time."

She had dreaded intimacy with the other Slades. Once the engagement committed her to it she made an earnest effort over them and found it full of surprises. She took up the question of Rocky's future with Winifred and asked her future mother-in-law candidly which of the various women's clubs around town would be most helpful. Winifred considered and shook her head.

"In the first place I can take care of that," she said. "In the second, it's very different for you, dear. You and Roscoe are going way beyond

Wiasota. People will want to look up to you. It's always easier to make the right new friends than to get rid of the wrong old ones."

She couldn't tell whether it was personal hostility, plain snobbery or practical politics. She could tell that Winifred did not want her involved in the local club life. She and Rocky were to hold themselves above that for the wider arenas ahead.

The personal relation was trying. They exchanged dinners and Archie made an effort when the Slades came to River House. No drink was served. The Reverend spoke grace. Winifred and Archie talked stiffly of old times. Hazel had gone to Des Moines with her chiropractor and Thelma was away at the State Normal School studying teaching. Veronica and Maybelle Lou, then in high school, gaped and giggled under their mother's watchful eye and said little.

"They were sweet," said Lucy, "and pathetic, too. They scarcely spoke when Winifred was in the room but they were friendly. They'd done most of the clerical work for Rocky's campaign and they showed me a lot. We addressed four thousand Christmas cards for him while they told me about their boy friends."

Winifred always tried to whisk the girls out of sight when Lucy went to their house. Lucy had learned to recognize this as prelude not to politics but to interminable tête-à-têtes which always came back to linen, silver and babies.

The Reverend, like the girls, kept much out of sight and presently desisted from his attempts to convert her to his congregation. She compromised the punctilio involved by asking him to perform their wedding ceremony at River House.

"He'll always think I snubbed their church," she said, "and I'll always think all churches are the same, but I couldn't say that to him."

Rocky had supported her firmly for a small house wedding.

"Mother would have to ask every female do-gooder in the state, otherwise," he said, "and we've got that vote anyway."

The length of the engagement revived sex. Rocky was still traveling the state or at Prairie several days a week. He returned increasingly ardent and expectant. She found herself indifferent and troubled about it.

"It will be better in our own house," he told her, but he steadfastly refused practical consideration of their own house. When she insisted that they should plan he was impatient and evasive. He told her it was impossible to plan in politics. He then had no inkling that Herman Brodbeck's retirement would open a Senate seat in the '48 election. His most tangible goal was election from our district to the U. S. House of Representatives in 1948; victory in that meant Washington.

"We can live with the folks till we see," he said.

She knew that meant living at River House. Archie had already invited them to live with him as long as they liked. Rocky had formed the habit of spending most of his week ends there instead of in the crowded rectory. She tiptoed to his room late and lonely through the drafty halls and returned to her own with the dawn, still lonely, perplexed and increasingly sadder.

"It frightened me," she said. "I used to tell myself that sex was the final gyp. All of history, folklore and literature insist that it's the summit of experience. But we had no real communication at all above the waist. It was just what you'd called animal fun; you couldn't build a lifetime on that."

Rocky himself was increasingly aware of their other incompatibilities. It made him restive and irritable. He had begun to feel in River House an oppression more serious than impediments to trysting.

Archie continued polite but Rocky found his unvarying formality chill and faintly mocking. The front door swung wide; he had to leave the Cadillac outside. Warming his hands at the library fire, he could feel the glare in Simeon's portrait. The only comfortable chair in the room was Archie's. He could dream of the day when he would be master there; the present reduced him.

"I want you to see my place at the Plaza," he told Lucy. She understood that he wanted her to see him where he was important. She hoped another perspective might convince her that he was. Trousseau shopping made an easy pretext. She drove up to Prairie alone, took a room for herself at the Plaza as they had agreed and sat in it, lonely and unsure of herself, until an hour after the appointed time her phone rang.

"For God's sake come up," said Rocky. "I've got some real wheels here to meet you."

In a fury she told him that however much she might be acting like a call girl she was not one. He could come down and escort her up to meet his friends. He came to the door, furious himself. He told her that no nice girl would use such language. If she was too good for his friends she should have stayed in the graveyard of River House. She was being disloyal and making him ridiculous.

"I promised Dennis Flynn you'd pour him tea," he said. "And I've got Anton Auerbach and the Senate majority leader and whip up there waiting to meet you."

She knew she had been overwrought. She kissed him, conciliated and hurried to the elevator with him as he frantically briefed her on her social duties.

A personal call from Dennis Flynn was a triumph Rocky had achieved only by promising the presence of Simeon's granddaughter. Flynn was over eighty then and had not gone out socially for years. He managed the party and received the calls he would accept from a secluded throne in the back office of his son-in-law's bonding and indemnity company, across the park from the state capitol. That day the whole town knew that he was calling on Rocky Slade in the hotel.

Anton Auerbach was the other extreme of state politics. He was the son of a large brewing fortune. He had never worked. He played the violin, dabbled in painting and entertained. He had first aroused public attention by gifts to the Prairie Art Museum. From that he had progressed to unpaid service on its board and thence, with Flynn's friendship, to the equally unremunerative Park Commission.

"Fairy, of course, but bright and hard to reach," said Rocky.

"His sister went to Smith with us; she's nice," said Lucy.

"Good God!" Rocky exploded. "And you never told me! That we can use."

Of the other two Senators she could remember afterward only that one was bald and one kept his hat on. Rocky's suite itself shocked her. Immediately after the war the hotel had been redecorated extensively. Rocky's parlor was the flower of that effort. It glittered with chromium, glass, mirrors, enamel and multicolored Venetian blinds. It had a complete bar, opening out of the shell of what had seemed to be a grand piano.

"I had to look twice," said Lucy, "to make sure the futuristic designs on the lamp shades were not dollar signs."

Rocky's visitors absorbed the first impact of her surprise. She liked old Dennis Flynn. He carried his eighty years with a spare, erect dignity. His red face, snowy hair and bushy brows over twinkling blue eyes suggested a benign, if skinny, Santa Claus. His memories of Simeon were grateful and affectionate. In spite of Rocky's pointed cues Flynn would talk over their tea of nothing else.

"Your grandfather paid me the first dollar I ever earned in politics, my dear. In fact it was twenty," Flynn told her. "In those days I always said we were three parties, for the banner at headquarters was Republican but the policy with aspiring statesmen like me was to be very liberal with advice and very conservative with party funds. I was just a hanger-on then with strong hands and hopeful but mostly hungry until the great navigation bill came up.

"Your river down there was part of the plan. It might surprise you, considering that a deer can jump it dry-footed some years and fish can't swim against it times of flood. But that was not known in

Washington, where we had loyal friends on the Rivers and Harbors Committee. So it was decided in caucus to open the West to navigation. When word of it got out every Republican contractor with one horse and a fresno took to pricing pianos in Chicago, for the prospects were good.

"Half the farmers down your way could see themselves as Mississippi planters, shipping hogs instead of cotton to Europe from their front yards. The other half were in stock and said the steamboat whistles would scare their cattle across the Continental Divide so it made for contention until your grandfather got wind of the project.

"Up he came to Prairie and said he'd have no fresnos hauling dirt over his front yards or steamboat whistles disquieting his sleep either. In the way of things I was introduced to him and when he spoke of qualifications I showed him my strong hands.

"'Violence is crudity, Flynn,' says he, very stern and reproving. 'And needless with whiskey at ten cents a glass.'

"So I got twenty dollars in gold pieces for my promise that the Senator from Sioux County would not vote at the crucial session. Your grandfather was very right, for even at ten cents a glass I served the party, made a fair profit for myself and protected the Senator from the violence he might have encountered in the street. He was agitated at times for his future but we put it in the papers he was in the hospital at death's door with the summer complaint. The story was easily believed for we had an epidemic that week. Half the Senate was right there in Afflerbaugh's saloon with us until it was safer out, for them and for your grandfather's bass fishing."

"He was a great old pirate," said Rocky heartily. "Pity we haven't got him for the freeway fight."

"Pity indeed," Flynn chuckled. "It's a mercy of God, if you'll excuse my saying so, my dear. Your grandfather would have run that thing in figure of eights until it crossed the sorriest acre of land he owned, for perpetual toll rights."

He chuckled again and patted Lucy's hand.

"I hope you'll forgive an old man's memories, my dear," he said. "For I came to admire and not to scandalize. Those were very different times to these. Your grandfather had a mind of his own when very few people in our part of the world had minds at all. But every stick of the Maynard Institute was honest contracts paid for with his own money. It made great indignation in the party."

Anton Auerbach separated Lucy briefly from the others for a private word she thought at once ominous and apologetic. Anton was middle-aged, frail, diffident and determined beneath a shy mask. He told her that beauty had always been the dominating force of his life. He found the whole freeway fight painful. No part of it was more repugnant to him than the inevitable prospect that beauty for all might mean destroying older and more private concepts of beauty for some. He hoped that she and Archie, whom he had always admired, would remember this no matter what happened.

The Senator with the hat told her that he had been in politics all his life. They all came back to friendship. He had served Wiasota for thirty years and still didn't own his house. When he looked around a room like this at friends like Dennis and Anton and old Rock and now, he hoped, Miss Lucy herself, he realized that politics came and politics went but no matter what happened friendship remained. He hoped it always would.

The other Senator said that nothing was better than old friends unless it was old friends *and* old bourbon. He was mighty glad to see a young man like Rocky with plenty of both and since there seemed to be enough he would, in fact, just have another. At the door, as they said their good-bys, old Flynn paused over his handshake with her.

"I wish you great happiness, my dear," he said. "And if you'll accept an old man's valedictory you'll remind this fine boy from time to time that football is fine for the starring and the applause and the cheers but politics is always a team game."

Rocky was exultant. She had managed them all perfectly; she had the real flair. Flynn loved her. She could beat Anton Auerback at his own snob's game. The two Senators had told him she would make the perfect wife. They were really operating now. He was going to buy her the damnedest steak in the history of Wiasota, as soon as he had checked his bar.

"Half those bastards will pocket a bottle, the other half use briefcases," he told her dryly as he counted his store.

"It's an investment, of course, but if you make it too easy for them they despise you for it."

The subject reopened doubts she had suppressed in the tension of entertaining the others. She studied the room and the bulging piano bar with troubled eyes.

"Rocky, isn't this all dreadfully expensive?"

"I'm not playing for peanuts," he told her.

She wanted to know more, to understand the details of what he called operating. She remembered that her father had given him nothing; that he had always been sensitive and secretive about money. To probe was to reduce and deflate him.

As they set out for the steak house she decided that she could at least understand another part of his life. It had not escaped her that in one way or another all four of his guests had warned her of impending disappointment for Rocky. She brought this up obliquely. He nodded with immediate, sober attention.

"Natch. That's politics, too, dear. Flynn already thinks enough of me to want to cut me down a little."

"Can he?"

"Maybe." Rocky shrugged. "Unavoidable risk, dear. I have some cards, too."

"What are your cards?"

"That plurality. Some goodwill here and there; some fear where it will help."

"What kind of fear, Rocky?"

"Auerbach," said Rocky. "They think he's invulnerable because he's rich but he isn't."

"Why not?"

"Because he's been on the police blotter, right here in town on a complaint from a bellhop in that hotel. Flynn had that page pulled out of the blotter but it's still a sweet piece of information."

"Rocky! You wouldn't use such a thing."

"You don't have to use such things, dear. It's like bridge. When everyone knows where the trumps are you just throw in the cards and count the score. Some of those boys will be very surprised at my score."

"Where on earth did you learn it?"

"Disgruntled reporter with a long memory and a longer thirst," said Rocky. "He's expensive, too, and worth every dime of it. If the boys want it rough, I can play it rough, too, just like your granddad."

The Prairie Steak Broiler was a horror of phony rusticity. It ran to wooden beams, copper hoods over charcoal grates, electronic spits and imitation candlelight. Lucy had to have her hair washed the next day to expunge its prevailing reek of burned suet and cigarette smoke. Rocky quarreled with a waiter over tables until the maître hurried up, all deference and propitiation. Of course Mr. Slade should have the center table, even for two.

She had hoped for the seclusion of a booth. She soon saw why Rocky had insisted on the center of the room. News of Dennis Flynn's visit to him that day had seeped into every back room in town. Throughout the meal they received a procession of homage. Half the visitors stayed to chat over a drink, on Rocky. Most of the men drank with their hats on and called Lucy sister. A girl with one of them asked her if she had got her mink from Rocky.

The men all slapped old Rock on the back and told him they were hearing great things. Was it true that he was just like that with Dennis and Anton? Those who thought of it assured Lucy that she was the luckiest girl alive and just right for old Rock. Many didn't bother to speak to her; in the confusion introductions were blurred and often simply omitted.

One man seated himself confidently close to her and demanded the best Scotch in the house: "On Rocky's bill, waiter; this is his night." Then ignoring Rocky, who was preoccupied with a whispering conference across the table, the man pressed an exploratory knee against Lucy's thigh and asked her if she had heard the one about the three nuns and the rabbi. She told him she did not like jokes about religion. He laughed and said that was okay he could find other things to joke about with a chick like her.

Rocky was still entirely engrossed across the table. Lucy returned the pressure on the man's knee until he winked. Demurely she asked him how he made little chicks laugh. He was half through explaining what a big bang it would give him to take a chick like her away from old Rock before her cigarette formed the strong hot coal she wanted. Then under the table she pressed it firmly into his intrusive leg. He jumped up and ran cursing for the men's room.

"What's wrong with Elmer?" Rocky was concerned.

"Overheated, I think," said Lucy. "Friend of yours?"

"He's big," said Rocky, with troubled eyes on the retreating figure. "Fronts for United Cement. You didn't insult him, did you?"

"Impossible," said Lucy. "He's probably looking for some of your other chicks."

He thought she was jealous. It flattered him and he enjoyed teasing her. She was not jealous. She was desolate. She asked him to take her back to the hotel as soon as they had eaten. Rocky wanted to stay and hold court there before progressing to the Fandango Club. He told her he wanted the rest of his friends to see them together.

They had intended to make the most of Prairie's limited night life. She couldn't bear the prospect of more Elmers. She urged him to drop her at the hotel and go on, if it was professionally important to him. He became sullen. He told her she was snooty and upstage with his friends; she was spoiling his contacts. He knew they were tough. So was all of life when you got out of a cocoon like River House.

"You don't make decisions, Jim," she said. "They're all made for you, perhaps long before you. You just have to grope around till you find them. Suddenly in that damned restaurant I knew it was all over. I didn't care what Grandpa had done or Daddy hadn't. I was still ashamed of myself but that was one thing I could control. And beyond it there was something else. I'd always have to live with myself but I wasn't going to try to explain Rocky to his children or to mine because there wasn't anything to explain. All that muscle and energy and ambition were just empty."

She was haunted by the memory that every decision she had made about Rocky had been wrong. She resolved to sleep on this one and to sleep alone. In the car on the way back to the hotel he was able to forget or at least to dissemble his disappointment in a resurgence of ardor. It was to be their first full night together. He was eager, caressing, confident. Everything would be all right when they were alone in his suite. It was what she had told herself on the lonely drive to Prairie. She knew now that nothing would ever be right for them.

At the hotel she insisted on going to her own room. He could not argue in the elevator. When it closed behind them he walked down the corridor with her, angry and insistent. She had promised him this. She refused to go up to his suite. He insisted that he would stay in her room. She told him she wanted to be alone. He grabbed her and kissed her and told her he would never let her go.

"The awful part was that I really did want him then," she said. "I could feel that kiss all the way down the backs of my legs. But everything above my waist knew that it could never, never work."

She got him out and locked the door and had the first solid sleep she had known for weeks. Her mind was made up; whatever happened it was over.

In the morning he had knocked at her door with an armful of flowers, tender, sweet, conciliatory. She refused to let him in but agreed to talk it all over at breakfast in his suite. He insisted it was the only place where they could have any privacy.

"If I'd been in any doubt," she said, "that breakfast would have ripped it. His idea of privacy is a parade."

She had dressed and gone up to the parlor of his suite to find it converted into a restaurant. There was enough food for a family on a sideboard full of silver dishes; a waiter was standing by to serve them.

"We can talk later," said Rocky.

She was grateful to have the waiter there. She did not want to talk. She wanted to give Rocky his ring and go home. When the waiter had finally cleared out his things and gone, Rocky tried to get Lucy to go to bed with him. She refused and told him that she had come up to return his ring. She was not the right girl for him. They could never be happy together.

He seemed stunned. He kept insisting that he had done it all for her. He could not live without her. His whole career was purposeless until their marriage crowned it. She reminded him that he had won his first election before he would even take her out. She had told him that she did not think she could love him. She had tried to make it up to him, to help him in other ways, to learn to love him. She knew now that other ways would never be enough.

They were arguing in circles when Ed Brady had turned his own key in the door and walked in on them. Rocky introduced him at once as a valued friend and confidant. Ed had winked broadly at Lucy and mimicked the pose of the discreet monkeys.

"Sorry to interrupt morning devotions, sister," he said. "But old Ed sees no evil, hears no evil, speaks no evil and has very urgent news for your boy friend."

Rocky retired to the bedroom with him, tense and silent. They were closeted for half an hour while she fumed and waited with the solitary thought of departing. When they emerged Rocky was aquiver with new excitement, Brady solemn and owlish as he kissed his fingers to her and hurried out. She had arisen; Rocky pushed her into a chair.

"Lucy, do you want to ruin me?"

Then, pledging her to secrecy, he told her that Brady had just learned of Herman Brodbeck's impending retirement. Brady had it straight from one of Brodbeck's secretaries. They thought that even Flynn had not heard of it yet; they had to make every minute count before he did, and Lucy had to help.

Her first sensation was overwhelming relief. She had dreaded hurting Rocky. His absorption in this news was a reassurance in double measure. He had no time now for pain; he had an outside chance at the United States Senate.

"How wonderful for you," she said.

"Unless you louse it up," he told her somberly.

In her relief she could even tease him about that.

"Every single girl in the state will vote for an eligible bachelor," she told him.

He shook his head earnestly.

"I thought of that. The shopgirl vote won't fetch this, Lucy. Those solid middle-aged suckers want to see the ball and chain on a candidate."

"Then you'll have to find another girl at once," she said. "I'm sorry,

Rocky. I don't want to hurt you but I'm not marrying you; that's final."

He told her it was not as simple as that. A public breach of their engagement at that moment would shatter his prestige, make him the laughingstock of the town and alienate Flynn before he could figure out new angles for this situation. She owed him at least a brief support. He had even gone heavily into debt to court her.

"You can return this ring," she said.

The ring was the least of it. His whole scale of living had been adjusted upward to his position as her fiancé. It had not mattered before that she and Archie had never helped him. People had drawn the natural inference of a loyal and powerful connection. Public loss of that now would cut him down just when he needed building up to this supreme opportunity.

With a little time he could find the angle to bring Flynn to heel; he could even find his own financial feet. The legislature was already convened. Passage of the freeway bill itself was a certainty. Rocky hoped for a powerful backstage voice in the choice of its route. He was already committed, with knowing friends, to legitimate speculations which would recoup his debts.

He told her candidly that he had been on the verge of asking her and Archie for a loan that week. He needed it to build solidly for their future together. The least she could do was to help him, now, through this crisis. He thought another ten days would settle it.

"You've either got to help me or ruin me," he said.

In her emotional relief at the end of the affair the financial and political details had seemed to her a blessing. She could help him about those; she would be able to remember that she had helped him. She agreed to postpone the formal breach of the engagement for a few days. She told him that she would try to get him a loan from Archie.

"I knew the truth would hurt Daddy," she said, "so I tried to shield him and ended up by killing him."

"You gave him the best moment of his life, Lucy. You justified it."

"He didn't need justifying; he was honest."

"He told me that morning that we make our own rules, Lucy. And he lived to be proud of yours."

Chapter Thirteen

I HAVE chronicled in sequence conversations that were interspersed through several days. They were broken by the presence of others and by the long hours Lucy insisted on spending at Archie's bedside, whenever a lapse in sedation offered even the faintest possibility of returning consciousness. They were broken also by the continuing sequel of events around us.

Rocky had not been boasting when he told us he had never thrown a pass he couldn't cover. At first some of his angles appeared asymmetric. Their subsequent manipulation provided us, and Dennis Flynn, with a masterful demonstration that politicians equal to the same thing are not necessarily equal to each other.

The morning after Archie was stricken, the Prairie *Times* printed Brady's editorial, substantially as he had shown it to me. Tom rose to the bait in the next issue of the *Sentinel* with a signed editorial on the front page:

> . . . insinuations against anonymous figures are unworthy of our contemporary and the American way of life. If the Prairie *Times* knows of misconduct in high places it should confront the suspect with explicit charges.

That night the radio pundits in both Torrent and Prairie had a Roman holiday with it. There was still no mention of Rocky's name. Every phrase was couched with the standard safeguards against libel. Mystery titillated the solemn allegations that forthcoming disclosures were believed by observers close to the source to be fraught with far-reaching effect on the political scene.

An element of luck prospered Rocky's efforts. In all that week there was no murder worthy of the name. A news audience blooded on six years of war was already yawning over the growing pains of the United Nations. They seemed very far from Wiasota. This was battle, of a kind, once more.

Whispering carried Rocky's name across the state with a velocity that mocked the legal timidities of the air waves and gained momentum as it moved. By the second morning the story had snowballed into the national wire services and broadcasts. After teasing them for another twenty-four hours, the Prairie *Times* released as a news story its capitulation of the demonstrable spendings of Councilman Slade.

I read them with partial relief. Brady had decided to add the contract for Rocky's Cadillac to the list so that it ran even higher in total than his editorial statement. But Lucy's ring was not itemized. The rest of it was bills from the places Rocky had mentioned to me, interspersed with bold subheads: Fifty-Dollar Dinner for Four . . . Uneasy Lies the Head, in a Thirty-Five-Dollar Suite . . . Was It All Hundred-Proof, Councilman?

With the suspense ended and the diversionary fireworks petering out, the main attack moved, with classic concentration, against Flynn himself. One word from Rocky at any time during the first two days would have terminated the affair with an editorial scolding. His steadfast silence ballooned it into national news. The much-augmented press corps at Prairie didn't quite dare to leave the thing unresolved.

The anonymous observers close to the source hinted darkly at a test of American political morality, fraught with momentous consequences. Wiasota might be pivotal in the national elections of '48. Destruction of Republican hopes there in consequence of the alleged scandal could be of incalculable moment. The people of Wiasota, wrote Brady, and many of the people of America would be satisfied with nothing less than explanation from the highest party levels. He hoped that Dennis Flynn would be sensible of his responsibilities.

Flynn endured it for another twenty-four hours and then, through a spokesman, announced his refusal to comment. Within an hour presses were rolling and air waves seething with delighted reprisal from the assembled reporters. Brady got the front page of the Prairie *Times* for his boxed questions in big type.

The people demanded to know whether this was a partisan or merely an internal issue. Did the Republican party accept or disavow responsibility for the ethics of its office holders? Was two payrolls for ever official a logical extension of two cars in every garage?

Flynn's announced refusal to answer the questions added the final touch. Democratic papers and statesmen crept forward to view with alarm. The glum Republican silence had begun to echo from coast to coast when, on the fifth day, Rocky covered his pass.

To a summoned press gathering at his hotel suite in Prairie Rocky issued an official statement.

"I have been the victim of a whispering campaign of smear and slander. For myself I can stand it because I know that no man can do right in public life without making enemies. I can even stand the reflection on my mom and dad because I have been blessed with parents who never feared to pay the personal price of a lifetime of service.

"What I cannot stand, what I will not stand, is the reflection of these cowardly slanders upon the good people of Torrent County who have entrusted me with public service. To them I shall make full explanation tonight at eight o'clock in the auditorium of my old high school in the most beautiful city in the world."

Rocky himself would not amplify with another word. A personal statement and abundant further information were, however, provided by Ed Brady. In his personal statement Brady said that he had fought his conscience for five days. He could not sit by and see an innocent man pilloried by press and politics. Mr. Brady had resigned from his newspaper to offer unequivocal support in his determination to see fair play for a Wiasota boy.

Mr. Brady was appearing now as spokesman and personal representative for Rocky Slade, without remuneration. He didn't have to defend old Rock. Some of the public might just remember that old Rock had defended himself before from dirty play. Mr. Brady stressed that special arrangements would be made for the press and that admission to the public would be absolutely free at the big, spontaneous Save Rocky Slade rally in Torrent that night. He was empowered to say that the *Sentinel*'s radio station would offer word-by-word coverage as a public service to community and nation.

At the time of the announcement Lucy was in Archie's room. He had not spoken since he fell to the floor but she would not abandon hope. I was pondering the potentialities of the Save Rocky Slade rally alone when Miss Premm appeared at the door. She had come daily throughout my long vigil, bringing fresh linen and mail. That afternoon she brought neither.

"I wondered if you heard the announcement," she said.

"Just now. Did you hear it driving out?"

"I knew of it," she said. "Our church group refused Winifred's request for official sanction."

"I'm glad to hear it."

"Some of us," said Miss Premm, "do not consider these proceedings religious in nature."

"Is that what you came to tell me?"

"Not entirely, Mr. James. Winifred has commendable, as well as other, characteristics. It would be deplorable to see political zeal degenerate into malicious personal gossip."

"I agree. Do you consider it likely, Miss Premm?"

"I should consider it less likely," said Miss Premm, "if she were advised against vindictiveness. Many of our generation, Mr. James, can remember a time when Winifred was less—far less—than antagonistic toward Archer Maynard."

Suddenly I remembered that spring afternoon on their verandah in Lucy's childhood. I could hear again Archie's unguarded chuckle and his dry comment that Mrs. Slade had slapped him about sex, once.

"A certain bitterness presently replaced Winifred's more generous instincts," continued Miss Premm calmly, "but one hates to see old gossip and grudges vexing a new generation."

"I think I see what you mean, Miss Premm."

"I was sure you would," said Miss Premm. She took off her hat and put it on the table and warmed her hands before the fire.

"You've been very confined here, Mr. James. I brought my knitting and I'd be happy to watch the phone and keep Miss Maynard company if you thought of going out."

A divinity student with dusting mop in hand let me in the door of the rectory before shaking her head. Rocky was not at home. Mrs. Slade and the girls had been at the high school all afternoon. There was no one in the house but the Reverend and she was forbidden to disturb him because he was meditating on his sermon. As her voice stopped we could both hear the rhythmic snores through the study door.

The high school auditorium as I entered it was seething with preparation for the big spontaneous rally. Boy Scouts, already in uniform, were dragging festoons of bunting down the aisles and teetering happily on high ladders. From the stage an earnest young man kept calling into a microphone:

"Testing—one, two, three, four; testing—one . . ."

In the center aisle down toward the orchestra well Winifred was concluding an argument with the unhappy leader of the American Legion band.

"You will *not* march in . . . we have exactly twenty-two minutes. You will be seated in uniform with your instruments—"

"How's this, Mrs. Slade?" called a janitor from the stage.

She surveyed the stage and shook a critical head.

"No. The seats are masking the flags."

Veronica hurried breathlessly down the aisle.

"Mother, the stick placards are here—"

"In the hall just outside the doors," said Winifred. "A stack beside each door where the scout ushers can give them out—"

"He wants to be paid before he unloads them, Mother."

"Tell him to charge them to me personally," said Winifred.

Veronica sped off and Winifred studied the stage again.

"Better, but I'd like the flags higher. Get a box."

Then as the man went for one I spoke and Winifred turned to face me.

"Why, Jim; what are you doing here?"

"I'd like a private word with you, Mrs. Slade."

"I'm busy," said Winifred, "you can see for yourself . . . No. No. State flag on the left, American on the right."

"This won't take long," I said. "It might save a painful mistake."

She scrutinized me more thoughtfully and then marched up the aisle ahead of me and beckoned to a relatively quiet row of seats.

"Roscoe was very disappointed in you, Jim," she said.

"I came to talk about Archie, Mrs. Slade."

She looked a shade less hostile but still suspicious.

"We heard about his attack. I must say, after the way he has behaved—but never mind. How is he, Jim?"

"Weak," I said, "but his memory is very strong."

"His memory?"

I nodded. "He's living very much in the past, Mrs. Slade. At lunch we fell to talking about old times and we both remembered the day Lucy bit your hand and he told you the truth was much too precious to be reckless with. Do you remember?"

"She jilted him," said Winifred. "She jilted my boy in his hour of need."

"Mrs. Slade," I said, "silence and forgiveness are not only the Christian way; they're the safe way."

"Jim." Her eyes narrowed. "What are you trying to say?"

"I'm reminding you, Mrs. Slade, that any small community is a glass house."

She cogitated, her eyes still suspicious but very thoughtful again.

"We heard Archie was unconscious."

"Only at first; his mind is very clear about the past."

"Jim, have you anything more to say?"

"I hope that covers it, Mrs. Slade."

"All right," she said. "And thank you, Jim."

She was rising as Veronica hurried back breathlessly.

"Mother, he says he charged 'em to you last time and unless he gets cash—"

"I'll speak to him," said Winifred, unhurried. "Jim, this is politics for you: leeches screaming for money from every side."

I walked up the aisle and out into the main hall of the school. Lucy had always warned me against lying in court but I thought that if I ever had to I could do it. Then at the door I met Tom Gilchrist hurrying to the auditorium. He paused to inquire anxiously for Archie. I modified the report I had given Winifred. Tom didn't have to tell me he was on his way to see her but she would not repeat our conversation. Then, as his mind came fully around to me, he frowned with perplexity.

"What are you doing here, Jim?"

"Research on bread and circuses," I said.

He shook his head ruefully. "Hattie would agree," he said. "She's sore as hell. They told us they had to have the radio time for a kind of old-fashioned town meeting—real working democracy—by God, Jim, it makes you wonder!"

He broke off and looked down the hall to where we could see Winifred haggling with the printer's truckman. From the auditorium the voice came clearly:

"Testing—one, two, three, four . . ."

We looked at each other and Tom shrugged and then his shoulders lifted a little; his face set defiantly.

"Damn it, Jim! I still say innocent until proved guilty!"

"Are you talking about Rocky or about democracy?"

"So democracy's imperfect," said Tom. "What's better?"

"Nothing, but that's the point, Tom. You can grow by making mistakes but not by denying them. It's about time we locked the stable door."

"That's up to the people," said Tom.

Since I didn't have to go back to the rectory, my return route through town gave me my first look at our main street in several days. From two blocks away I could see the new sign covering Ed Delany's show window. From a block I could read the foot-high lettering: SAVE ROCKY SLADE. I counted five more such signs before I was stalled by a minor traffic jam at the square.

There a radio truck with another SAVE ROCKY SLADE sign emblazoned across the top was purposely creating the jam. Through the horn tooting of its indignant victims I could hear Freddy Eastman's voice, magnified by the microphone, reverberating through the square with angry sincerity:

". . . so we can sit here and watch the politicians and papers give one of our own boys the business or we can show those big shots and the whole damned country where Torrent stands. It's up to you, folks, and I want to see every Torrent man with guts at the big Save Rocky Slade rally tonight."

A bored cop admonished the driver of the truck again. It rolled on, the line began to move and I drove past the old statue of Simeon and the new one with Artie's name on the scroll back to River House.

In the library Miss Premm told me that Lucy had not come downstairs during my absence. Dr. Jamison had just arrived and gone straight to Archie's room. I helped Miss Premm into her coat and watched her methodical gathering of bag and gloves.

"I hope you found your outing beneficial," she said.

"I hope it was. And—Miss Premm?"

"Yes?"

"Will you take a transcript of the broadcast?"

"I intended to," said Miss Premm. "I have noticed that news accounts are not always accurate."

Lucy and Jamison came down to the library together. One look at their faces told me the unchanging news of no change. Lucy always insisted on his having a drink after his last visit of the day. That night he shook his head over it sadly.

"Archie always gave me one," he said. "Now you're doing more for me than I can do for him."

He sipped again and spoke casually.

"You've not going to the rally, are you, Lucy?"

"No. Rocky and I aren't engaged any more, Arby."

"Oh." He smiled. "Mrs. Jamison did say something about that. Saw it in the paper. Changed your mind, eh?"

"Yes."

"Well, young people do," said Jamison. "Did your daddy know it, dear?"

"Yes."

"It should have cheered him," said Jamison. "He used to fret to me about that. I told him to quit bothering his head; nobody likes their in-laws."

"Are you going to it, Arby?"

"Lord, no!" Jamison chuckled comfortably. "I never bother with politics. I guess they'll make quite a show at that. Rocky always was slick. But I listen to a quiz program unless I have to go out. Those quiz people give away their own money."

On the previous evenings we had had visitors. That night there were none. I think every radio in Torrent except Dr. Jamison's was tuned to the rally. Lucy and I went up to Archie's room for a long look at him after dinner. His eyes were closed; the rising and falling of his chest was even but barely visible. He was a long way from our world. As the radio brought it into the library I was grateful that he was.

Before me as I write lie three versions of the rally: Miss Premm's copied transcript, the newspaper accounts and one of the mimeographed press copies which Brady distributed to all reporters. Tom saved one of the latter for me. It is of interest only in one unexplained detail. The mimeographed pages were numbered. In the section devoted to Mrs. Slade's remarks, there was missing about a page. A penciled note explained the gap as "Omitted." Otherwise there are few and minor variations in the three reports. The Slades had rehearsed with care.

Rereading the accounts now I marvel at the difference between the cold black print, with its insulting omission of fact, truth or relevance, and the emotional fervor that throbbed across the air waves into the library.

By seven-thirty, as the announcer exulted, there was not a seat left in the high school auditorium. It had been chosen for more reasons than economy. A small auditorium is easier to fill. That night there were standees in aisles and halls. At a temperature just below freezing a crowd estimated as several hundred listened from cars and curbings outside to the loud-speakers placed for their convenience.

Just before eight o'clock the newscaster announced that owing to the unprecedented gravity of the meeting it had been decided to dispense with customary formalities of introduction.

"Torrent needs no introduction to Rocky," he said.

Precisely at eight the Reverend and Mrs. Slade, followed by Rocky, filed onto the platform to a tumult of cheering. They let it last while the newscaster described again the waving of banners and the SAVE ROCKY SLADE stick placards. He turned his microphone toward the house for a second during this. The sound of the ovation had a waterfall density. Then Rocky's parents took their seats, the announcer told us tremulously that Rocky was holding up his hands for silence and, as the noise abated, we heard his easy familiar voice.

"My fellow citizens, I have broken a promise to you tonight. I expected to fight this battle alone. That was why I declined the offers of support that have been pouring in to me through this dark time. That is why I told the officials of the great party whose banner I am proud to bear that I did not want their support tonight. I wanted to stand alone in explanation to the friends and neighbors who have believed in me.

"But I had to break that promise. I had to break it or to break faith with the greatest mom and dad any American boy ever had."

The text reads "Applause." Over the radio it sounded like an explosion. Then, adjusting his mike, the newscaster informed us excitedly that Rocky had gone over and kissed his mother.

"My mom and dad," continued Rocky, "reminded me that I was theirs before I was yours. My dad reminded me of something more fundamental to our American way of life than that. He reminded me that there is a Higher Force above the little struggles of our time, a Force that must guide not only our striving for the right but our hope of forgiveness, for our enemies as well as for ourselves. My dad, ladies and gentlemen, asks your permission to invoke that Force."

The text reads "Applause, quickly muted," for the outburst scarcely survived the Reverend's quick step to the rostrum, the raising of his big arms.

"Oh, Lord . . ."

His prayer had the merit of brevity. The twenty-two minutes were ticking. Earnestly the Reverend assured the Almighty that He was Almighty and would, accordingly, not disappoint the justice expected of Him tonight. His voice trailed off into silence and then through it we heard the ringing, militant accents of Winifred.

"Ladies and gentlemen, I would like to hear 'The Star Spangled Banner.'"

The Legion band was prompt on cue; the house responded with roaring fervor.

"Folks," said the newscaster, "this is mighty stirring. The song is over but they're still cheering and clapping and now Mrs. Slade is holding up her hands for silence and your big happy neighborhood network is bringing you—Mrs. Slade."

"Neighbors," said Winifred, "I'm not going to speak to you about politics because I'm not a politician and I don't want to be. I'm here tonight because I'm a mother."

The text reads "Prolonged applause which Mrs. Slade had to quiet by raising her arms again."

"When my Roscoe told me he didn't want his mother fighting his battles for him, I laughed at him. I never have fought his battles. He does that himself. Anyone who wants to investigate *that* is in the wrong place. They should be asking our friends at Notre Dame."

The text reads "Brief applause, some cheers."

"I came here to fight the continuing battle of my whole life—for the women and mothers of Torrent. You may think these smear attacks on Roscoe are just a cheap political trick to keep a poor boy down. To me they are attacks on the womanhood, the motherhood of Torrent, attacks on our homes, our churches, our schools, attacks on our country itself because although some of the menfolk don't act like they've learned it yet, our country is half women. The other half is only the men we women make."

Laughter was noted with the applause here.

"So I have nothing more to say to the men. But to you women and mothers like me, I say this: when rich and ruthless people, when power politicians set traps and tricks for a poor boy, they are setting them for you. When they insult a life of service, they are insulting you. When they try to crucify innocence, they are crucifying womankind!"

The text records "Wild and prolonged applause." At the time I scarcely heard it. I had begun to relax. Winifred was done and I knew that she had understood me that afternoon.

"Now folks," said the newscaster, "Rocky's mother has gone over and kissed him and is leading him up to the mike and here is Torrent's own Rocky Slade."

"Neighbors," said Rocky, "the issue tonight is very simple. It is whether, in this great democracy of ours, plain people have the right to elect a poor man to represent them.

"When you chose me to get Torrent a freeway I never doubted that. Perhaps I was too innocent but I knew that freeway was going to be built with state money, with your money. So I took your mandate and went up to Prairie and started trying to make sure of what we were getting for our money. What I got was—nowhere, and very fast. I was up against local selfishness, sectionalism, factionalism and—I'm not pulling any punches tonight, folks—just plain dirty power politics. I'd been elected to speak for you. The men with the power and the purse strings up there practically told me a County Councilor wasn't much punkins in their little games.

"I was pretty nearly licked, folks, and there may be some of you who can remember that Rocky Slade doesn't like being licked. I don't like it for myself. I don't like it for any team I ever played on. But that didn't really matter. What mattered was that if they licked me, they were licking you; they were licking democracy. When I got back from that first failure I told my old dad how hard I had tried for you. He just shook his head.

" 'Son,' he said, 'you haven't really tried at all. You haven't tried prayer.'

"That night in my little room at the rectory I got down on my knees and prayed, like I used to pray before football games but a lot harder because I knew how important this was. The next day, folks, my prayer was answered. It was already being answered while my old dad reproached me, if we had only known it. A little group of public-spirited men here in Torrent had subscribed a fund of a few thousand dollars to assist the legitimate promotion of Torrent's interests.

"Now, folks, I got to say something that might sound irreverent. I was suspicious. I know from Scripture that 'He worketh in mysterious ways, His wonders to perform,' but plain, poor hard-working people like you and me also know that you don't get something for nothing in this life.

"This money was offered me by one of the most respected and public-spirited men that we all know here in Torrent, but I knew I owed it to you to ask more about it. So I did. To put it real crude, I looked that gift horse right in the mouth. I asked that fine man who these public-spirited citizens were and what strings they wanted on their gift.

"Now, folks, I'm giving you and the whole world his answer: *I don't know who those men were and there weren't any strings.*

"Sound funny? It did to me until I realized what that fine man's refusal to give me their names meant. It meant that I wasn't ever to know. It meant there couldn't be any strings 'cause I didn't even know who was helping me . . . and *I give you my word of honor I don't know right now!*

"My prayer was answered anonymous. It let me save your money, save public expense, by using their fund to get you *your* freeway. That's exactly what I did and let me tell you all right here again that I am still going to get that freeway for you.

"In fact, that's the whole trouble. Certain interests never wanted to see Torrent get a freeway. Certain people would like to see all America in the mud and themselves the privileged ones on horseback, riding roughshod over democracy. Certain newspapers would rather see the state's money, your money, spent nearer them.

"When they saw that I was going to get that freeway for Torrent and Torrent County and all of southern Wiasota, the best they could think of was to attack me personally. I guess you read in one of those papers the wicked uses I made of that public-spirited fund.

"I spent some of it in restaurants, but of course, a poor boy shouldn't eat. I went to hotels instead of just sleeping under a bridge and keeping quiet about Torrent's rights. I even traveled. I went to Washington with the State Chairman of our great Republican party, to demand that Wiasota get back some of the money those leeches tax you out of. Maybe that was wrong, too. Maybe poor boys should stay home and keep quiet instead of working for their neighbors.

"Now here is the wickedest part of all, folks. I bought an automobile. Of course it was only a second-hand automobile but poor boys shouldn't have cars. I guess they ought to go round the richest per capita state in the whole Wiasota Valley fighting for a freeway from a horse and buggy. Maybe it's too efficient for a poor boy to drive sixty thousand miles in six months getting you your rights.

"The funny part of it is that I don't even own the car. The finance company owns it, just like it owns most of the ones you other poor people drove here tonight. But just for the record I'm proud to tell you that I did buy a car to represent you. Maybe I never will own it— you know those finance companies—but here you can see with your own eyes my payment checks for it, drawn by a Torrent boy on a Torrent bank to a Torrent car dealer. If that's a crime all I got to say is there's an awful lot of us criminals supporting the American economy and standard of living with checks like these. . . ."

We could hear the slap of papers on the rostrum and the roar of laughter, followed by rolling thunders of applause. Then we heard another sound. The door behind us opened swiftly. We looked around to see the night nurse standing there, her face as white as her dress.

"Miss Maynard—Miss Maynard—"

I followed Lucy's flight up the long stairs. Behind us Rocky's booming voice receded until we could hear the nurse's frightened accents:

"Doctor said I could have my portable in the bathroom to hear the rally, but I did go back in to look at him every few minutes and—"

Archie was lying at peace in the bed in which he had been born. I wondered whether he had heard any of the rally over the nurse's radio. We would never know. His eyes were closed. His face, in death, had taken on that faintly quizzical smile with which he had tried to shield himself from life.

How long we stood beside him I do not know. Lucy said nothing. Presently she bent over and kissed his forehead and then I took her hand and led her back to the stairs.

I had slammed the library door as we ran upstairs, but in my haste I had forgotten to turn off the radio. I opened the door again to the

blaring strains of the Legion band, just concluding "Onward, Christian Soldiers" against a resounding tumult of song and cheers. It
stunned us so that we gaped a second and through that second we
heard the newscaster's voice.

"A triumph, folks . . . a vindication of Rocky Slade and the American way of life. Now he's kissing his mother again and . . . OH—OH
—FOLKS! Dennis Flynn has come out on the stage and put his arm
around Rocky and the crowd is going wild—"

I got to the radio and turned it off. The silence hit the room with a
nearly physical impact. Then through it I heard another sound. I
looked around and saw that Lucy was crying.

I I I

The rest of Rocky's speech is not worth quoting. With minor modi-
fications it is still the first, the only speech he ever bothered to make.
He was still Robin Hood, stealing the freeway from rich interests for
poor voters.

A last summary of it lies before me now, the black ink as cold and
forgotten as Rocky's defiant evasions. He had covered his pass with
noise and emotion; all the ink in the world would never change the
effect. The Prairie *Times*'s final editorial is uncomfortably suggestive
of an obituary.

> The emotional orgy which Torrent miscalls a town meeting in
> traditional American style has truer antecedents in the jungle.
> It solved nothing, answered nothing. Torrent was on the evident
> route of the Freeway before Mr. Slade began his noisy and expensive
> exertions. It is still there.
> Our concern was not and is not with the Freeway. It is with ethics
> of politics. Mr. Slade is a public official, elected and paid by the peo-
> ple of Torrent County to serve Torrent County. Not until this paper
> demanded public explanation would he admit that following his elec-
> tion to office he began systematically receiving private money offered
> surreptitiously by private people. He boasts that this saved public
> expense. What evidence there is shrieks that every accountable dime
> of his known subsidy was spent on the advancement of Mr. Slade's
> personal career.
> Such explanation as he has deigned to make of this subsidy is as
> irrelevant as a prostitute's price. The interests of his purchasers may
> or may not have coincided with public interest. Mr. Slade was still on
> two payrolls. He was still serving two masters.

Hewitt was very bitter. Tom had been able to persuade him and his
fellow contributors to permit the printing of the names and the

amounts they had given. There were few surprises in the list. Six of its members had the undeniable financial interest of residences on one of the two proposed routes of the freeway; but, as Tom's paper reiterated, Rocky would not vote on that. The *Sentinel* contented itself with a mild admonition to misplaced zeal.

Hewitt and Madge drove Lucy and Mother and me to the cemetery. Details of the funeral had preoccupied us to the exclusion of everything else until then. When it was over Hewitt and I found ourselves face to face in the dining room at River House, completing the arrangements Archie had ordered for pallbearers and a few friends. When the last cork had been pulled we had a drink to Archie and then Hewitt took the Prairie *Times* editorial from his pocket.

"Did you see this, Jim?"

"Yes."

"Did you ever hear of anything so outrageous?"

"I'm not sure I did, Hewitt."

"I've been wondering," said Hewitt, "whether I don't owe it to this community to sue that damned paper. I suppose there's just enough truth in it to protect them for libel but it's certainly an invasion of my privacy. What do you think, Jim?"

"Are you seriously asking advice?"

"Indeed I am."

"You'd better keep as quiet as the Lord will let you."

He gave me a long angry stare. Then slowly the anger faded out of his face. He poured us another drink and when he spoke again his voice was measured and rueful.

"You may be right, Jim. I'm thinking of washing my hands of politics. When an honest attempt to exercise a stabilizing influence can be perverted like this, I think it's hopeless.

"After that clambake was over and Dennis had come out with his arm around Rocky, I turned off my radio and did some pretty hard thinking. Dennis had never come to town without dropping in on me but I hadn't even known he'd be there. So next morning about eleven I went to the hotel.

"I knew perfectly well why he had to make that show of support there at the last. After all, he's got the whole party to think of. But I know he hates Rocky and I wanted to remind him that even if things hadn't worked out exactly as we planned, we'd accomplished our basic purpose. We'd kept the bastard in line with something to lose. When this hullabaloo, for which I was taking most of the rap, was forgotten, Dennis could just quietly drop him out the nearest window. But when I tried to point this out what do you think Dennis said?"

"I can't imagine, Hewitt."

"He looked me right in the eye, and said to me, 'Hewitt, what you bunglers have done is to tie that son of a bitch around the party's neck for life.'"

Chapter Fourteen

IT was several years before the freeway reached River House. Those who blame it for the final ruin of the place are scarcely correct. Long before I had done the last arithmetic on the inheritance taxes I knew it was doomed.

I even made an effort to find Mr. Franklin again. He was not hard to find. He wrote me an unexpectedly jocular letter saying that he had put off all further consideration of a country estate until he got out of the penitentiary.

Do what I might, I could find no other purchaser. Announcement that the freeway would take the river route, which meant through Simeon's rose garden, destroyed the last possibility of sale for residential purposes. The lengthy wrangle over the precise survey chilled even the lukewarm interest of potential subdividers.

Slowly the place lapsed into a ruinous total decline, devouring every dollar of the estate in its protracted agony, decaying before our eyes in inexorable reversal of the processes of its creation. As the house died, the grounds came back to life with the resumption of the natural growth from which they had once been cleared. Yard, lawns and terraces bristled with weeds, underbrush and second-growth trees, springing strongly from the storm havoc that littered the landscape.

Slingshots and air rifles presently left the windows gaping and spectral. Owls and bats shared the inner darkness of the house with trysting couples and tramps. One of the latter, who may have found an overlooked bottle in the flooded wine vaults, finally accelerated the unrelenting combustion of time with a historic fire.

Now of Simeon's pride there remained only blackened walls, a glitter of sharded glass where the greenhouses had been, a collapsed boathouse sagging over denuded pilings and a melancholy collection of bills and taxes. With luck, belated proceeds from the freeway condemnation might pay off the deficit some day. The taxes would continue until the new life of the freeway itself generated a new crop of subdivision houses to shoulder them.

The best I could hope for Lucy was to wind up out of the debts which were her inheritance. I was scowling over the figures in my office one afternoon when she came in with the *Sentinel* in her hand.

"Jim, they've reached the house."

I hadn't realized they were so close. The work had been done in sections; this was one of the last. Now the machines were at the boundaries. Tom had sent out a reporter, who took pictures of the blackened walls and summarized his findings under the headline "An Era Passes."

"I want to see it once more," said Lucy.

We drove out together through the late spring afternoon. Honeysuckle was heavy and sweet in the air again as we turned into the lane. A descendant of the bobwhite I had heard so long ago was reproaching another wayward harem with plaintive lament.

Rain, snow and ice action had made the old driveway impassable to cars, even where you could clearly see it. Grass and brambles and underbrush were already hiding most of the bluestone in fresh warm green. We walked down it slowly through new hazelbrush and cockleburs, exploring until we found traces of the old walk around the east side of the house.

New leaves on the trees had already cut off all sight of Hewitt's abandoned place. To the eastward, with the house at your back, you could almost imagine that nothing had changed. Then we rounded the ruins and looked west.

There for a mile and a half stretched the gaping brown gash of the new road itself, through orchard and west copse and on through the woods to where the moraine began its slow bend. The raw earth crawled with tractors and carryalls snorting and puffing along the whole length of it. One enormous diesel had chugged up to the very boundaries between what had been gardens and orchard. As we blinked at it we heard the last reprieve of that day's quitting whistle. Men descended from the machinery all along the line and began to trudge off to their cars at the far end of the stretch.

Unconsciously we both turned from it and looked again out over the valley to the south. The river was high with spring, the fields beyond waving green and blossoming. In the distance a freight train left its long white plume of smoke over the fertile serenity. Then we both heard the sudden, self-conscious voice close at hand.

"Oh. You folks live around here?"

One of the workmen had walked over from the nearest diesel,

through Archie's sagging pergola, and had begun to cut roses with a pocketknife, his face uncertain as he eyed us. We told him that we did not. The knife came out again. He resumed work but he felt the necessity of explaining himself.

"The missus wants 'em," he said. "Used to be a big shot's rose garden here."

We said nothing. He cut industriously for a moment and then held up his bouquet for us to see.

"This was one of them places made all the row about Rocky Slade here a while back, remember?"

Rather curtly, I said that we did remember and took Lucy's arm. We started off together but the man smiled at us reassuringly.

"Don't get me wrong," he said. "I got nothing against Rocky; used to play football against him, for Union. I could of told them big shots they'd never work no tricks on Rocky. I'd tried that myself. It's all just politics anyway, like I told my missus. We watch him every time he's on television. We get a kick out of seeing him push 'em around in the Senate."

He waited, tentative and still a little concerned about the roses. Then he closed his knife with a snap.

"Might as well get some yourselves; they won't be here tomorrow."

He waved and walked off toward the scar of the road. Lucy stood as she had been standing, her face set toward the lowering sun on the horizon. I had wondered if she might be crying. I should have known better. The eyes she presently returned to me from the past were serene. Her voice was clear and lifting to the future.

"Now kiss me and let's go back to the children."